BORN
EVIL

BORN EVIL

THREE SISTERS

Mechelle Davis

authorHOUSE®

AuthorHouse™
1663 Liberty Drive
Bloomington, IN 47403
www.authorhouse.com
Phone: 1-800-839-8640

Published by AuthorHouse   05/23/2012

ISBN: 978-1-4520-9870-8 (sc)

Any people depicted in stock imagery provided by Thinkstock are models, and such images are being used for illustrative purposes only.
Certain stock imagery © Thinkstock.

This book is printed on acid-free paper.

Because of the dynamic nature of the Internet, any web addresses or links contained in this book may have changed since publication and may no longer be valid. The views expressed in this work are solely those of the author and do not necessarily reflect the views of the publisher, and the publisher hereby disclaims any responsibility for them.

Written in the memory of my father Elroy Smith

Dedication

When the road started to get rough, you were there for me. When it seemed like I've had enough you put your arms around me. When I lay awake at night and cried you consistently told me things would be alright; for this, I will always love you.

I will like to say a special thank you to JeVarn Harris and Lisa Mitchell, who have been in my corner cheerleading for me every step of the way. I love you both.

I grew up fine, I mean my life was one to be desired by all those around me, but there was something missing. I didn't know what it was or how to find out what I have been missing all I knew was that this life I was living wasn't mine.

All of my life my parent's expected perfection: top of my class, popular, liked by all, choiced, dating the most popular girl, applying to top colleges, ultimately following the family legacy, graduating at the top of my class from law school and finally passing the bar examine the first time around.

I lived their life and experienced success at every turn, but I still felt empty, imperceptible; as if I did not exist. I graduated college and on my graduation day my Mom and Dad gave my girlfriend and myself an all expense two-week paid vacation to Paris France. They'd hope I would have proposed to her by the time we'd returned, but she was their girlfriend, not mine.

The third day into the trip, Marisa had our day planned: there would be no breakfast at the Four Seasons Hotel George V Paris, instead we ate breakfast at a pavement café, Café des deux Moulins and then on to visit the Arch de Triomphe Louvre Museum. Marisa was enjoying the fruits of my parent's labor, but I, with each passing day became more and more disinterested in her and this life.

Day seven, I did not want to get out of bed and my mood was ruining the trip for Ms. Tomae'. I encouraged her to view the vineyards alone or with the snooty couple two sweets below us. My suggestion was still attached to my tongue and lips when she accepted and was out the door. Moments later I heard laughter, loud smooches and a man's voice asking if she were ready. The voice caught my attention, but my heart felt nothing. I laid in bed attempting to sleep my emptiness away until an alarm of some sort forced me to throw the covers back, swing my feet over the side of the bed into slippers I quickly kicked off and to the side, stand to my feet to annoyingly search out the melodic noise.

I found it in the bottom drawer, right hand corner, under the 42 pairs of socks my mother's assistant had packed, three pair for each day, exquisitely wrapped in silver stripped paper, sealed with what looked like some 18th century style candle wax and some sort of carving in the center. I immediately thought of my mother. She was notorious for replicating the old. I pulled the edges to free the corners trapped beneath the wax and the wrapping eagerly fell away and landed on top of my bare feet. As I picked up the wrapping what I thought was a card fell to the floor. Instead it was two pieces of wax paper sealed together to somehow display the most scintillating thing I had ever seen on paper; a Black Stallion made purely from candle wax that smelled of Black liquorish, the beauty of it drowned out the noise. I smiled; I knew the gift was from my mother: silver my favor color, the uniqueness in which the gift was sealed and the Black Stallion a perfect replica of the horse that grew up with me. She had known that I had been struggling with something and had always known what and at which point to do something, anything to make me get outside of myself for a moment and enjoy life. She was once again successful, the mood I was feeling when my feet slid into my slippers was gone and I felt a relief.

I reluctantly laid my miniature Black Stallion on the dresser and flipped open the box, pressed the miniature sticky note that said, "Press here" and the noise silenced. Folded in the lid was a note, I retrieved, open and read the black letters printed on red paper that said,

"My son I have watched you grow into someone exceptional, far beyond your years. As I tried to guide you throughout your life with small gifts of encouragement this is one of my final gifts to you. It is time for you know who you are, where you come from, who your true parent's are . . .

I could not breath; my true parent's? This letter was insinuating that I was adopted. If it is true, this explains my emptiness as the feeling arose in me full force and slowly began to settle because something inside of me knew what I was reading was true. I continued to read.

. . . and the legacy by birth you are to live. Open the lid.

I lifted the lid and perfectly positioned with the opinion of 12 men was placed a Porsche Designed Indicator P'6910 watch. I pressed the button as directed and a voice said,

"In due time you will know me, but right now it is time to search out who you really are; I am your father, but I would rather you know me before we meet. I left something in your dressing room for you. Until we meet face-to-face enjoy the pages that tell the true story of who your family really is.

I ran to my dressing room and the only thing that was out of the ordinary was what appeared to be Marisa's diary. I felt guilty with the thought of reading her personal thoughts. I stood over the book lying there emitting so much temptation and I couldn't resist as I slowly picked it up and opened the cover. I was relieved the woman's name written with so much pride was not Marissa. I hungrily turned the pages, skipped a few, then a few hundred, and then back to the beginning to fill in the blanks. As I turned the pages a note fell to the floor directing me to the shower room, and stacked on the sink were three more diaries. Tears poured from my soul as I cried I do exist! I do exist! I gathered myself from the bathroom floor and did as the note suggested, I showered and then dressed. Picked up my early return tickets and the diaries and jauntily and surreptitiously left the hotel, without warning or notice and followed the path the owner of these diaries laid to finding my parent's.

I settled in my first class seat, buckled in so that I would not be disturbed later, pulled the diary with the perfectly bolded number four in the lower right corner on the cover from my duffle bag, turned to the last few pages and began to fill the emptiness. I know no matter how difficult the challenges were the girls went through I heard Monica say it best. "I've learned three things by my 26th birthday and that is true love comes once, happiness comes at least twice and good friendships last forever. I know the challenges each of us faced increased our faith in GOD and each other and taught me that family isn't just biological. I found friends, protectors, confidants, I found . . . sister's . . . I found family. I am truly blessed to have two great sisters, not by birth but by grace, chance, and choice and from now until the end of my days I will always have sisters and I will do anything to protect them.

The three of us have and share secrets that we will have to carry to our graves and though our secrets haunt us they undoubtedly make us closer. We learned that without hesitation we will kill for one another, die for one another and we also learned the hard way that we put each other before our own children. I have never been loved and was not quite sure how to give, but I had an idea, my sister's helped me put the feelings that were in my head and heart into them . . . . for so many reasons, we will forever be changed, but somehow remain the same. Humph, one chance encounter challenged and strengthened our love for each other.

As I sit in the dark and think about the past 20 years of our lives I can't help but laugh, cry, be happy, angry, frustrated, encouraged and whatever other favor-opposite emotions one person can feel. I am different now, even more than my sisters know, more than I realized and it scares me each time I think about our lives I become more different. I mean, a change is expected when you have been through what we have been through, but my change is compiled with my childhood. My sister's remind me of the good life I now have and I need to move in one direction; forward. I need to get over it, the past that is, but how can I when the ultimate betrayal has been committed. They're right, in spite of our past we do have a good life . . . What do you think?

Mechelle Davis

Kim stood in the kitchen of her immaculately clean and decorated condo, talking to Monica and Eryka as she have every morning for the past 20 years nibbling on her famous breakfast half-paying attention, half-responding to the topic of the week.

"Kim, Kim, Kimberly Ann Marie Jenkins, are you listening to us?" Monica loved calling Kim by her full name it always annoyed her.

Slowly, responding annoyed, "You know that I hate . . . forget it! Yes I'm listening, don't I always?"

"What's on your mind?" Monica continued.

"Nothing . . . Really." Kim responded; clearly the sound of thought in her voice. Using her upbeat man-down voice, Monica laughed, "Uh oh, man troublllle."

"No that's not a "Nothing . . . . really, man trouble, that's a "Nothing . . . . really, I am on the baby kick again, tell me I'm wrong." Eryka playfully demanded but immediately regretted her response.

Monica squealing from excitement, "You're really ready to have a baby?! Wait a minute, how does Eryka know about this and I don't?"

"Because I am only thinking about it and I wanted to share it with you too, but Monica you know how you harp on things and I just did not want to feel pressured about such a big decision. You know how I am about my career, how selfish I am with my time and how I want to do things when I want to do them. Not to mention that I want to have a child without the complications of a man. I still feel that a man is not needed to raise a child, especially a girl. Monica you and I strongly disagree on that and I really did not want to get into a debate about how a child needs to have two parents to become well-rounded and well-balanced adults."

"Whatever. I always knew that you liked Eryka better than you liked me."

"True, but I love you both the same!" Kim said teasingly in a semi-high pitched voice to return the sentiment Monica had just given her.

"Look Monica, like I said, I told Eryka because I thought she could hold water, but apparently I was wrong. My time is running out and I want to enjoy the ten minutes I have left eating my bran muffin and hot milk before I go to work. I will talk to the two of you later. Love you both. Eryka . . . like you more" Kim's joke hurt Monica's feelings, but before Monica could express her hurt Eryka started with her dreams.

"Kim?" Eryka called.

"Yeah?"

"I had another strong feeling last night."

"Oh come on Eryka with the dreams; nothing is going to happen to me."

"I mean it Kim something really bad is about to happen to you that will change your and our lives for the rest of our lives. Just don't do anything from the ordinary and change your schedule up some."

"Now Eryka, how could I not do anything from the ordinary AND change my schedule?"

"You know what I mean. If you leave the building call one of us until you get where you're going, please Kim, I am really scared."

"Stop it Eryka, Monica said, you're scaring me now." Truth be told, she was scaring Kim too. Eryka's dreams have only been wrong once and that was because she got the twins mixed up, or did she?

"Don't worry your pretty little head off, I promise I will call either of you if I leave my office, this also means going to the Lady's room and water fountain."

"Kim you don't drink from the water fountain and you really shouldn't make light of Eryka's dreams they have saved our butts a lot." Kim now knew for certain she hurt Monica's feelings because

Mechelle Davis

she was defending Eryka. Kim made a mental note to talk to Monica later.

"They're not dreams," Eryka retorted.

"You just called them dreams!" Monica shot back.

"No I didn't, I called them . . ."

"Then what are they?" Kim asked cutting off Eryka's rebuttal.

"Feelings . . . . Intuitions . . . Premonitions . . . . Ugh whatever they are Kim isn't important, they're telling me your next move would map out all of our lives, test our friendship and it won't be for the good. More importantly, I am not sure if WE will survive this one." There was dead silence on the phone. Eryka continued, "So please Kim, all I am asking is that you keep one of us informed if your schedule happens to change, at least for a little while, Okay? We are just getting some normalcy back in our lives, promise me that you will call either of us if your schedule changes!"

"Okay, Okay enough already, I have already promised that I will let either of you know if my schedule changes. Okay? Why do we have to have the same conversation every morning? Look I have to go I can't even enjoy my breakfast. Bye ladies, move in one direction." Kim hung up leaving Eryka and Monica on the phone.

"Monica you know that she is not going to call either of us if her schedule changes."

"Yeah, I know."

"Get ready for a short life."

"Come on Eryka it can't be that bad whatever is going to happen to her!"

"Us . . . !"

"What?" Monica questioned for clarity, secretly hoping that she heard Eryka wrong.

". . . Whatever is going to happen to us, Monica, you couldn't even imagine. Remember what happened to us the last time Kim did not listen, the hell we went through for over nineteen years, what we lost and the secrets we have to keep for the rest of our lives? I don't think I could forgive her this time."

"Eryka, don't you really mean, you don't think she could forgive you this time? All we went through was not at the hands of Kim but that emotional con-artist and you. You committed the ultimate betrayal and she has not once said anything about it. Give her the

Mechelle Davis

same kind of love she gives you. Because if you don't and you hurt her like you did last time I won't be able to forgive you for sure this time especially since I still don't trust you. You must think that I have forgotten that it wasn't just Kim you betrayed; you sacrificed me and it is because of Kim that we are even speaking." The silence on the phone, over the dial tone made the sister's extremely uncomfortable. Eryka replaced the receiver on its base and Monica appeared in the doorway adjacent to the den looking down the hall that made a clear path to the kitchen to reinforce her warning.

Kim stood in her kitchen visibly shaken by what Eryka just said. Briefly thinking about the last nineteen years of their lives and all they had lost. Taking a deep breath, Kim said out loud to give herself the encouragement she needed, "I am not going to let one sick bastard direct my life again. I am going to work and on with my life, I've learned how to fight back, I am stronger now, definitely made up of stronger stuff. Hell I teach self-defense, silently Kim repeated to herself, 'move in one direction, move in one direction, move in one direction. Sighing with determination Kim nervously walked toward the door of her rented company condo, move . . . in one . . . direction!" Kim opened the door, allowing the cool morning Pennsylvania air to greet her, stepped over the threshold and closed the door behind her, stood on her porch, put her head to the sky, shoulders back with a smile and took a deep breath . . . "Bring it on!"

Eryka met Monica half way down the long hallway a gentle and cautious determination in her steps. Carefully choosing her words because she knew though Kim's wounds may have scabs Monica's were still very fresh. "Seriously Monica all blame aside, considering where we come from and what we have loss I don't think that I will be able to forgive Kim this time."

"Seriously Eryka it's impossible for me to put blame aside, but Kim some-how managed to and took on the blame herself. She still unfairly feels some responsibility for the hell we've been through so I don't think that she would be able to forgive herself, she heard you."

"Yeah, she heard me, but will she listen?"

Irritation and contempt now erupted in Monica's voice, "Yes she will listen. I have to go, love you. Move in one direction!" Eryka did not feel that Monica's words of affection were sincere, but routine and that hurt more than anything, more than if she had not said it at all.

"Love you too, Monica. Move in one direction! Monica?"

"What!"

"I really do love you and I hope that we could one day work through this." Monica did not respond though she extended Eryka the courtesy to stand and listen to what she had to say, but Monica's body language told Eryka that she did not have much time to speak her peace, then without a word Monica opened and closed the door behind her.

Sitting in traffic frustrated, Kim could not get what Eryka said off her mind. Her palms became sweaty and the cool car felt sweltering hot as she looked at the next exit ramp half mile ahead. "I will not let him win, I will not let him win," she kept repeating and crying to herself and gripping the steering wheel of her new black BMW, as traffic began to slowly move. Kim cautiously reached out to turn off the heat she never turned on. She could feel the panic setting in. "I can beat this, I will beat this . . . I will beat him, again taking a deep breath . . . . I have to!" Kim looked in her rearview mirror and froze . . . "oh my GOD not again she screamed!"

She stood behind her mother afraid because after all the years of her mother's boyfriend looking at her and touching her he had just gotten bold. She prayed that all the times her mother said she loved her she would prove it right now.

What could you possibly see in her, she's only nine?" Eryka's mother asked.

"But she is not built like a normal nine year old, look at her she is already tall as you with breast and a back side that would make GOD forget he created it!"

"Forget it, you are not touching my baby, you are not taking her innocence, I will leave you alone before I let you do that!"

"So be it!" James said in a successful attempt to call Angela's bluff.

"Wait-wait-wait, how could you look at her like that, you raised her since she was six months, her whole life?!"

"Yeah I did, but it doesn't change the fact that she is not my daughter and I am a man, I have needs, all I want to do is touch her, I won't hurt her, I promise."

Eryka watched the man she called Daddy plead with her mother to take her innocence. Plead the way he had so many times when her mother came home from work and caught him in bed with another woman. Just as he did all those times he put his hands on her mother's caramel face and ran his hand through her beautiful, thick, long brown hair and Eryka knew what was coming.

"Baby, you know I love you and nothing will ever change that. You know how I am, I like to try new things" he said as he lustfully looked at Eryka, kissing her mother on the lips while never taking his eyes off her. Eryka could see him salivating when she allowed her eyes to drop to avoid his stares and they accidently fell halfway between his seven foot one inch frame at the large bulge. Her heart dropped; she knew what that bulge was, the girls in school told her when nasty Thomas caught one in his pants after Tiffany let him touch her boobs. Her thoughts were interrupted when her mother turned to her and stroked both sides of her face, and playfully put a phantom strand of hair back in place Eryka knew what her mother was about to say.

Eryka's knees grew weak and she could not move, her legs became lead and her feet cemented where she stood. She could not believe her mother lied all those years with such sincerity. She thought to herself, *"She never loved me at all."* Tears welled in the ducts of her eyes and her attempt to close them before they fell was fruitless.

Wiping her tears her mother gently kissed her cheek and sincerely looked her in the face, "Look baby all he wants to do is touch you, I will be right here, I won't let him hurt you, I promise. Just let him touch you," she said. Eryka could hear a greater desperation in her mother's voice than there was fear in her. "Just do this for Mommy just this once, she continued as she reached behind her, took James' rough hand and placed them on her breast. See Mommy's here, I won't let him hurt you, I promise."

Angela stepped aside and James forward as he bent down and slid his tongue in Eryka's mouth. She could not see where her mother went because her eyes were closed hoping this would end soon. Then she felt her mother behind her removing the ponytail holder she had managed to squeeze her long, thick hair into, Eryka could not believe this was happening. James slid his hands under her shirt and with one hand unclasped her bra; she knew he heard her heart pounding because she heard it herself. Her mother said nothing when he put his mouth on her chest. Freeing his hand he tried to slide it down her pants. Eryka pushed him away, ran out the back door to her Aunt Jessie's house. Her mother's words reverberating in her head.

"I won't let him hurt you. I won't let him hurt you."

There was nothing James could have done to her that day or in a lifetime that would have hurt her more than her mother just did.

Mechelle Davis

Eryka burst through the kitchen door of her Aunt Jessie's house out of breath, faced soaked with tears and sweat from running in devastation through the hot sun. She could not tell her Aunt fast enough what had just happened to her. She just knew her aunt would not believe her because even though it happened to her she could not believe it.

"Girl what is wrong with you?" Aunt Jessie asked in a way that showed no concern, just a seemingly routine reaction to someone bursting in her door, out of breath and scared to death.

"Momma and, Momma and . . ."

"Momma and what?" Aunt Jessie asked with mild concern.

"Momma, Momma and James tried to . . . she wanted me to . . . he, he, wanted to . . ."

Aunt Jessie did not want to hear the sordid details of her niece's trauma she knew there was nothing she could do, James still had many secret over her head and the devastation of them getting out would be greater than the devastation Eryka was experiencing. She hoped that her niece would forgive her one day. She tried to choke down her tears as she forever surrendered her nieces trust and admiration.

"Your mother called before you got here she said when you arrive to send you back home, because you were full of lies. What lies are you telling now?"

Eryka told her aunt everything just the way it happened and she did not believe her, at least the words she spoke proved she did not believe her, but the tears in her eyes said otherwise. Aunt Jesse reached over into her freshly folded laundry basket, ran the thick cloth under cool water and cleaned Eryka's face. Eryka was relieved; she knew the routine before her aunt gave her solutions to all her problems.

"Now this is what I want you to do." Aunt Jessie said securing Eryka's cheeks like a sandwich slightly squeezing, gently shaking her head side to side, just before she kissed her on the lips. Only this time she did not kiss her on the lips.

". . . are you listening?"

"Yes." Eryka replied as she looked at her soon loss hero.

While Aunt Jessie shined Eryka's face and put her hair back into a ponytail she said, "I want you to go back home—Eryka's heart sank—and do what your mother tells you to do, and stop making up tales, you are going to get somebody in trouble." Aunt Jessie washing Eryka's face was pointless because fresh tears replaced the old. Eryka was devastated . . . Devastated and alone.

"What am I going to do? I have no place else to go"

She went back home, took the long way, three times and when she got there James was gone, her Momma was sitting in the corner crying and to Eryka she didn't look the same. The beauty she had seen all her life was gone along with the security and comfort a child seeks and feels with their parents.

"Come here girl!" her mother said in a tone that Eryka had never heard her mother use with her before. When she got to her, she reached up and grabbed Eryka's shirt in an attempt to pull her down to her level, for more reasons than one Eryka vowed she will never stoop to Angela's level. Eryka steadied herself and her mother responded by using her shirt and arm as leverage to pull herself up. Staggering to her feet her mother stepped back with her finger pointed at Eryka, another first for her three times over, she was drunk!

"I will not lose my man because of you."

Eryka turned her back to her, a first for Eryka. Her mother continued with Eryka's ponytail gripped tightly around her hand pulling her backwards shorting her height about a foot and Eryka felt her mother's hot liquored breath on her neck and the side of her face.

"When he comes back you will do whatever he says and you will not tell anyone, do . . . you . . . un . . . strand me?"

Eryka did all she could do to nod yes but the hold her new mother had on her hair restricted her movement. A new kind of anger swelled up in her as she took her drunken mother's hand and distorted her fingers to loosen the grip on her pony tail.

"Let go Angela!" Eryka saw the hurt on her mother's face as she towered over her she wanted her to feel what she was feeling. "Yes Angela, after what you were willing to let him do to me, you will always to be Angela to me." Eryka said in a tear and contempt-filled voice as she walked away. The night and the days after were long and getting use to the new drunken woman of the house scared Eryka, the unexpected terrified her. James never came back, at least while they were at home, and Eryka's mother never let her forget it. Angela went to work one Friday, where she did well as an IT Director, and when she came home everything was gone. For the next three and a half years Angela treated Eryka as if she hated her for James leaving and taking all of her things with him. She sold Eryka to all her new boyfriends and beat her at night because they desired Eryka and not her. After awhile Eryka began to like the feelings her sexual Dads gave her especially when they did what Angela called 'The Big Girl Thing.' Angela taught Eryka how to move, what sounds to make and when and how to fake an orgasm. Eryka's mind drifted during lesson 101, "How to Fake an Orgasm.' She learned early on that she is highly climatic and so did her sexual Dad's, it was their little secret, a secret that made Eryka's young, tight body a little bit more attractive. Angela's voice became loud and clear as Eryka briefly redirected her attention to her and just as quickly Eryka thoughts drifted as she reflected on that horrible day in the kitchen, *"I believe this is really why Angela screamed at night."* She thought back to the time when Angela and James were together. *"I mean, how could she not when something feels so dam good?"*

By the time Eryka was 12 she was a different person, even she didn't recognize herself. She had had two abortions and 10 diseases. Many of her sexual Dads refused protection, demanded none be used. Eryka became an expert at triple-sex and led a life that no one would ever suspect. She had to maintain the look and act of innocence, her honor roll status and the normal, or close to normal life of a happy, well-adjusted preteen. It was kind of fun to her because she was able to create the perfect home-life and the perfect parents. The hard part was holding on to friends after so many excuses of why they could not come over her house.

It wasn't long before Eryka grew to look forward to the meetings Angela set up for her. She could not wait until school was out many times she knew who she was meeting even before she made it home; at eleven years old she had regulars. Eryka thought this was the way of life for her at least she had convinced herself to believe that it was until she met a new friend.

It was May 17, 1989 Wednesday morning, the sun was shining, the warm breeze felt good blowing through the window, the birds were singing and dancing on the branches of the trees and Eryka could hear the laughter of the twins next door as they piled into their parent's truck to be taken to school; even with all that beauty Eryka's day started ugly. Eryka forced her feet to the floor, sat up on the edge of the bed, her eyes still closed as she thought back to what felt like an eternity ago to when her mother would wake her up with smiles, kisses and the smell of breakfast in the air. Only now it was the alarm clock that woke her up and the only smell that was in the air was sex, sweat, and stale hate. The only smile she sees is life laughing at her for thinking that there is something better than this.

Glancing at the clock Eryka quickly stood to her feet, body aching and tired from the strange positions one of her regulars made her tort her body into. Quickly showering and dressing equally as fast, Eryka knew better to check the refrigerator for anything to eat. She grabbed the overstuffed gym bag and the book bag she had hidden in the front closet. Her Daddy's did not want any trace of her adolescence in view as if that would change the fact she's young enough to be their daughter or granddaughter. She closed the blood stained door behind her, never bothering to lock it she walked off the porch and never looked back.

Eryka stopped at the Sugar Shack halfway into her four block walk to the bus stop for chili cheese fries and a Hawaiian punch. Like clockwork, just as she arrived at the spot where the bus met she saw the loud, yellow breadbox turn the corner. She put her breakfast in her book bag and worked her way to the curb. She wanted to be one of the first to load so that she could claim her seat in the back, scarf down her breakfast and catch a nap. Eryka stepped on the bus and was greeted by the sign that displayed without words, a circled hotdog, soft drink and fries with a line through the middle. Flopping down in the seat in the last row of the bus behind the driver, Eryka took out her breakfast, loaded the chili cheese fries with ketchup and salt and ate quickly, but slowly. By the time she finished and looked up she saw anorexic Annie staring at her whispering to a friend but quickly ceasing her chatter when her eyes met Eryka's. Anorexic Annie began quickly fixing the blonde hair she took pride in, not out of vanity but of nervousness for making eye contact with Eryka.

Eryka slide down in her seat, positioning her pony tail to one side for comfort, she clutched her book bag, leaned her head against the window and quickly fell asleep. The forty-five minute ride felt like five minutes when she heard the bus brakes squeal the bus shake as

Mechelle Davis

it rode over the big, yellow school zone speed bumps and come to a jolting squelching halt. She kept her eyes closed as the kids rustled to get off the bus to beat the bell. She decided she would claim the opposite position to when she loaded the bus; this would give her the few extra minutes she wanted—needed to knap.

Eryka had not realized that she had fallen asleep again until the bus driver called her name in a tone as not to scare her. She slowly opened her eyes to a massively built, attractive man standing before her firmly giving direction to wake up and get off his bus, then admonishing her for ignoring his big red sign and eating on his bus. Eryka followed his eyes to the seat and saw her empty containers nicely placed next to her. She liked this man, he looked at and talked to her like a man should look at and talk to a child.

Eryka grabbed her trash, book bag and repositioned her large pony tail to the back of her head. She thought '*I'll get anorexic Annie later.*' When she got off the big, yellow box she saw a girl about her age and there was something about her that caught her attention. Something about her that she recognized immediately that she did not know she missed or wanted until she seen her. The girl seemed to be happy, but sad at the same time. As if she had a good life, but there was a secret that she was keeping, Eryka wanted to be her friend, for the first time she wanted to be friends with someone, allow someone to get close to her, know the real her and Eryka knew that day she saw her that she would tell her all her secrets. She felt she needed a friend, wanted a friend and even from a distance she was perfect!

Monica heard her mother scream again and then glass shatter. "Please, tell me what you want and I will get it, jus . . ." She never finished her pleas when Monica saw the shadow of her body slide across the floor from under her bedroom door. She saw two feet then one, the other was kicking her mother while she lay on the floor, in her forced fetal position protecting her organs. She could not help, her mother told her hundreds of times to stay in her room, but her mother's screams outside her door were different than they were before, Monica felt she had to do something.

She ran out her bedroom with her ice-skate and it was as if her Dad was waiting for her. She caught a left hook across the right side of her face and she felt her entire back half meet the wall with a vengeance, her head hit with a thud, pain shot from the back of her head out of both eyes and blood poured from her nose and mouth. She felt the same light-headed feeling she felt before when her Dad punched her in the stomach and knocked the wind out of her, but this time the room spun and with each spin it was getting dark. She knew what was happening and if she allowed herself to go dark her Mom would be in the dark forever.

She struggled to her feet and just as she stood up her Dad prepared himself to hit her again but Mrs. Hargrove, drove the blade of Monica's ice-skate into his back and it did not faze him. He turned, secured Mrs. Hargrove by the neck, took the ice skate from her and ran the blade of Monica's skate down the side of her face, blood splattered, she screamed and so did Monica at the sight of her mother's blood. Her Dad threw her mother across the room and tried to go after Monica again. Quickly getting to her feet her mother ran toward her father and did the only thing she could do to slow him down, she held on to his leg.

"Run Monica run!" Her mother screamed to her with a fear in her voice that she thought was only in movies. Monica attempted to run but slipped in her mother's spilled blood. Regaining her footing, Monica ran through the living room that connected the entire house, pass the dining room table, through the French doors, down the stairs and out the front door leaving her mother's screams behind, each scream chasing behind her like a dagger hitting her in the back until she was too far to hear. Now they echoed in her mind. Monica ran and ran the two miles, across their farm, pass little Ms. Perfect Hailey's house, pass the spot where little Jon-Jon loss his arm driving, then falling off his father's tractor trailer, across the bridge where she had her first kiss, through the field where old senile Mr. Berkovich laid himself down and died and pass the spot where she get on the bus to go to school—to the neighbor's house at 3 am for the sixth time that month, in her nightgown, no shoes, but this time soaked in her and her mother's blood. She woke up the neighbors pleading for help; "he's killing her." Hurriedly Mrs. Jenningson opened the door to the familiar plea's and began to scream, the blood on Monica made her injuries appear crueler than they were. The words in her head were not escaping her lips as clearly, the right side of her face had swollen severely, partially closing her right eye and swelling her lip.

"Please help me my Dad is beating my mother again, this time it's worse, Dad tried to come after me again and Mom stabbed him in the back with the blade of my ice-skate. Please Mr. Jenningson he's killing her." She added the last part-truthful line for effect because for years Mr. Jenningson has been running to their aid with the promise that he will never get involved again if her Mom continued to stay and or go back. Monica and her mother even stayed with the Jenningson for two weeks so that they would leave her Dad alone. During those two weeks Monica's Dad never called or ever came by to talk or apologize even with his disregard to them, her mother still went back. More horrifying to Monica, her mother asked her father if they could go back home. Monica wanted to stay with the Jenningsons', but her Mom was not willing. Monica felt safe with the Jenningsons' like a child should feel. A picture of security by all definition was not the family she was born into. She was living the shattered dreams of a once happy family.

Mr. Jenningson was a well-built, stocky man in his mid to early forties, with jet-black hair that grayed around his temple, his golden skin made his powder blue eyes jump out from his face. His hands were strong from farming and he always smelled good no matter what time of day it was; like a fresh bar of soap and a mist of cologne. Monica remembered she would have loved to have Mr. Jenningson as her Dad. She would always stop by the Jenningson's house after school because Mrs. Jenningson always had pie and milk ready for her when she arrived. Monica was never hungry she just loved the warm feeling that she felt when she walked in the house. It felt like home, just like the hugs Mrs. Jenningson would give her everyday and Monica would eagerly run into her arms. Mrs. Jenningson for whatever reason could not have kids of her own, which was okay by Monica because somehow God knew Monica would need them. She felt loved when she was with the Jenningsons' it was different from the feeling that she had with her parent's. She knew her parent's loved her, but she could not ascertain if it was because they were her parent's and they felt obligated or if it were because of her.

Monica and her family lived a very comfortable financial lifestyle; according to her friends they were rich. Though all her friend's family farmed Monica's Dad farm proved time and time again to be the most lucrative in the area, in the state of North Dakota. Monica quickly learned early on that being rich with money had nothing on being rich in love.

Mrs. Hargrove did all she could to show Monica love, but the years of beatings had made her timid. When Monica arrived home her Mom had cookies and milk waiting for her, but it wasn't like the Jenningsons', she could smell that Mrs. Jenningson pies and cookies were freshly baked and warm when she bit into them. Her Mom cookies were store bought, made for profit not from love. She ate them anyway because she did not want to hurt her Mother's feelings and she grew pudgy for awhile. Her Dad complained about her pudginess as he did about everything; the only time Monica could remember him smiling was when he was plowing the fields. He became a different man, even more so after his Dad died he started plowing the fields more heavily with a huge smile on his face.

Mechelle Davis

Monica remembered her Dad's eyes even lighting up from time to time. She believed it had something to do with the disappearance of her grandfather's body.

The day before Monica was to say her last goodbye's to her granddad she was sitting at the dining room table looking through the pictures she and her grandfather had taken over the years. Slowly turning each page as to remember the details of each moment the picture captured. She loved her grandfather dearly and even though he had not been the best father to her Dad he was a terrific grandfather to her not because he spoiled her with things, but with love.

Monica heard her mother and father discussing what she thought were funeral arrangements until she heard her Mom asked her Dad, "What are we going to do without a body? Monica needs to say goodbye." Drunkenly her Dad responded, "He don't need no funeral that bastard just gone up and die before I had the opportunity to tell him how I fell, I mean feel; he died out of spite. Now he needs me and to hell with him." Staggering unsteadily on his feet he continued, "As they say in the fertilizer world, he's fertilizer!" Toasting his glass in the air to whatever drunken god her serves. Shortly after the death of his father her Dad started drinking and beating her mother more heavily, as if that were possible, a year later he started beating on Monica. She was nine when he first hit her and eleven the last time she allowed him the opportunity.

Mr. Jenningson passed Monica on to Mrs. Jenningson "Get her cleaned up!" He quickly dressed in his work coverall over his pajama pants, grabbed his shot gun and headed out the door. Monica was scared for her Dad because Mr. Jenningson was angry . . . and big and the years of drinking and self-pity had really abused her Dad's stature and strength. Twenty minutes later in the quiet of the early morning air, even so far away Monica and Mrs. Jenningson heard the blast of what they knew was Mr. Jenningson's shot gun and Monica felt a mixture of happiness and sadness because she knew . . . hoped her father was dead. Mrs. Jenningson dressed and drove their truck to Monica's parent's house only to learn that the gun blast did not take the life of Monica's father but the leg of Mrs. Jenningson's husband. When Mrs. Jenningson arrived the ambulance and police were already there, someone had called when they saw Monica run across the field heading to the Jenningson for help; Mr. Hargrove had become known for beating his family, but the person that called for help did not call soon enough.

As Mrs. Jenningson hurriedly ejected herself from the truck she knew that something was not right she looked back at Monica who was cowering on the other side of the truck Mrs. Jenningson attempted to gather herself before she moved toward the house. Then she saw her husband, exhibiting strength and courage being rolled out on the stretcher with his leg following in what appeared to be a large Ziploc bag with ice. He looked up at Mrs. Jenningson with a smile and said, "Don't worry honey it is not as bad as it looks!" All Mrs. Jenningson could do was hold her husband's hand and cry through a smile that courage timidly hid behind.

Mrs. Hargrove stood in the door of her home beaten, battered and bruised with her arms around her very intact, drunk husband. Through angry eyes and horror Monica stood mortified; she felt so guilty, if only she had not run to them. She blamed her mother because she kept putting up with it and now Mr. Jenningson will never walk right again.

Mr. Hargrove was never punished for attempting to destroy the Jenningson's life because Mr. Jenningson's shot gun was found in the Jenningson house and her Dad, though drunk claimed self-defense. Mrs. Hargrove never told the police what really happened, that Mr. Hargrove was waiting on him at the door with a hammer, invited Mr. Jenningson in, swung the hammer hitting Mr. Jenningson in the arm. When Mr. Jenningson dropped his gun Mr. Hargrove picked up the gun, ordered Mr. Jenningson to stand up. Mr. Hargrove drunkenly saying, "I ought to kill you I have that right you know, but I won't, I promise, but I ought to coming in my house with a shot gun. What if I just shot you in the arm, you think the ambulance would make it waaaaaay out here in time? Slowly swaying the gun he tauntingly asked Mr. Jenningson "What if I shot you in the hand? Put your hand up let me see if I am still a good shot. His words slurring just like his stance if not more.

"You think I could hit just that big toe on your right foot? Well I'm not as good a shot as I used to be I need a bigger target and that right leg looks to be just . . . about . . . the right size. He aimed, drank desperately from his flask, repositioned Mr. Jenningson's heavy shot gun under his arm, pulled the trigger and Mr. Jenningson fell.

Mechelle Davis

Mr. Hargrove stood over Mr. Jenningson with the tip of his boot in the pool of blood that poured out from where Mr. Jenningson's leg used to be. Monica's Dad continued swaying his body, gun and slurring his words, "I have never been good at keeping promises, so I lied, somewhat. Let me see you farm now, coming to my house, with your shot gun, in my business. Always coming over here thinking you are better than me, who do you think you are? Telling my wife to take care of herself as if I can't take care of my own family, let me see you take care of your crops now, how quickly will you run to their aide next time or them to yours now that you need them? Good luck with keeping your family alive, holding on to that farm and that hot ass woman of yours. Now that you're half the man you use to be she won't be around long, tell her to look me up!" Looking over his shoulder with a drunken snarl his words continued to slur. "I've got no use for this one right here, she's just useless. Look at her!" Mrs. Hargrove hurried past her husband silk scarf in hand, kneeled beside Mr. Jenningson and tied the silk scarf around Mr. Jenningson mangled leg as he winced in pain but never let out a sound.

Mrs. Jenningson climbed into the back of the ambulance with her husband as the doors closed Monica shamingly looked up at the departing truck to catch what she thought was a glimpse of hate in Mrs. Jenningson eyes. Monica closed her eyes briefly to wish away what she knew in her heart she saw but wished she didn't. Catching one last look Monica saw Mrs. Jenningson smile slightly letting her know it would be okay. She stood in the middle of the driveway and watched the ambulance until the red lights blurred by her tears, extinguished in the distance.

The sounds of her mother's voice echoed in her head. Monica sweetie come on in . . . Monica . . . Monica . . . Monica . . . Monica! The echo grew closer then there was a hand on her shoulder. The touch felt like the dirty hand of betrayal, immediately after her mother touched her Monica vomited and each time those hands of betrayal touched her she was unable to keep down whatever she had consumed or not consumed. Monica pushed her mother away with the back of her hands and instantly the illness faded.

Pulling herself together Monica walked past her mother without a word, distain in all her being toward her. She walked up the front porch stairs into the house to the loud sounds of her drunken father's snores coming from the recliner in the living room never looking behind her she closed the front door. The smell of the house was putrid as she turned the corner to see the pool of blood where Mr. Jenningson has fallen, the discarded gauzes, rubber gloves and paper seal that came from the bag that contained Mr. Jenningson's leg. The sound of the door gently opening then closing behind her startled Monica and without looking back she continued on to her room, closed the door and placed a chair under the knob, not to keep her father out, but her mother and the insecurities and weakness that came along with her.

Monica lay awake half the night crying, feeling guilty, let down and determined not to be like her mother, to be better and stronger. After a long sleepless night, Monica went to school the next day and days thereafter as if nothing happened. She told her friends and teachers she had a not so uncommon tractor accident. Those who knew her family knew better. Afterschool she would take the long city bus ride to Trinity Hospital, the hospital that could not save Mr. Jenningson's leg, only to learn that the Jenningson's would refuse her visit or at least the visit of anyone with the last name of Hargrove. Monica did not give up, she went everyday for the six weeks Mr. Jenningson was in the hospital and physical therapy learning to walk again with his prosthetic leg.

Six weeks, three days and eighteen hours that is how long Trinity Hospital kept Mr. Jenningson. One day, after school Monica took the long bus ride to learn that Mr. Jenningson had been released that morning. Eagerly she ran to the city bus stop, boarded the bus, took the two hour journey home and ran the two and half miles from the city bus stop to the Jenningson. Anxious and out of breath she excitedly . . . impatiently rang the door bell and no one answered. Monica heard the happy sound of laughter and music through the door. The Jenningson's always played music and danced and laughed and talked and danced and laughed and talked some more. She ran down the stairs and around the back, Mrs. Jenningson always left the back door open for her to let herself in; it was locked. She was being ignored, pushed away and desperation, desperation much like her mother's but totally different set in.

Monica laid her head on the back door. "Please Mrs. Jenningson, Mr. Jenningson let me in, I'm sorry you were hurt. I'm sorry for what my father did to you and I'm sorry that I came to you that night, I didn't know. Please don't push me away, you're all I have. What will I do without you? You guys are the only peace in my world, please, please, please, let me in."

Monica begged as she cried and softly pounded on the door. The music stopped and with much hope in her eyes and heart Monica looked up through the space that the curtains provided to allow her to see in and there stood Mrs. Jenningson in the kitchen staring at the door. Monica could see that she wanted so badly to let her in, but the voice behind her called her attention, she slowly turned away, never looked back, slowly closed the kitchen door and disappeared into another room. The music resumed but louder than before and definitely louder than normal. Monica understood and in loss despair she dawdling walked away.

Monica walked the long way home, around the field instead of through it. The walk was a blur mostly because her tears obstructed her vision as she walked out of routine. At the edge of the driveway she heard the familiar sound of shouting and screaming. She went around back to enter into the kitchen in an attempt to get to her room unnoticed. Little did she know the fight this time was about Mrs. Hargrove's store-bought cookies and Monica's weight gain. Monica's plan to go unnoticed failed; Monica opened the door and to her surprise there were her parent's, her father that is, screaming at her mother who instantly seen the deep sadness in her daughter's face. Ignoring the fact that the screaming man behind her could turn violent at a moment's notice Mrs. Hargrove, in hurried pace went to Monica in an attempt to console her daughter. With deep sincerity in her voice her mother asked, "Sweetie, what's the matter?"

Mrs. Hargrove's concern for her daughter was interrupted by the pain in the back of her head. Mr. Hargrove had fiercely grabbed a handful of bronze, wind-blowing hair and angrily slammed Mrs. Hargrove to the floor.

"Forget that bitch, don't you hear me talking to you!?"

Mrs. Hargrove did not respond the assault rendered her unconscious. Monica's father continued to scream at her unconscious mother and when he noticed she was not moving her kicked her; out of anger or to learn if she was being deceitful. She didn't move and out of fear and disbelief Monica didn't either. For the first time she saw a brief glimpse of fear in her father's eyes. He quickly recovered from the show of something human, went to the refrigerator, retrieved the pitcher of ice cold apple juice and brashly threw it in her mother's face; still she did not move. Monica looked at her father in disbelief as she ran to her mother's aide, shaking and calling her mother's name only to get the same response as the apple juice. Monica's father stood frozen in his steps as she ran for the phone to call 911, the call was answered quickly.

"911, what is your emergency?"

"MY MOTHER IS NOT RESPONDING, PLEASE HELP ME!"

"What happened to your mother?"

"MY FATHER ASSAULTED HER AND NOW SHE WON'T WAKE UP. PLEASE HELP ME!"

"Put your face to your mother's mouth and nose. Is she breathing?"

"I DON'T KNOW, I CAN'T TELL!"

"The ambulance is on its way, but I need you to relax and do a couple of things for me."

"OKAY, WHAT?"

"I need you to find a mirror and put it to your mother's nose, can you do that?"

"YES!" Frantically, Monica reached for her purse, pulled out the black mirror with the colorful flowers Mrs. Jenningson had given her and put it to her mother's nose.

"OH MY GOD SHE'S NOT BREATHING. WHAT DO I DO? DAD DO SOMETHING!"

"What's your name?"

"MONICA. SHE'S . . . SHE NOT BREATHING, SHE ISN'T BREATHING!"

"Monica I am going to need you to perform CPR until help get's there, okay?"

"WHERE ARE THEY? MY MOTHER IS DEAD, PLEASE HELP HER!"

"Monica you mother is not dead and we're both going to help her. You are going to save your mother's life. I need you to relax and listen to what I am saying. You need to give your mother air if you don't she will die. Now listen, pinch her nose with one hand between your pointy finger and thumb, with the other hand, tilt her head back and put your mouth over her mouth, making sure no air escapes and blow." Monica put the phone on speaker and did as the operator instructed.

"OKAY I DID THAT!"

"Did her chest rise?" Monica pinched her mother's nose again and blew into her mouth.

"NO IT DIDN'T, NOTHING HAPPENED, she cried as she screamed MOM PLEASE!"

The operator yelled quietly over the speaker phone and over Monica's panic. "Monica . . . Monica. I need you to do it again, this time blow twice and then find the dip in the middle of her chest, clasp your fingers, lock your elbows and press down two inches, bout 30 times, tilt her head back, hold her nose, cover her mouth with yours then blow two times if her chest does not rise do the compressions again. Got it?"

"I GOT IT. I REMEMBER THIS. WE DID SOMETHING LIKE THIS IN SCHOOL LAST YEAR. WAIT A MINUTE." Monica did what she was told with new confidence adding two additional breaths combined with what she remembered and begged her mother to breath between breaths.

The operator came over the speaker phone, "How is she doing Monica?"

"WHEN I BLOW AIR IN THERE IS A WHISTLING SOUND THAT COMES OUT BUT SHE'S STILL NOT BREATHING. SHE'S STILL NOT BREATHING. WHAT DO I DO NOW?"

"I need you to check and see if there is anything in her mouth. I need you to open your mother's mouth, look in and if you see anything, anything at all, use your pointing finger and pull it out!"

"THERE'S SOMETHING WHITE IN THERE!" Monica put her finger in and pulled it out. She shook and repelled her throwing the object across the room as if it were hot coal. "IT'S HER TOOTH, HE KNOCKED HER TOOTH OUT!" She screamed as she looked back at her father.

"Is there any blood in her mouth?"

Mechelle Davis

"NO. NO BLOOD!"

"Start the steps I told you all over again. Pinch her nose with one hand, blow two quick breaths and do the chest compressions." Monica began to panic again.

"SHE'S STILL NOT BREATHING. DAD HELP ME! . . . HELP ME PLEASE!"

"Monica, you can do it, you can save your mother's life, just do the compressions just as we discussed you're doing fine."

"IT'S BEEN SO LONG, SHE'S . . . SHE'S . . ."

"She's depending on you Monica, you can do it, do the steps again. Come on you can do it!

Monica continued, but the breaths were not as powerful. Monica was weak from panic, fear, and the failed attempts to save her mother's life and then her mother coughed.

"SHE'S BREATHING, I DID IT, WE DID IT! SHE'S BREATHING!"

Mr. Hargrove heard the operator sigh in relief saying, "Thank you GOD"

"Great, I knew you could. Now roll her over on her side to help her breath. Is that sirens I hear?"

Through her sobs Monica responded, "Yes, the ambulance is finally here."

"Good when they get in the house I want you to give one of the Paramedics the phone. Can you do that?"

"Yes. Yes I can do that, thank you!" Monica said as she repeated to herself, she's breathing, she's breathing. Oh my God you almost killed her." She glared up at her father.

The paramedics entered the house through the front door and worked their way through to the kitchen. Monica handed the first Paramedic she saw the phone and attempted to console her mother who was now coughing heavily and drooling some kind of thick mucus. The second Paramedic yelled almost immediately, "she's going into shock!" Monica didn't know what that meant, but in the hasty way they moved she knew it could not have been good. She looked at her father who was now sitting at the kitchen table with disbelief and regret on his face. Monica walked over to him and he mistook that as her attempt to console him. Instead she said, "You almost killed her, just like you did Grandpa and put him out there in that field. Her father looked surprised and neither acknowledged nor denied Monica's claims.

What are you trying to do, kill us all? You wouldn't even help me save her life. I will *never* forgive you for this!" Monica did not notice the police standing in the kitchen until one called her father's name, Richard Hargrove?'

"Yes?"

"You are under arrest for the attempted murder of your wife, Madeline Hargrove. Please turn around, "You have the right to remain silent, anything you say can and will be used against you in a court of law. You have the right to have an attorney present now and during any future questioning, if you cannot afford an attorney, one will be appointed for you free of charge. Do you understand your rights as I have explained them to you?"

"Yes, I understand them."

Monica looked at her father feeling vindicated because now he looked like the helpless one. The other officer caught Monica's attention as they rolled her mother out with needles and cords coming from her nose and arms. Monica was consumed with anger, it would be the second time within two month her father would have put someone she loved in the hospital in serious condition; at least this time he will pay.

Startled by the officers voice the officer asked, "Young lady is there anyone we can call to come pick you up? If not, I am going to have to take you to the children's center until we can find you suitable care?" Monica knew there was no one she could call, but it did not stop her from thinking about the Jenningson'.

"Can I ride to the hospital with my mother and call my aunt from there. I want to make sure my Mom is alright?" The officer looked at the Paramedic for the okay.

"Sure but when we arrive we have to call someone to be with you. Okay?"

"Okay." Monica knew she had no one, but this would give her a little more time to figure something out, all she knew is that she was not going to a foster home for any length of time. Thankfully her mother became lucid in the ambulance. As the ambulance pulled up in the emergency entrance, Monica noticed, her fourth grade teacher Mrs. Taylor standing there waiting for the doors to open. She ran to

Monica as if she thought she was hurt and relieved to learn she was alright.

"Mrs. Taylor, what are you doing here?"

"Your Dad called me and told me that you needed someone and here I am. He said you needed to be with an adult until this small misunderstanding is all straightened out."

Monica knew who she was, the kids taunting was true, and didn't like her there pretending to care, while her mother fought for her life. Mrs. Taylor made herself scarce when they began to lower her mother from the emergency truck. Monica didn't look back as she trotted behind the gurney that wheeled her mother down the hall and through the doors that read, 'DOCTORS AND PATIENTS ONLY BEYOND THIS POINT' and like Houdini there she was again. Mrs. Taylor put her hands on Monica's shoulders and gently steered her away from the doors. She handed her a fruit punch and sat in the waiting room with her. She never asked any questions just kind of gave Monica her space. Two hours later the doctor appeared in the waiting room.

"Is the family for Melinda Hargrove still here?" Monica immediately jumped up and rushed over to the doctor, "I am Madeline Hargrove's daughter, how is she, is she going to be okay?"

The doctor looked at Mrs. Taylor who gestured for him to speak directly to Monica.

"She is going to be fine. She had another seizure and I suspect that she will have them off and on for the remainder of her life, but they will be manageable with medication."

"What do you mean another seizure? My mother doesn't have seizures."

"She does now, the trauma from the head injury brought on the seizures, which again she will have the remainder of her life. As time progress she will learn the triggers of her seizures and manage them with medication. But for now her throat is a little sore and will be for about a week because it sounds like a piece of her denture broke off and lodged itself in her throat. I want to keep her here for a couple of days for observation, but I expect a full recovery." The doctor smiled down at Monica, "Do you have any questions?"

"Can I see her?"

"Yes, but only for a moment, like I said she had a seizure and she is pretty wiped out. Now I want to warn you, her head is bandaged.

Mechelle Davis

It is not as bad as it looks the bandages are there to hold the cold compress on the back of her head. She has a pretty bad bump and we removed her plate."

"Plate, what plate?"

"Your mother has a plate in the front and a tooth from that plate broke off. We removed the remainder of the plate so she may look a little different to you, but I promise you she is much better than she appears."

"What happened to her front teeth?"

"Tooth and I am not sure Little Miss, perhaps you can ask your mother when she is feeling up to it. Come on I'll take you to her." Monica followed behind trying to figure out when her mother got fake teeth, she's so young.

She walked into the room lined with strangers and was led to bed six. When she pulled back the curtains it was just as the doctor said, she looked bad. Monica almost did not recognize the once visually flawless dark-skinned woman with hazel brown eyes as she gasped. The doctor did not warn her about her mother's two swollen eyes.

The doctor put his hands on Monica's shoulder. "I promise you she isn't as bad as she looks. The swelling is from the trauma to her head, but she will be fine, you have my word." The doctor felt more compelled to be honest with Monica, to him she act more like an adult than a child, he knew she could handle the truth as he recognized that her childhood days ended a long time ago.

Monica smiled up at the doctor she appreciated his honesty despite her age. She stepped inside the curtain, took her mother's hand and through tears gently called out to her.

"Momma? Momma, are you awake?"

The grip on Monica's hand tightened and a smile came to her mother's face, she slowly turned her head and her blood-shot eyes met Monica's.

"Have we had enough yet? Are we going back? We don't have to go back Momma!" Monica pleaded as she sobbed.

Her mother shook her head no and Monica briefly displayed a smile for what she thought was her mother saying she had had enough.

"I love him. Maybe this will force him to get help. I don't want to be without him." She said as the swollen lip and missing tooth provided a passage way for the tea kettle sound to accompany her words. Monica pulled her hand back as if she were touching hot coal. She starred at her mother in disbelief and disgust and then turned and walked away. She heard her mother calling her name in a tired whisper, but Monica did not answer instead she whispered to herself, *I've had enough!*

Mrs. Hargrove was in the hospital for fourteen days, five days seizure free before she was released. Monica did not know her mother had been visited by the police and she had dropped all charges. Mrs. Hargrove felt two weeks in jail was enough for her husband to realize the magnitude of what he had done to her. Her mother took a cab directly from the hospital to the jail and bailed her husband out. Mrs. Taylor took Monica home the following night after her mother's release to pick up fresh cloths where she found her parent's sitting eating dinner. Neither had bothered, especially her mother, to come get her from the outdated woman.

Monica could not believe her eyes as she stood frozen in the doorway of the kitchen starring at her mother who quickly removed herself from her chair and ran to hug Monica who rejected her affection.

"How could you get him out of jail after what he has done to you? He tried to kill you!"

"Monica honey, no he didn't it was an accident."

"Are you crazy, he wants you dead, just like Grandpa? Mom if he didn't try to kill you, why wouldn't he help me save your life?"

"He panicked Sweetie; he didn't know what to do."

"Neither did I, but here you stand and with him. What were you going to do, leave me with his mistress and her husband and go on with your lives just the three of you?!" Monica shot a disgusted look back at Mrs. Taylor.

Her parent's paused as well as Mrs. Taylor, shocked that Monica knew about the affair between her and her Dad.

"No Monica honey no, we needed to talk some things through before we brought you home. We both know some things have to change and we both want those changes."

"Are you insane, he tried to kill you and you put yourself back in danger by being here alone with him? What if he had done something to hurt you again and I wasn't here, your stupidity and his 'panic' could cost you your life and I would not have gotten the chance to say goodbye, again. Mom he doesn't love you and I hate that you feel so alone and lost inside that you don't see that or don't want to. He tried to take your life and I gave it back to you and you chose him to come home and left me with his mistress." Monica said sobbing.

"Monica it wasn't like that. It wasn't like that at all."

"It sure looks like that." Monica was crushed and could not believe that her mother just left her out there. She sighed as she wiped her tears, and in that moment she truly decided to give up.

"Look Mom you were just released from the hospital and I don't want to stress your day so I am going to get some things and go back to Mrs. Taylor's for a couple more days to give you two time to work things out, Okay?"

"Okay Sweetie. I love you."

Monica thought. *How?* That was two weeks, six days and fourteen hours ago that she last seen her mother and breakfast the following morning that she last seen Mrs. Taylor.

Monica went to school as usual and she was grateful she had met a friend walking across the courtyard coming from one of the buses that brings the city kids that are too far too walk. She saw her get off what looked to be an empty bus it was the huge, thick ponytail that caught her attention then her. Like Monica she had a sense of sadness and loneliness that she covered with a smile, unlike Monica she stayed to herself, but everyone knew her in a positive way. They met at the walkway just before entering into the school. Monica spoke first, "Hey."

Eryka replied, "Hey, you new here?"

Monica smiled, "No this is my second and last year, Are you new here, I have never seen you before."

Eryka looked down at Monica, "No this is my second and last year too." The two remained quiet for a moment and then started talking again it was something about one another that made them want to keep talking.

"How old are you," Monica asked

"Eleven and a half."

How old are you?"

"Eleven and a half, When is your birthday? Monica questioned.

"June 16, 1977."

Mechelle Davis

"When is yours?"

"June 30, 1977."

The two smiled, it was as if they were long lost sisters separated at birth and from day one of meeting each other they told one another everything. They kept talking over each other as the relief of their secret lives spilled out, they cried, hugged, laughed Monica needed her that day and Eryka needed Monica too. For the first time Eryka had shared the secret get-away she found on the abandoned side of the school with someone else.

The two settled into the quiet of their secret hide-a-way and Eryka told Monica about the last time she will ever see her mother, about the night before she came to school. Her mother sent her to the store for cigarettes and her daily lottery tickets and when she got home her mother was gone, but there was a 200 pound man waiting for her. There was something familiar about him but, the smell that emitted from him was unforgettable and unforgivable. The years of abuse had matured Eryka and in a calm, demanding manner that showed no fear she asked, "Where is Angela?"

"She had to step out for a moment." The man replied.

"Then why are you here?"

"Don't play shy you know why I am here."

"I don't do anything without Angela being here."

"You're not still on that, are you? I thought we've been through this before." The man replied in a husky voice from the chair.

"Eryka instantly knew who he was."

"James?! It was Angela's boyfriend part of the source for her living nightmare.

"What happened to you? You look and smell awful!" The comment angered him.

"Never mind how I look or smell, get on your knees!"

Throwing her mother's cigarettes on the table, "I know the routine, Eryka replied, I'll be right back." Continuing sharply shouting on her way to her bedroom, "You need to have your money ready by the time I come out of here!" Eryka dressed quickly, returned to the living room usually dressed in the lingerie and hills her mother bought for her sexual Dads. This particular outfit she bought in secret, put it between the box spring and her mattress, took it out periodically to look at it but held on to especially for James. She knew that he would come back and wanted to give him something special. Eryka planned this night for a long time and thus far it was going just the way she dreamt it; minus the odor.

Eryka reentered the living room and immediately re-dimmed the lights James had brightened and used the sexy voice her mother taught her to use. Seductively, "You know James I have been waiting a long time for you to come back, we have not been happy since that day you changed things, the day you stopped wanting to be my Daddy and want to fuck me! I learned that day that Angela loved you and not me, knowledge that I definitely could have lived without. With that knew knowledge and now obvious new skill's come new curiosity. I've wondered about you, what you did to Angela behind that closed door to make her emit screams and moan like that. Can you show me, will you make me scream like that, moan like, cum like that?

James eyes fixed on Eryka's womanly breast as he began to massage his erect penis and slowly walk toward her. Eryka wanted him to stick to the script that he was oblivious to and to ensure that he did before he picked up his right foot again and placed it down she got on her knees and crawled to him her hair falling down her back and behind her arms turned him on. She knew it would, the older men loved when she crawled to them and he wasn't any different. He dropped his pants and she was somewhat turned on, by the size of his erection, but the smell was unbearable. She was appreciative that she had her oral piece in when she took him into her mouth and as he closed his eyes, dropped his head back, took hold of her head and began to screw her mouth and moan from pleasure, she bit down. He screamed and punched and oddly enough, his hitting her turned her on even more than his screams. From the look in Eryka's eyes as she told the story Monica knew Eryka was different from her, Eryka's experiences had done something to her, created a sink hole in her soul.

James's penis separated from his body, he fell to his knees and while he was screaming Eryka stuffed his dick in his mouth the look of horror was still on his face as she warned him not to talk with his mouth full. She pulled a gun from the front of her lingerie put it to his head while he pleaded through a full mouth; she looked at him for a while and thought about all the things she had been through since he showed his genuine colors. Squatting down and blowing her breath in his face she said, "See I have no love in my heart for you, you have a better chance getting warmth and mercy from this bullet." She pulled the trigger, brain matter covered the very entrance that imprisoned her so many years ago and the same entrance that just set her free.

When Angela returned home, half hour later, there were police and yellow tape everywhere. Eryka was sitting in the ambulance with a blanket around her concealing her victory lingerie under a T-shirt, jogging pants and gym shoes, her years of practice to play innocent for her sexual Daddies finally paid off. She told the police that her mother went to the store and she heard glass break while she was in the bathroom when she came out 'that man' was in the house and made her crawl to him to perform oral sex. Her mother kept a loaded gun under the coffee table for protection and while she was doing what he ordered she knew that her only chance of surviving was killing him so she bit down, reached under the table for the gun, he kept hitting her but she did not let go until 'it' separated from his body. When he fell to his knees he reached for her and she shot him in the head.

Angela stood not recognizing the monster she created, but she dare not poke a hole in her story because that meant disaster for her. Instead she played the loving concerned mother who was just devastated by her young daughter's experience and Eryka allowed her. When they returned from the hospital Angela was very different almost as if she were afraid of Eryka and Eryka liked it. Eryka knew and admitted to herself that she would eventually hurt Angela, the hate and resentment ran too deep so she told Monica that the night before was her last night with Angela.

Monica told Eryka about her Mom, Dad and the Jenningson's and she knew she was never going back. Her mother was not the person she wanted to grow and become and if she stuck around it would be an up-hill battle on roller-skates to prevent that from happening. Months went by and Eryka's mother left her alone, she allowed her to do whatever it was that she wanted for obvious reasons, but Monica's mother was not so relaxed. After Monica did not go back to Mrs. Taylor's house for two days after school friends told her that Mrs. Taylor took the rest of Monica's things home to her mother and warned Mrs. Hargrove to leave Monica alone because she did not want to be found and it was best that she wasn't. This was a failed attempt to punish Monica for telling Mrs. Taylor's husband all about her and her Dad. Monica's mother and the Jenningson's immediately started looking for her. The third night Mrs. Hargrove placed a missing person report. Monica called the Jenningson's to let them know she was alright and to tell them she was never going back. She thanked them for showing her what parent's are supposed to be like and expressed she will forever treasure what they have taught her and one day express the same love and affection to her children. Mr. Jenningson tried to get Monica to return home but all she could think about was why couldn't her mother be like Eryka's mother and just leave her alone?

"I will keep in touch Mr. Jenningson, Mrs. Jenningson, I love you both. Eryka knew what Monica was feeling but did not understand how she could walk away from what she considered a happy home.

"You know Monica; it isn't like your mother sold you whenever she could for whatever reasons I think that she genially and genuinely loves you." Monica did not acknowledge Eryka's comment instead she expressed, "I am happy that the Jenningson's forgave her she really need somebody. Mr. Jenningson said that unfortunately Mom and Dad are still together and that they do not go to her rescue or allow her to come to them for help." Eryka saw the tears of resounding sadness in Monica's eyes but she could not tell if they were for the separation of a friendship or the death of ideal parent's. Monica mourned the shattered dreams of a happy family.

Eryka and Monica became inseparable: they were hungry together and afraid together, homeless together and together they were determined to make it without the small-portion of the parents' they left behind.

Eryka had secretly saved over $8,000 dollars from the money she made and for awhile she and Monica stayed with friends and in hotels that randoms' would get for them. Even with their conservative spending the two exhausted money quickly.

Eryka knew that the only way for the two of them to survive was to go back to her source for money. She persuaded one of her many political sexual Dads into transferring their school and they continued to go to school every day as if things were normal as long as they kept their grades up they did not have a problem; people really didn't pay attention. But things became difficult because Monica's Mom kept pressing the issue and showing up on television with her picture. Eryka suggested she never recognized herself when she dressed up for her sexual Dads so the girls worked on changing Monica's appears. Amazing what a few extra pounds, a little make-up and change of hair style can do. The two laughed at the transformation and Eryka joked, "Now you look like a true Politician, you can go back to being the true you when the cameras are not around."

Contributions from the politician fund eventually ran out, but Monica and Eryka legally founds ways to make money whenever and however they could think of and managed to survive from place to place for seven months, nine days and two nights. Eryka's many sexual Dads were more than happy to help out in whatever way she wanted in exchange for her silence. A $10,000 pay off allowed the two to concentrate on the remaining four months of school and just before their money ran out, the school year ended and the two bought two tickets, boarded a bus that took them as far away from Monica's mother as it could get them; Houston Texas.

T he summer in Texas was challenging, Eryka promised her most prominent political supporter that she would leave him alone until he won his seat, which meant no more money for Monica and her. The two managed to work under the table at small restaurants to support themselves, but when they realized that the money the two of them were making was barely enough to pay for the run-down, roach-infested room, cloth themselves, eat and emergency money to run if needed. Eryka came up with a very old but new plan, an attorney.

Eryka promised herself that not another man would use her. It was her turn to do the using. She contacted her lawyer friend who was all too happy to hear from her until she told him the new terms of their relationship; her silence for his financial support. She knew he would agree especially after she saw a brief excerpt of him on MSNBC competing for a judicial seat. Eryka wasn't greedy . . . at first. She had bigger plans for him she felt he underpaid for her contorting her body they way she did and it was time for him compensate her, retroactively.

His first installment was transportation and unlimited access to his assistant, whom did not like Eryka at all, but she dare not overstep her position, Eryka ensured then assured that the repercussions would be devastating to an aspiring young politician. It was time for Monica to earn her keep if they were to survive.

Eryka explained her plan to her attorney financier and two days later Monica and Eryka were on a plane to the windy city. As planned his assistant retrieved the two from the airport posing as their cousin, screams, hugs and kisses the whole political act.

Mechelle Davis

She took them back to her place and remained with them all day. Her downfall was she was a creature of habit: a warm bubble bath, with a glass of champagne and to save time, a quick nap while she soaked.

Eryka crawled into the beautiful candlelit bathroom, jazz and lilac filling the air, across the pristinely cleaned ceramic floors, retrieved the glass from the platform of the Jacuzzi bathtub and slipped into her glass two of the pills her mother use to give her to help deal with the men crawling in and out of her. The liquid fizzled and Eryka placed her hand over the glass the quiet the sound, swirled the liquid with her finger and timely returned the glass to the exact spot she reached out to retrieve it.

The assistant mistook the effects as tiredness and exited the tub, wrapped the towel around her and tried to make it to her bed. Never making it out of the bathroom Eryka and her attorney financier caught her before she aggressively kissed the floor. He carried her to the bed where a blind folded man, with a well-defined body and tattoos was tied up waiting to do what he was getting paid to do lie their blind-folded, bound, naked and with plenty of drugs. The attorney situated the assistant's naked body across the man in a straddle position, Eryka held his love stick as the assistant was slid down onto him, the act and her moaning turned Eryka on, but disgusted Monica. The assistant's body fell forward onto his chest landing into the powered danger Monica had poured onto him, a perfect set up for the next picture. The camera flashed taking pictures from every angle.

She was repositioned, face on his stomach, with her hand wrapped around his erect love stick, Monica stood naked in a body length mirror with the jeans that had been draped covering her face and Eryka spooned behind her. Just as Eryka began to move her hair from her face the final click of the camera sounded. Monica and Eryka redressed their actor and he was led back to the waiting car by the attorney. The two girls dressed themselves and then the assistant in the comfort wear she had laid out for herself and went to bed. The assistant did not remember the effects of the night before, but she did the following night.

Eryka spent time with her attorney financier and the assistant returned Monica and Eryka to the airport late the following night.

Mechelle Davis

She kissed her cousins goodbye as Eryka handed her a yellow envelope strongly encouraging her not to open it until she arrived home. Disciplined in all she does she followed Eryka's instructions from that moment forward.

Eryka's stature allowed her to drive without being noticed, so Mr. Attorney bought her a new-used car, a new car attracts attention. Eryka and Monica remained in the motel, and were able to put away emergency money and enjoy their summer at the beach, parks and sneaking into the swimming pools of the more upscale hotels. Eryka's Financier loved hearing from her and did what he could to keep the smile in her voice, until he learned of her riskier demand.

School was to start in one week, Monica and Eryka knew that Monica could not attend public school, her mother may find her, nor could she attend a small private school, she could be noticed. She needed a school recognized enough that it would look impressive on their college application, large enough not to be noticed, but small enough to not to be forgotten by teachers, private enough that her mother would not look and expensive enough that the money would do the talking: The Awty International School with 1180 students was perfect. Eryka's lawyer friend was happy to pay for her and Monica, but under two conditions. He sent Eryka a video camera, she knew what he wanted and enjoyed doing what he requested. She had missed him he was warm, gentle, kind, and understanding. Eryka loved talking to him, spending virtual time with him. She liked the way he treated her and made her feel. He had a balance of recognizing she was a child in some instances and making her feel like a woman in so many others. To her this medium did not allow her and his relationship to feel perversely wrong. His give made her want to do more than even she realized.

Eryka's financer had taken care of everything for both: Monica and Eryka, the first day of school was worry free and amazing. He had arranged for the two to be picked up and dropped off in front of the school. The story was their never-married parents were out of the country on business, the two are sisters connected by fathers but different mothers, this somewhat explained their different last names, closeness in their birthdates and the difference in their appearance.

The two quickly established themselves as fun-loving, exciting and friendly in school, but private, very private after school. Their explanation was that the strict rules of their parent's would not allow the company that their magnetic personalities invited. The lack of outside relationships reminded Eryka of her former life and the once friendly girl soon became recognized as standoffish, but still yet a good person with a no non-sense attitude. Monica could see Eryka missed something, but could not determine what it was and never imagined that it would be Angela. Eryka scolded herself for missing something that was so wrong for so many reasons and she knew she could not have for even more reasons. She could not surrender and show her emotions, so she took a page from the assistant's book and took a hot bath, added the music, minus the Lilac and cried heavily and silently by herself as she conceded to his second condition and never contact him again.

Five months into the school year things could not have gone any better if the two had planned it. Their lives were drastically different, but their secrets made their lives similar to the one they left behind until they met Kim whose life was very different from theirs.

Eryka met her first, she was being bullied by the biggest girl in school and she looked so pathetic. There was something about her look; it showed sheltered, but not homely. She looked as if her parent's really cared for her, spoiled her with love and things. The look of her told Eryka that her happiness was not an act; it was genuine and Eryka and Monica admitted they were kind of envious, not of her but the good, happy life her face proved she had even while being bullied.

Suddenly Eryka said to Monica, "Stay here."

Eryka ran across the field, around the maze fence and pushed the one way looking clamp gate that led to the big kids area and grabbed the huge girl by her super fly cut afro, kicked her in the back of her right knee hard enough to get her to the ground but not break anything, pushed her on her back and then put her foot on the big girl's neck. Eryka issued the girl a strong warning, violent enough that afterward the girl reported Eryka, but she never bothered Kim again.

Monica was so proud of Eryka the way she stepped in and beat the hell out of the bully that was twice her in size and weight. Over the months Monica gained a greater respect for Eryka and Monica had grown to depend on Eryka even more, Eryka stepped up every time. Monica wished she could be like Eryka, she was strong-willed, book-smart, and street-smart and she did not let her past or what her mother made her do affect how she looked at herself. Eryka was beautiful, she was tall and thin like a model, she was the darkest brown, the shade right before you get to dark-skinned, with long, thick, wavy, jet-black hair but the anger she tried to hide made her physically strong, her small frame and gentle face and demeanor definitely had many people fooled. Monica loved her dearly, but she was terrified of the evil-anger Eryka held inside. Eryka's face and demeanor was so gentle that the only way to accomplish such an emphatic and sympathetic deception was through years of practice. Monica prayed continually that her soul would never become that dark.

"Thank you, but I could have handled her." Kim said.

"You're welcome, but it didn't look like the other side of your face was up for the task." The two laughed.

"I'm Eryka Bronson she said waving Monica over and this is Monica Hargrove."

"Hi, I'm Kimberly Jenkins, but I go by Kim, I don't like being called Kimberly."

"I thought about waiting until you were finished beating Helga up with your face before I came to introduce myself and my sister, but you were merciless on the girl, I had to jump in." Eryka teased.

"Ha-ha. Kim teased back. She has been after me for the past six month's I don't have a clue of what I did to the girl."

"Well don't worry about it, she will never bother you again, I will . . . we will see to it."

"Thanks. What do you want?" Kim asked

"What do you mean what do we want?"

"Everybody in this school is so self-serving nothing is done for free. So what do you want?"

"Nothing, seriously we just don't like violence, especially when it is clear that the victim is not fighting back."

"Really?"

"Really!

Kim sighed as she fixed her clothes. "You may not want anything now, but I am sure at some point you will and I am not sure if I will be able to pay such a huge debt."

Mechelle Davis

"I was wrong about you Kim Jenkins I pegged you as trusting." Eryka said.

"I usually am until something sets off a red flag, and you two not wanting anything in return are definitely a red flag. I try to listen to my gut feelings my mother said they're GODS whispers, his way of keeping you safe. Monica and Eryka looked at each other and giggled to try and break the uncomfortable stares and silence Kim's comment sparked.

"What, you two don't believe in GOD? The two stared at Kim and did not offer an answer. Kim drew her own conclusion and did not press. Eryka and Monica uh? I heard about you two through my brother he said if ever I met you two to stay away. The two of you are something else. Not in a bad way, but more like out of my league."

"What's your brother's name?" Monica asked

"Cameron. He's my twin older brother; 22 seconds. He knows a lot of people and always knows what he's talking about. I trust him beyond reproach."

Eryka smiled at Kim's choice of words. "Reproach huh? Well Kim if . . . Cameron knew so many people, why didn't he put the word out to that bully that you were not to be messed with?"

"Cam says I need to toughen up that I am too girly to the point that I am helpless outside of him and school."

"We can see how he could come to that conclusion, but you kind of held your own which means your brother is partially always right." Kim shot a semi-infuriated look at Eryka for doubting her brother.

"Yes, I guess you can say that he is *partially always* right. Kim responded picking up her book bag "because together we are completely right."

"Kim I am not reproaching him nor lifting him up, I just want you to know there are . . ."

Monica purposely interrupted Eryka. "We have heard a lot about the Jenkins duo, Monica said as she quickly diverted her eyes toward Eryka and back to Kim, so you are pretty popular here, why are you by yourself?"

"My brother was supposed to meet me here ten minutes ago, instead I ran into that Helga looking girl or should I say she ran into me."

"Well it doesn't look like your brother will be showing up, how about you hang with us?"

Eryka punishingly nudged Monica.

"Okay." Kim said skeptically she had heard a lot about the two, but nothing too bad that she felt she could not deal with and she wanted to know what they were hiding, why they never invited anyone to their home and now they were inviting her. Cameron said they were runaways and homeless and warned Kim to stay away, only saying that a friendship with them would be costly. That the life they created or presented is a lie!

"Where do you live Monica questioned?"

"Why do you ask?"

"I am just wondering if you knew how to catch the bus home since you've been abandoned and all." Eryka asked Kim before she could answer Monica's question. Kim focused her attention on Monica as acknowledgment to answer her question first.

"On the bus, I live a little over an hour from here—too far to walk." Now focusing her attention on Eryka, "I have caught the city bus with my brother but never by myself, can't say that I am comfortable enough to do that just yet."

"How old are you?" Monica asked. Kim glanced in her direction but did not answer.

". . . but we have a driver, if you would give me a second from the Spanish Inquisition I will call him and he will come pick us up."

"Us?" Monica and Eryka asked in unison, turned to one another at the same time, "Pinch, much love, you earned a hug." Kim laughed with them and admired their closeness while they shamelessly hugged each other.

"Anyway Pete is really good at coming when I call so he won't take long. Mom and Dad always tell him to stay close to the school when we get out in case Cameron does one of his disappearing acts like now."

"You have a driver?" Monica asked with a surprised, excited and impressed voice.

"No, my Mom and Dad does, they just make him available to us just in case something goes awry." Before she could finish her statement Pete drove up with the back windows down in the shiniest limousine that either Monica or Eryka had ever seen. As Pete pulled up Kim began to approach the vehicle and asked in a matter-of-fact way, "Where do you two live so Pete will drop us off?"

Folding her arms Eryka replied, "I'm not getting in that!

Kim paused, "Why not?"

"It looks like a hearse!"

Kim's feelings looked hurt and Pete chuckled as he opened the doors for the girls.

"No it doesn't. It looks almost like the one we came to school in." Monica replied in a voice that immediately softened Eryka's jealoused disposition. Monica grabbed her sister by the arm, eagerly passed by Kim and Pete and slide into the back seat. Once in the back seat Monica whispered to Eryka, "Why would you do that?" But before Eryka could answer the question she never intended to answer anyway she heard Kim thank Pete for picking her up.

"Does your parent's know that you are bringing two strangers home?" Pete asked firmly. Initially, the machination was to go to their house, but you know how Mom and Dad are about outside activities on school days so

"No it's a last minute thing and their not strangers to me. Cameron did not show up and they saved my butt, big time. I'll tell you about it later, just don't tell Mom and Dad about Cameron not meeting me or me bringing Monica and Eryka home. I will tell them in my own time. Okay?"

"You got it, but you have until dinner to tell them." Pete said with a smile tapping the tip of Kim's nose with his index finger. "Will I be taking them home later or are their parent's picking them up?" Kim sighed.

"I will tell Mom and Dad at dinner because I want them both to stay the night, so I plan for us to go to school together in the morning."

"Be sure to tell your parent's, don't disappoint me."

"I won't." Kim replied as she slid next to Eryka and then transferred to the seat in front of the two. Pete had the gentlest, most handsome face to be a man of his massive size and stature. Even though he looked as though he could take out an entire football team by himself he still had gentleness in his eyes that attracted people to him immediately, everyone except Eryka who made a mental note, *watch him!*

The ride lasted a little longer than Kim thought because of rush hour traffic. But the girls did not notice the extended ride because they sampled everything, except the liquor within the limousine from the refrigerator, the virgin bar, the candy bar and the music channel.

"Oh my goodness Kim you have it made." Monica stated as she stuffed her mouth with a peanut sneakers bar and Eryka drank her fruit juice. The girls felt the limousine turn and all fell on top of each other in the direction of the turn laughing. As they adjusted themselves to get off the floor, Eryka still with her arm in the air to keep from spilling her juice in the nice clean car. Kim announced. "We're here." Just as Pete pulled the door open. "Oh my GOD Pete Mom and Dad are home, you have to drive me around back to the delivery entrance!"

"Now's a better time than any to tell your parent's there's guests in the house."

"Oh come on Pete, remember in my own time?" and Kim pulled the door closed. There was a brief pause; Kim heard the driver's doors open and close and then the limousine jolt forward. With a sigh of relief Kim relaxed in her seat. The ride around back seemed like forever to Monica and Eryka, but was far too quick for Kim.

The two girls stepped out of the limousine behind Kim, smiled at Pete as he stood so obediently holding the door open. Eryka laughed and sarcastically whispered to Monica, as she slightly tilted her head to look Pete in the face, "I have to get me one of those." Pete felt something out of kilter about Eryka, turned to Kim and reinforced his earlier direction.

"Be sure you tell your parent's you have guests." Kim did not respond she just nodded. Her mind was on hoping that her parents were in the front of the house and not the back. She was jolted out of her thought when Monica asked in wide-eyed amazement, "This is where you live?"

"Yep, nine months out of the year. We stay at my Nanna's beach house during the summer."

"How many houses did your parent's put together to make this one?" Monica asked and Kim smiled, "this is just one house, we all had input in its design, even Pete, he's like part of the family." Eryka shot a cautious look at Pete and he returned the sentiment.

"Come on let's go inside quietly." Monica politely demanded.

"Okay, this is what we are going to do. When we get inside we are going to the left up the stairs . . . quickly. I need to tell my parent's that you are here before they see you. They are, especially my Dad extremely strict . . . okay anal about having people over during a school night. Education is paramount to them and they won't allow any distractions during the school week. So remember as soon as we get in the door go to your left and up the stairs . . . quickly! I will be right behind you."

Before Kim could double back from the delivery entrance and open the Kitchen door Pete had gone through the side door and met her at the kitchen door.

"The Jenkins are in the family room and the kitchen, you are sure to get caught if you go in now with them"

"No I won't get caught I sent them up the stairs by the delivery entrance. Thanks Pete"

"Your Dad will be up a while he is working on a new project, he's been at it all afternoon. So you will have to tell them at dinner."

"Okay done, Thanks Pete."

Pete smiled and winked his eye, "that's two you owe me and I like payment in full, on demand."

Pete's statement made Kim feel uncomfortable, but she shook it off as his quirky humor and walked into the kitchen, "Hi Mom, and then the family room, hey Dad." kissing them both on the cheek neither noticing her new facial decorations.

"Hey sweetie, are you hungry?"

"Starving, feel like I can eat enough for three people."

"Where is Cameron?" Mr. Jenkins looked at Kim for an answer. The twin's parent only called him Cameron when they expected that he would have done something contrary to what he has been taught. The Jenkins was in constant fear of Cameron's actions.

Kim averts the question and asks, "What's for dinner?"

Her mother allowed Kim to avert she knew it put Kim in an awkward position to tell on her brother, but Kim's lack of response told more than she knew.

"Lasagna." Her mother responded while her quick gaze quieted Kim's father, but only for the moment. Kim got out while the getting was good; she knew her mother saved her.

"I'll be right back; I need to take my book bag to my room." Kim trotted the distance from the kitchen, down the hall that lead to the stairs, which she took two, by two in anxious anticipation to see her new friends. Kim walked into her bedroom to find Monica and Eryka had already made themselves at home. They had raided her refrigerator of her midnight snacks. When they noticed Kim standing in the entrance of the door they quieted themselves fearful that they were making too much noise.

"Were we too loud?" Monica asked with concern.

"No the bedrooms are pretty far off from the rest of the house so you don't have to be too quiet, but not too loud either. Dinner is in about fifteen I will offer to clean the kitchen and bring up you two some lasagna. Please don't roam the house, stay in my room my Dad has cameras everywhere and he view them frequently to keep an eye on Cameron, there is the bathroom. Kim gestured toward the fuchsia door. That refrigerator has drinks and snacks help yourself, whatever is in there should hold you two over until I come back." The two laughed because Kim was much too late with the suggestion and the flash tour.

"I will be back as soon as I can."

"Okay." Monica said gleefully as she made her way to Kimberly's closet. Eryka look at this, some of this stuff still has tags on it!"

Kim smiled at the two and closed the door behind her, returned to the kitchen and positioned herself on the stool to talk to her mother as she did every day after school. Only this time she had to explain the cut next to her right eye. "Mom come on it's not that bad, please don't over react, I am alright!"

"Who did this to you and why? What happened? Should I come up to the school? Do you need a doctor?"

"Okay Mom, first question, It's that girl I have been telling you about she just got violent today, but it's okay a couple of friends helped me out so I won't be having any problems out of her anymore, second question, no I do not need you to come up to the school that would only make things worse. It's resolved, I am certain of it. Last question, no I do not need a doctor, I am not the first nor will I be the last girl on the planet with a black eye."

"Kim look at your face there is a cut there; it is not just a black eye. It could get infected."

"Where was Cameron when all of this was happening?"

"Probably with his friends, besides Dad she's a girl, do you really expect him to beat up on a girl?"

"With a name like Helga, How much of a girl can she be?"

"Dad her name isn't Helga that is a name the kids at school gave her because she is so big. It used to be Hefty Helga, but she lost a few noticeable pounds so Hefty was dropped and Helga kind of stuck. Her name is Hannah Brightenson."

"Well Hefty, Helga, Hannah, whatever her name is she sounds like she is too big to be bullying you. I assure you if you come home with another bruise or scar I will have no other alternative but to come to the school. You're far too small for anyone to bully."

"Dad I may be small but my face packs a mean punch." Kim teased as she spun around on her stool.

"Kim this is serious, I agree with your Dad honey. She really got you good, look at your face. I am really upset; I think we should pay the school a visit."

"Mom it's usually the small ones that are bullied. What's for dinner?" Kim asked again as she walked over to the pot and lifted the lid.

"Did she knock you deaf? I told you lasagna. Get out of that pot. Did you wash your hands?" Her Mom asked as she playfully hit Kim across her backside with the towel she had thrown across her shoulder.

"Yes Mom I did and then sanitized with the convenient hand sanitizer you have mounted on the wall right before I came into the kitchen."

"Are you sassing your mother?"

"No Dad I'm not. I'm just saying I washed my hands. I know the rules."

"Good, there will be none of that sassing in this house! Where is Cameron?" Kim had prepared her answer on the way back to the kitchen.

Mechelle Davis

"I need a book on geography and he went to get it for me I was ready to come home after that Helga thing." Kim crossed her fingers as she lied she always felt bad when she lied to her parent's, her Dad was different from her mother he would not allow her to divert from his question; she had no choice but to lie. Kim reasoned to herself that she was only partially lying because she did need a geography book and the Helga thing did have her pretty shaken up.

"What's for dinner Mom, you never said?"

"Sure I did, but I made beef stew for the homeless and lasagna for the family. What do you have a taste for?"

"Lasagna's good, I love it when you put cottage cheese in it. Can I take mine to my room I want to get a jump start on my homework for next week, there's a lot of research I have to do?"

"After you sit for a bit with us Kim you know we don't allow eating in the rooms."

Turning her attention to her father Kim in her 'con Daddy' voice said, "I know Daddy, but my homework load is large this week and I can eat and research. I promise I will bring my dishes down as soon as I'm done." Mr. Jenkins agreed and Kim knew he would, he was a stickler for education.

". . . But after you sit for a bit with your Mom and me."

Dinner was quiet as usual when Cam was not home, not quiet from lack of conversation but the fear of someone knocking on the door or the phone ringing and the person on the other end saying that Cameron has yet again been involved in or done something nefarious. Kim, in a huge way, resented her brother for making her parents worry like he does. But the love she has for him is far stronger than the resentment she felt.

Kim sat for ten minutes, as long as her excitement would allow her. She asked to be excused again, pleading her case, "Mom, Dad can I finish my dinner in my room, I have a lot of homework I need to do and complete?"

"Complete what do you mean complete? You've been avoiding doing your homework?"

"No Dad, I started some of it in study hall today, I told you I have a heavy load this week." Anticipating their questions Kim walked over and kissed him on top of his head. "I know how important school and my homework are, not only to you but to me and my future." Mr. Jenkins smiled with approval.

"Mom do you need any help with the dishes?"

"No honey that's okay, go ahead I'll get it."

"Well let me help you put away less food," Kim said as she piled her plate and another with enough food for a football team, filled her glass with water, slid two forks into her sweater pocket and put the food on a serving tray.

"Kim it's easier to put it on than it is to take it off." Her mother warned as she looked on at Kim with concern piling her plate.

"Don't worry Mom I have enough energy for three people it won't stick around." Kim said as she hurried to her room tossing her words over her shoulder, "Besides a little weight may help me ward off the Helga's of the world." Kim smiled back at her mother. Finally arriving to her room Kim opened the door and the two lighten her load by grabbing their plates.

"Did you get something to eat with one of the girls asked?" Kim retrieved the forks from her pocket and joined the girls on the floor.

Kim did not know so much fun existed as the three stayed up half the night eating, laughing, talking, playing games, braiding and beading Eryka's hair, oh and knocking down some of the weekly workload.

Kim broke her promise to Pete and hid Monica and Eryka in her bedroom for three weeks after school thinking her parent's never knew. After her Mom went to sleep each night and her Dad to his office that he built off from the house the two were able to move around without care; hours at the Jenkins home always felt like minutes. Eryka and Monica had found their way to the upstairs sun-porch, stood enjoying the view of the forest and marveling at the apartment like tree-house.

"This house feels like the Jenningson's, full of love in everything you see and touch; it smells like . . . it smells like . . ."

"It smells like what?" Eryka asked irritated, a part of her knew what Monica would say because she felt it too.

". . . home. It smells like home." Monica responded with tears in her eyes realizing she missed her parent's and pseudo parent's alike. Emotions instantly running wild, she missed the Dad she had before he became an abusive and disgusting, drunk. The mother she had before she became a battered woman and the people who showed her what loving parent's could be. Eryka's reply forced Monica to get it together.

"I don't know or can't remember what home smells or should feel like, but if this is it, we are never leaving." Eryka replied displaying the amazement Monica had when she got out of the limousine four weeks earlier.

Kim looked at Eryka and Monica she did not understand the excitement the two seen in her lifestyle the school each of them attend was designed for children whose parent's could afford it.

"Kim you better take those dishes down before one of your parent's come up here looking for them." Kim continued to braid Eryka's hair as she glanced over her shoulder at the empty plate, abandoned on the other side of the room, in the middle of the floor.

"Thanks Eryka, I forgot all about that." Kim quickly picked up the plate and went to rush out of the room as if she could see one of her parent's in route and she was heading them off. She paused before she opened the door the sounds of Monica and Eryka's laughter landed on her back and bounced to her ears. Kim turned for a moment to watch the two continue to enjoy each other's company. She liked having them there and decided that she would do all she could to keep them. They made her feel less lonely and definitely not as awkward.

Humming Kim, walked to the kitchen, placed the plate, and silver wear in the sink she heard her mother gently say, "Make sure you wash and dry your plate." Sighing because she hoped that she would make it out of the kitchen and back to her friends before her mother noticed that she had put the dirty dishes in the sink.

"Okay." Kim filled the sink with warm soapy water to wash her plates and the few after dinner dishes her parent's had used. Kissed her parent's good night and returned to her room. She turned the knob expecting her new friends to still be in laughter mode but they were both comfortably asleep on Kim's floor pillows. Looking at the girls briefly she was jealous of their relationship, she wanted what they had. She covered them both, with an extra comforter from her linen closet, changed into her pajamas, washed her face, brushed her teeth, tied down her hair and climbed into bed. It felt to Kim that

Mechelle Davis

soon after her lids met her alarm clock blared forcing the three girls to join the morning sun.

Kim had not noticed that she really did not like getting up going to school until she had Monica and Eryka to possibly go with her she was eager and she wanted to rub her newfound friends in Hefty Helga's face. Kim felt like for the first time in a long time she would be safe and could actually enjoy going to school again at the very moment she realized she didn't like it. By the time Kim went downstairs for breakfast Cameron was waiting for her.

"Why do you take so long getting dressed?"

Kim smiled at the sight of her brother, "Wow good morning to you too. Beauty is an art that can't be rushed. It takes time to put on the finishing details, besides it would be disrespectful to my creator if I didn't take pride in his work." Cameron smiled and didn't offer a rebuttal, at first.

"Kim?" Cameron called as Kim finished pouring herself a glass of orange juice and began gulping it down.

With the glass to her lips, Kim turned her attention to Cameron pushing out a soft, "huh" from the back her throat, past her tongue and over the liquid pleasure that filled her mouth.

"Looks like you missed a spot on the right side of your face." Kim didn't respond as Cam continued. "I talked to Pete this morning while he was cleaning the car." Kim turned put the glass on the counter in alarm afraid that Pete had told him about Monica and Eryka.

"I am not going to ride with you this morning to school. I have something that I need to do. I will see you this afternoon."

Relieved Kim took a seat on the stool at the kitchen counter. "What's so important that you have to miss school and do Mom and Dad know that you are taking the day off?"

"No and they are not going to know are they?"

"Cam is you trying to get sent away? You know if you are caught skipping or getting into any type of trouble, especially playing with fire, Mom and Dad are going to send you away. What will I do when you're gone?"

Cameron walked over to console his sister, but he knew that there was not much he could say because he was having difficulty consoling himself; he had known, but come to accept that he was not at all normal. He could not help what he was feeling and he needed to do things his way. He felt his parent's didn't and don't want to understand the things that he is going through so they turn a blind eye and blame him. He secretly wished they would take the time because he did not know what to do with the small monster that was rapidly growing into a large demon.

"Look Kim, you know that I won't do anything to willfully or purposely pull us apart, but there are just some things I have to do that I can't tell you about and don't know how to explain. In fact, I think that it is better you don't know."

Standing up to gain her brother strict attention Kim asked, "Why Cameron? I think I could help you figure it out."

"Come on Kim no questions please. I promise I will be there when you get out and stop worrying about me, you are beginning to act like Mom."

"That's not possible; Mom wouldn't lie and keep covering for you." The two paused, then Kim continued, "More secrets and lies huh Cameron?" Cameron bent his five foot eleven inch frame down to kiss his sister on the forehead.

"I love you Kim that is neither a secret nor a lie. Go ahead, Pete is waiting for you."

"Where are Mom and Dad?"

Sounding slightly annoyed, not at Kim but at the fact that his parents are never there for him as he would love for them to be, needed them to be but understanding the reason. "Where else are they Kim at this time?"

Kim ignored Cameron's irritation, partly because she knew what it was about, but mostly because she needed to sneak her friends out.

"Oh Cam I forgot something, in my room tell Pete I will be right down." Not allowing Cameron to respond in one way or another Kim quick stepped toward the front of the house. Cameron yelled behind her his voice echoing.

"I'll tell him, but don't have him waiting too long. See you later I won't be here when you come back down." Kim did not respond she just waved her hand.

Cameron stood for a moment watching his sister, protecting her from so many secrets, he wasn't sure was real or imaginary. He turned to exit the house as the sound of his mother and father's voice begun to reverberate in his head, the very day his demons intensified.

Cameron had come home early from school, something inside of him was redirecting his destination, but he ignored it. He walked up to the back door and the door was open but the screen was locked. He knew his parent's were home and started to leave until he heard rancor in his father's voice as he said,

"We made a mistake we should have only taken her. I told you when I looked at him that there was something wrong with that boy!"

Cam removed the magnet from his pocket, placed it on the handle of the screen door and slid it to the left. He heard the lock click and normally so would the person inside. Their parent's had designed the lock so that no one would get lock out, when the magnet was used it clicked on the outside and beeped inside so that the person inside would know they are no longer alone. Cameron stood for a second to see if the arguing would stop, it did briefly but resumed in the same raucous tone that it had ceased.

". . . He has got to go I did not sign up for this!"

"Yes you did Henry, you can't throw him out like trash when things get rough; he's going through something. He is a smart boy and needs your direction, you need to be lither with your schedule and spend more time with him."

"Are you blaming me for his neurosis to all things unholy? He is a sick boy and his genetics don't have a dam thing to do with me! What happened to him, his mother or father doesn't have any of him noted in their history?

"You don't know that honey they were young and may not have known all of their history or have been shielded. How he is may not be his fault."

"I understand that Grace, but Kim is not that way she is smart, beautiful, kind, understanding loving . . ."

". . . and loves her brother deeply. If she detects that you loathe him we will lose her too."

"If I didn't know better, I'd swear he was born evil. He's the devil in carnet Gracie and frankly I am afraid of him. I am afraid for you and for my little girl. What if one day he does something and I can't protect you or my little girl how do you suppose I live with that?"

Cameron's Dad's words were quelling it was like putting petrol to his behavior. He felt hurt, angry and devastated as the final words of his mother and father's argument filled the air.

"I am afraid of him to Henry, but he is still our son and we can't be selfish, he needs us. When we signed those papers 10 years ago that made him ours not by birth or blood but from the heart. I love him just as much as I love Kim and I will not have you emotionally abandoning him. You will free your schedule and spend more time with him or so help me Henry I will take my children and leave!" Henry's demeanor suggested that he was not opposed to the idea. Grace paused hurt with disappointment in her eyes as she placed her hands on her husband's shoulder. *Was I wrong about You? Are you not the strong, loving man I married? Are you giving us up, Henry? Are you telling me that you no longer love me or our children enough to fight for this family? Is that what you are telling me Henry that after all of these years I was wrong about you?*

"Gracie I love you will all my heart and soul but I am willing to go if he stays. I don't want to lose you or my daughter, but Cameron is a different. You ask me to be agile with my schedule so that I can help him. Now I am asking you to be agile so that we both can help him. Let's send him away to school to a place where no one knows him. Maybe a new scenery will help him because I can't I am neither equipped with the skills or the will."

"You really don't know what to do, do you? Grace asked rhetorically. Okay let's find him a good school . . ."

". . . far enough away from here that he can't come home on his own at will, but you can easily get to him if needed."

"Okay with a good distance and a strong psychiatrist that can help him with his problems. Henry I love my son and I don't want to lose him completely, so if you believe this will help, then let's research schools."

Cameron wiped his tears and shook his head as if doing so would have the effect of an Etch-a-Sketch. He would wait for the day to come when his parents shipped him off, but in the mean time he had screaming *demons* to pacify.

When Kim walked in the room Monica and Eryka were dressed in the clothes she had laid out for them. She found herself a little bit jealous of Monica because her clothes looked better on Monica than they did on her and Monica had found a creative way of putting her accessories together to make what would normally not work, work. Good thing it was kind of warm outside that day because Kim's pants on Eryka were like Capri's, her small frame made the look, look good.

"You two ready?" Monica and Eryka looked at Kim and smiled as a way of saying yes.

"Good. Mom, Dad and Cameron are gone and Pete is downstairs waiting for us so we are in the clear. Grab your breakfast dishes and come on."

"Will we have time to wash them?" Monica asked.

"Don't worry about it, we have a cleaning assistant that comes while Mom and Dad are at work and we are at school. I will put them in the sink and she will take care of them."

"A 'Cleaning Assistant', don't you mean a maid?" Kim ignored Eryka's question and Monica helped her.

"I wondered how your mother kept this house clean all by herself." Monica added.

"She doesn't, we have chores to do and we are required to take initiative and do something extra without their direction. Even though we have people to take care of certain things Mom and Dad said that they don't want us to grow up lazy and abusing people profession because it is not at the standard they expect us to be when we start our lives independently from them as adults and to them that is at age 25."

"But looking at this house Kim, the driver, a maid—sorry, Cleaning Assistant-, your room, do you really think that you and Cameron will ever have to work if you don't want. Your parent's are loaded!"

"No they're not Monica they just work really hard to provide and we have to work for the things we want. They are always talking about how little money we have and that the extra things we want we have to work for them" Kim knew her parent's financial position, but she would play the naive role for the two of them just as she does for her parent's. She felt it would be insensitive to speak about how much she has when they apparently had so little. "Enough about money go ahead through those doors I have to set the alarm."

Kim pushed in the code, it beeped Monica and Eryka looked in the direction of the sound to see Kim trotting to catch up.

Kim joined the two girl's conversation while the three walked out the back door, down the short walkway and to the car laughing with anticipation of what their day would be like now that the school had time to hear that Eryka whipped the pants off Helga.

The ride to school was just as fun as the ride to Kim's house the days and weeks before. Pete had restocked the items the girls had used from the refrigerator with new items, preteen favorites. Eryka and Monica both opened their book bags and began to fill them with the things from the small refrigerator. Kim again encouraged them to take all they wanted except from her parent's refrigerator.

The girls did not realize the limousine came to a slow stop until Pete stood with the door open. Startled Monica and Eryka turned and ceased filling their bags with the goodies.

"Why does the ride seem to always go so quickly?" Monica asked. Excited, the three paused to gather themselves before they stepped out of the limousine. Monica first, then Kim and finally Eryka and the cheers ensued surprising them all. This was the reception the three were expecting weeks ago. They were instant celebrities and immediately neither liked the attention as they thought they would for their very own reasons. Pete was astounded by the reception, he knew that it only meant trouble and pulled Kim aside to ask her about what was going on.

"I will have to tell you later, Okay?"

"Okay, but this doesn't look good! Looks like your time's up, your parent's will know about you three today." Pete gestured toward the school's entrance.

The three walked side-by-side looking like the trouble two of them weren't, through the sea of people as they parted with applause. Their smiles mixed with secret emotions as the three reached the closed door the principle stood in front of; He greeted and escorted them to his office. Worried about the outcome the three walked behind Principal O'Malley making a pact to stick together reasoning that if each took the blame neither would get suspended.

Each of them told the truth as to what took place, deceptively splitting the assault on Helga between the three. They thought the plan worked until the principal showed the security video of Eryka laying Helga on her back and holding her hostage underneath her right foot.

Principal O'Malley looked at the three girls as he began his speech, turning his attention solely to Eryka. "This young lady's parent's are threatening to take actions against the school and pressing assault charges against you Eryka; I have no other alternative but to expel you. I'm sorry." But before Eryka had the opportunity to speak in an attempt to defend herself Kim spoke for her.

Abruptly standing and totally out of character for Kim she started in a calm and assertive voice. "Principal O'Malley you watched the same video that Monica, Eryka, Helga, Helga's parent and I watched and I am sure you saw Helga assault me first, waving her right hand toward Eryka and shrugging her shoulders, Eryka was just defending me. She did what any friend would do against a bully of Helga's size. Now let's be reasonable and talk about this. My parent's has encouraged many corporations to invest in this school and their investment has generated enough funds to bring this school from red to black, established enough funds to help student's remain whose parent's may not have enough finances to pay their tuition. Now, you must agree that this school has been better, in better standing with an established outstanding reputation, all because of the efforts of my parent's. It would be a shame if I went home and told my parent's that you knew Helga was bullying me and each time I came to you for help, you did nothing."

"Ms. Jenkins, it sounds to me that you are trying to blackmail me and that is definitely cause for expulsion. I will not tolerate such behavior!"

Leaning over the front of O'Malley's desk, "And my parents' will not tolerate sending me to school for a reasonably expensive education only to be assaulted by girls such as Helga, you and your camera's knowing about her felonious behavior toward me and others and you do nothing." Kim moved her hair from her face so that Principal O'Malley could view her fading black eye and healing scare. I am sure that something could be worked out where we all could be happy." Kim looked back at her friends, "Don't you lady's agree?"

Monica spoke up, "We do agree Kim. If you must save face by punishing Eryka fine, give her detention, but to expel her is a bit harsh. She will accept only one week detention on two conditions: One, that Helga is suspended for three weeks longer than Eryka's detention for initiating the fight. Two, you must convince Helga's parent's to drop any charges or potential charges against Eryka because if she doesn't Kim's parent's will then take the same actions against the school and Helga's parent's, you will lose your biggest financial supporter. Three, Helga must apologize to Kim, or all deals are off!"

"One month suspension that is a bit harsh ladies, Hannah parents will never agree to that or the apology!"

"It isn't as harsh as expulsion and we are confident that you would figure out a way for Helga's parent's to see this is best for everyone." Eryka stated sharply as she gestured toward the video screen.

Principal O'Malley looked at the three girls searching his mind as to when the three became so close. Quickly abandoning the thought he wondered how they hid it so long and became such adult negotiators. He briefly reasoned with himself that each of them had valid points and he would lose his job if he lost funding. "Okay ladies, it's a deal. Ms. Bronson you will have one week detention with the condition that your detention ends with me seeing an adult. And as agreed Helga . . . I mean Hannah will be suspended for four weeks with an apology to Kimberly. Your detention starts tomorrow. You three may go to class."

The three walked out of the office amazed at Kim who was completely amazed at herself. Then the realization of Eryka not having parent's set in.

"What are we going to do you have to have a parent or parents at the end of your detention?"

"Monica do not worry you worry too much, we will cross that bridge when we get to it, I have one week so just relax I will take care of it."

Mechelle Davis

The eight hours of school went by quickly and strangely enough the three were elated. They immediately grew exhausted of the congratulatory smiles, pat on the backs and could not bear telling the story again. In route to their lockers Monica noticed Hannah and her parent's exiting Principal O'Malley's office with Hannah in tow.

Kim heard Hannah's mother say, "You will work like a slave to pay for the tuition the four weeks you are out of school I will not pay for tuition that you are not using. You owe me four weeks of hard labor while you stay on top of your studies. You didn't tell me you assaulted that girl and blackened her eye. If there is fallout from this you are going away to boarding school!" Helga and her father's large frame followed behind her mother's petite frame as she yelled at the two for being a disappointment. Kim, Monica and Eryka almost felt sorry for Helga, but quietly decided to save their emotions for someone more deserving. Helga looked back and saw Kim standing with her friends and approached her without warning her reprimanding Mother.

"Kim it is a part of my suspension that I have to apologize to you, but setting that aside I had no real reason for attacking you it was ordered. I knew it was wrong, it felt wrong and you are the kindest person I have seen in this school. I wish that we could have been friends instead. I am really sorry for what I did to you and in the future I hope that we can be friends." Hannah did not wait for a response and Kim was grateful that she did not because a friendship now or in the future was not going to happen.

Kim exited the side door with Monica and Eryka, walked across the elementary school kids' playground to meet Cameron on the Southside of the school. A meeting place she and Cameron established three and a half years ago. True to form, Cameron was not there and Kim was over being disappointed. Eryka tapped Monica to cease her never-ending lips and motioned in Kim's direction. The disappointment of something was all over her face and the hurt of whatever it was was in her troubled demeanor.

"Kim who are we waiting for?" Monica asked.

"Apparently, nobody," she responded solemnly.

"Cameron stood you up again, didn't he?" Eryka chimed in. "Why do you keep allowing him to let you down? Why do you keep believing and trusting what he says?"

Kim turned around to face Monica and Eryka but directed her eyes at Eryka, "Because he's my brother, I love him and I can't give up on him. He's feeling alone right now and he's going through something that he thinks I don't understand. I can't allow him to be out here . . . there, turning to the streets, all by his self I love him too much for that."

"But . . ."

Annoyed at her persistence Kim walked closer to Eryka, "There's no but Eryka, there are no conditions on love, no limitations, you protect the one's you love without hesitation even if that means you will be let down sometimes and maybe completely in the end."

"Kim, Cameron is not who you think he is and if he loved you the way you love him then he would be out here right now and would have been out here when Helga attacked you. Instead he had . . . ." Kim ended Eryka's bashing of her brother.

"Eryka I don't think Cameron is anymore or any less than what he is. He's my brother, not my boyfriend we have lived in the same house all of our lives' so there are or will there be any surprises. You should know I am not as naïve as you think I am. In every relationship, relationships of all kinds, one person is going to love the other more. The person who loves harder is the one who somehow felt they lacked love or something in their upbringing and the one who loves less may simply not know how to love, been taught not to love or are genetically incapable of showing, expressing or sharing such an emotion. Cameron loves me and neither you nor anyone else can convince me otherwise. Look Eryka . . . Monica, I love that you two are in my life, it makes me feel safe and happy and we share a lot about the way we feel, what we have been through, whatever; but my brother is off limits. Anything about him or towards him is not a conversation we will have. I know who he is and when he is ready to change who he is I will be there just as I will be there while he is trying to figure some things out."

Monica and Eryka wondered how much about Cameron did Kim really know. Both stood silently until Monica pointed to the limousine coming around the corner. "Look Kim that is one of many persons' that seems to or will never disappoint you."

Kim turned her attention to the street and looked back at Monica. "One of many, what do you mean?"

Mechelle Davis

"Eryka and I promise to never disappoint you. Kim smiled shyly. We are sisters now and forever, you can depend on us for and through anything."

Kim hugged Monica and Eryka, ". . . and I promise to never disappoint either of you. The two of you can definitely depend on me for and through anything, but I mean it my brother is off limits." Hugging and laughing, Monica said, "Look at Pete standing there waiting for you, he is so loyal to you and your family. He really loves you Kim and you can see it."

"Yeah he does and soon he will love the two of you the same." The Three headed for the limousine.

"Do you think Pete refilled the jar of Sour Cherry Balls?"

"I'm sure he did Monica."

"Hey Pete."

"Hello Monica."

Eryka walked pass Pete and shot him an untrusting look.

"Hello to you too Eryka."

Shocked that Pete remembered her name, "Hey Pete."

Before Kim could get into the car Pete pulled her aside and question if her parents knew the two were coming over again on a school night.

"It has been weeks since you promised me that you would tell your parents that they are in the house. It started out as spending the night now they live like stowaways in your bedroom. I can't trust that you will do the right thing anymore, I have to tell your parents I have helped you deceive them long enough."

"No Pete you can't. Something happened in school today and I am afraid that if Dad meets them he will think that they are a bad influence on me and they are not. They really saved my butt."

"What do you mean?" Does this have something to do with your black eye?"

"I'll explain later Pete.

"No Kim you will explain now."

"Pete I am cold." Kim danced around to exaggerate how cold she was.

"Get in the front seat and I will close the glass."

"Then they will think we are talking badly about them."

Mechelle Davis

"Okay we will all sit in the back and we all will discuss what has been going on. Either way Kim I will know what is going on before we pull into the driveway. So you tell me now or we tell your parent's when you arrive home then you're on your own."

Kim slid into the limousine with her two new friends with Pete behind her. Hours had passed by the time Monica finished telling him how she and Eryka ended up in Texas living in a motel and now in Kim's bedroom. Pete was heartbroken and could identify with the life they had run away from because it was similarly horrible to the life he had run away from as a child and decided that even at the cost of the Jenkins trust he had to help Kim help them.

Unknowing to the three Kim had begun to worry and feel guilty for deceiving her parent's which meant the two had been deceiving her parent's long enough and definitely hiding the girl out in her room for far too long. Leila, the Cleaning Assistant was beginning to complain, but Pete quickly quieted her.

The four days of detention went well, but on the fifth when Eryka was to bring a parent she and Monica stayed home that Friday to give Eryka a little more time to recruit a parent.

Kim went over the morning routine. "Did Leila bring your breakfast up?"

"Yep." Monica said cheerfully.

"Good. Mom and Dad are gone to work as usual, but that does not mean go wild. Remember Pete was able to get the Leila to keep quiet about you two being here as long as you two clean up behind yourself, this means my room too. Remember my Dad sometimes come home around one and two and stays for about half an hour. Please don't make any noise, play loud music. If you get hungry tell Leila she will bring you whatever you like and please stay on this end of the house. It will give you time to get back to my room fast just in case Mom, Dad or Cameron comes home unexpectantly. Finally, when Leila leaves please do not disengage the burglar alarm Dad had a sensor built into his cell phone to allow him to know each time it is disengaged and by whom. Unless you are my Mom or Dad we will get busted, so only disengage it for emergency purposes, just push *911! I can't keep hiding you two out here if you don't help me keep you hidden. Today is Friday; I plan to leave school a little early, I am feeling sick already. Pete said he would take us to the movies and the mall. Daddy leaves his card every other Friday for me to shop as long as I keep my G.P.A between a 3.5 and 4.0 and stay out of trouble I have built up enough reserve to take you two with me for some new clothes."

Clearing her throat and sarcastically raising her hand Eryka interrupted. "Umph, excuse me Miss Jenkins? Kim did not respond and Eryka continued. "Would hiding us out in your room constitute staying out of trouble or getting in trouble if Mommy or Daddy found out?" Kim did not respond she finished her comments and direction. "When Pete picks me us this afternoon you two come with him and we can go straight from school to the mall."

"How much does Daddy allow you to spend?" Eryka asked in a jealous tone.

"He never gave me a limit, but that is because I know my Dad and what he considers a sufficient amount to spend at one time. I have not been since you two have been here so whatever I spend I think he'd forgive me just this once, it looks like you two can use something new." In a hurried tone, heading for her bedroom door, "Hey I have to go Pete is a stickler for punctuality. See ya later!"

Kim did not close the door good before she heard Eryka part rhetorically ask Monica, "Why does she listen and strive so hard to please and reason with that man he's just the family driver? I don't trust him there is something about him that makes me uncomfortable, something he is hiding I can't put my finger on it, but there is something not right about Pete; something seriously not right!"

"Eryka she loves him, she has said it so many times he's family. Look at all of them when he is around her, he protects her as if she is his own. I think she's blessed, she has two Dads, and us . . . we have none. There is so much love in this house, in everything you see, it feels so good here and it feels like love here because there is so much love in this family. Even her messed up brother Cameron, he loves Kim. Love is what drew your attention to her, made you help her, she exudes the kind of love we want the kind of love that is poured into a person their whole life so much in fact that it spills out even when they are being bullied and flows over to people around them. So much that a person like you who never had it or have forgotten what it is or feels like can recognize it and for reason you don't even know want it, need it, desire to be a part of it. I want to be a part of it, you want to be a part of it and Pete has a lot to do with it. This is the family we have been looking for, stayed up so many nights talking about and like or not, Pete comes with it." Kim smiled and continued down the hall without hearing the final conversation.

"Whatever it is that you don't like about Pete, whatever it is that you can't put your finger on wait until you know for sure before we bring down an innocent man. You could be mistaken because of your past."

"No Monica it is just the opposite, it is because of my past that I know there is something not right about him. I felt it when I first laid eyes on him. I felt it so strong that it almost painted a picture. I am not mistaken. Remember around the first time we met and we were trying to get into an adult movie after dark and without a parent?"

"Yes." Monica said smiling as she remember the events of that day.

"Remember Old Golden?"

"Yeah? You said you named him Old Golden because he's old and we just hit the jackpot." The two laughed.

". . . and remember you thought that he was the nicest person because he posed as our father to get us into that movie?" Eryka didn't wait for a reply. "When he walked up to us I told you something was not right about him and when we found our seats in the movie I couldn't enjoy the movie because that feeling kept intensifying to the point it made me throw up all over him? What did we find out about him two months later?"

"That he was a man with sick standards, he only "dated" what he called women five and under, the news said he was a serial killer that lured kids in by befriending the family and he targeted us because he heard you talking about the twins that lived next door to Angela and thought they were your siblings. You said he had a sick taste for killing."

"Was I wrong?"

"Sadly no, about him or all the other people you kept us safe from."

"Right, I am not wrong about Pete! Eryka said aggressively. You should have learned to trust me by now. There is something not right about him; I just don't know what or how I am going to find out, but I am."

The two were so engrossed in their conversation that they did not hear the footsteps coming down the hall.

Cameron heard voices coming from Kim's room and as usual, Cameron walked in without knocking to find the two girls sprawled across the bed enjoying one big mixing bowl of cereal, cartoons and homework. Cameron immediately knew who they were.

"Why are you in my house, in my sister's room?"

Intimidated by Cameron's strong presence and face that contradicted his small frame, Monica lay with her mouth open, Eryka enthralled by the person standing before her demanding answers. A smile curled up in the corner of her mouth and she spoke first as she, sat up, swung her feet and legs over the length of Monica's body and planted her feet on the floor and looked Cameron in the eye from across the spacious room.

"Your sister invited us here. What are you doing here?"

"I live here and Kim would have told me if she had invited you, how did you two get in here?!" He asked as he glanced at the window.

"As for your first question Eryka replied, "You don't live in this room, so why are you in Kim's room and she's not home? As for your second question, you guessed it; Kim brought us in through that window; five months ago—she lied. Lastly, I know why we are here, why are you?"

"I told you I live here!"

"No I mean shouldn't you be in school?" Eryka questioned

"What are you a Truant Officer in training?" Eryka smiled because she recognized the same darkness in Cameron that she felt in herself when she looked in her minds mirror, not just at her face but the pit of what she felt when she thought about doing or did different things to people. That mirror in her mind reflected through her eyes and produced Cameron.

"We are here because I was suspended for beating up that Helga looking girl you sent after your sister." Monica sat up in attention.

"What makes you think that I would send someone after my sister?"

"You haven't said you didn't, which is usually what an innocent man says the moment he is accused of something he did not do."

"I'm Ery . . .

"I know who you two are and I don't want either of you around my sister, she is a good girl!"

"Is that why you tried to make her go bad by having her beat up?" Monica loved to see Eryka at work. "You still never answered my question."

"Which is?" Cameron asked

"What aren't you in school?"

"That's none of your business you're in my house, so you don't get to ask questions, demand or even expect answers!" Eryka continued as calmly as though Cameron had offered her a seat and she declined.

"Is it because you have not been to school since nearly the beginning of the year?" Cameron looked surprised. "What a colossal waste of Daddy's money." Cameron was just as fascinated by Eryka as Eryka was by him, but he also recognized that he was way out of his league. Pride forced him not to back down.

"You see Cameron I know who you are too, good to put a great body with such an infamous name. Look I'll tell you what, you let us ride it out here until . . . whenever and I will prevent Principal O'Malley from calling to check up on you all of a sudden. Deal?"

Cameron stood shocked and captivated at the same time, she was much like him and he liked it. "Whatever, just don't make a mess, my sister's is a neat freak."

"Neat freak . . . Got it!" Eryka smiled acknowledgingly and sarcastically as their eyes locked. Cameron blinked first and Eryka smoothed his defeat with a reiteration. "You still never said."

"Never said what?" Cameron questioned.

"Why you are in Kim's room and she is not here."

Cameron put his hands behind his back, rocked heel to toe, and tilted his head in a downward motion only to look partially up at Eryka in an attempt to sound as clever as Eryka apparently is. "I know." He stepped backwards into the hallway closing the door in front of him. Cameron stood in the hallway outside the closed door and smiled. He turned and walked away slightly looking over his left shoulder as if he could see Eryka though the door, "welcome to my home Eryka." Cameron walked the long hallway that led to the back stairs—reset the alarm using his Dad's password—and exited the service entrance to continue his day.

Mechelle Davis

Eryka smiled at the door and pulled it together before Monica could notice her interest and reclaimed her spot on the bed, she retrieved her spoon and resumed eating her soggy cereal.

Monica, now completely out of her vegetative state, "How did you know he sent Helga after Kim? And how did you know he hasn't been to school all year?"

"Why did you stare at him as if he were some sort of legend?" Eryka paused to enjoy a little of Monica's discomfort, then continued smiling exhaustingly. "I hacked into the school's system and changed his attendance record and grades so that he would not get a phone call. You heard Kim, she loves him and he definitely has issues that school will not allow him and can't resolve."

"I didn't know you were that good with computers?" Eryka smiled at her sister taking in spoonful of cereal, thinking to herself, *there's a lot you don't know about me."*

K im thought school seemed to take forever to let out all she could think about was spending time with her two friends who were quickly convincing her that they were all equally sister's and their secret was important for them to remain together. The lunch bell rang. Kim headed through the side doors and ran across the field to wait for Pete. As she stood she thought about the unfair position she was putting Pete in and decided that that night, at dinner was the time to tell her parent's about Monica and Eryka. Her thoughts were interrupted by a familiar, friendly voice.

"Hey Skinny Minnie?" Kim turned around with a smile.

"I told you to stop calling me that. You know I hate that name."

"I know and I'm sorry, but you look so cute standing there all alone, huddled up in yourself. Skinny legs covered in those awful black tights and the only thing you could see are your knees banging together."

"Why are you standing here all alone? Why are you standing here, school isn't over and I told you to stop waiting for me!" Cameron went to his sister and wiped her nose with the sleeve of his hooded sweater. Kim didn't have the heart to tell him she was waiting for Pete.

"You heard Mom and Dad. If I make it home without you you are going to be in big trouble. Cam I think they are talking about sending you away. What would I do if they send you away?"

"Cameron did not answer the part rhetorical question he asked one instead. No secrets?"

"No secrets, Cam you know that!"

Mechelle Davis

"Then what you would do is rely on those two girls you've been hiding in the house. Are they secrets?" Kim did not respond Cameron did it for her. "Kim we are all we have, Mom and Dad are old and if we can't trust and depend on each other then who can we depend on? Do you trust me?"

"What?"

"It's a simple question Kimmy, Do you trust me? You know I will never let you down . . . right?"

"I don't understand Cameron what you mean when you ask, Do I trust you and I know you will never let me down? No secrets right?" Kim did not wait for a response she was ready to get out a lot of what she was feeling. "I mean, how many times have you put me in the position to cover your butt with Mom and Dad and I never once knew what I was covering your butt for. Trust you? How many times have I stood out here in the heat, cold, rain and you never showed up after you told me you would be here. It is because of you that Monica and Eryka found me because, like so many other times, you told me you would be at this bus stop waiting for me when I got here and you weren't. This day, the day I met Monica and Eryka, Helga was there waiting for me instead to pick her teeth with my skinny bones and I find out later that you sent her there after me. Trust you? Secrets? Don't I have reasons to lack trust and have a couple of secrets of my own?"

It was a side of Kim Cameron did not know existed and he was not sure if he was responsible for her alter ego or those girls back at the house. "I'm sorry I let you down, that I disappointed you?"

". . . and set me up to be assaulted?"

"That too, but Kim I was trying to . . . have I lost you?"

Kim ignored Cameron's incomplete statement and smiled at her brother who now shared her runny nose. "I learned a lot these last five months and I like the person that's developing. So, yeah to a degree you've lost me, it's just sad I wasn't able to share the new person I am becoming with you."

Cameron stood nodding his head responding in a slow thoughtful tone, "Yeah . . . yeah it is. I would have loved to see it." With an unspoken, but spoken understanding between the two and a renewed bond Kim looked at her brother shivering and cleaning her nose she asked. "Should we call Pete to come pick us up?"

Mechelle Davis

"No how about we catch the bus. Spend some more time together."

"Are you crazy Cam, it's cold out here, there is not a bus in sight and I have been out here a lot longer than you have, I'm calling Pete! Besides he's taking us to the mall." While she dialed the number to learn his ETA she looked at Cameron and laughed, "I bet you wish you had on that big heavy coat Mom and Dad bought. My knees may be knocking but your chattering combined with the waves that your body is producing from shivering I am seriously expecting a winter tornado."

The two laughed and Cameron responded, "You are so corny, hurry up and call Pete I'm freezing. Not expecting an answer he looked toward the street. When did it start getting this cold in Texas?"

Cameron helped Kim continue hiding Monica and Eryka, he supplied them with their parents pass code so they may move around the house freely. Their presence actually caused him to be home a lot more at night. During the day while Kim was at school, the Jenkins at work and Cameron off doing only God knows what, the girls had the whole house to themselves. They were verbally fantasizing about what it would be like to live with the Jenkins permanently, in the open. Verbally regretting that the months had gone by so quickly and expressing the realization that it would come to an end soon. When they smelled smoke and then heard a loud boom, followed by glasses shaking. Monica was terrified, but Eryka was rapt by the sheer force the boom gave off. Eryka and Monica went to investigate and in the forest the Jenkins called their backyard they found Cameron laying on the ground laughing hysterically. He acknowledged Eryka and with extreme excitement he tried to give a detailed description of what he had just done, the way it felt when the blast hit him and how far in the air he went before he came down. He started pulling off the heavy, smoking black jacket, gloves and pants that hit the ground with a thud when he dropped them.

"Blast gear, isn't the internet wonderful!" He said with wild excitement in his eyes flashing a perfect set of teeth.

Monica stepped forward to claim a position next to Eryka only to find Eryka's eyes lit up and with a half smile on her face. Monica feared Cameron and was beginning to wonder if she should fear Eryka.

I want him, Eryka thought *he is far more mercurial than me.* "Show me how to make one of those bombs!" Eryka said with excitement and the look of greed in her eyes. She positioned herself in front of Cameron who stood exactly two inches taller than her, placed her face next to his and asked, "Ever felt an o-bomb?" The look on Cameron's face proved he did not have a clue of what Eryka meant; it was evident that she was far more advanced than he and she could not wait to show him the o-bomb.

"I'll show you my bomb, if you'll show me yours." Eryka continued, Cameron agreed and she and he were inseparable for the next two years, they shared a bond that neither Monica nor Kim could recognize; it was as if they needed each other on a deeper level and their attentiveness to one another said it loud and clear. Without a doubt they had cemented. Monica didn't mind, Eryka managed not to leave her out and at the same time not make her feel like a third wheel. Things were going well for all: Kim told her parent's about the girls being in their home; the Jenkins allowed them to stay and after hearing about their daily life, quickly became their foster parent's.

The background check of the family revealed a lot of Cameron's misdoings forcing the Jenkins to see more of him as he is. The Jenkins was grateful that Monica and Eryka's parent were willing to terminate their parental rights. Neither parent showed up in court both sets of termination papers came back signed within days of going out. Monica was hurt, upset, but Eryka told Cameron her mother did just what she thought she would and she was thankful because it was the second best thing she had ever done for her. Cameron briefly saw Eryka's softer side, she was hurt but with the help of their family the girls worked through once again feeling unwanted with an ever stronger determination to be a part of a happy, healthy family."

" **M**om can you believe I am going away to college already, time went by so fast?"

"You don't have to go away right now, you can wait two years for your sister's and go to community college here you're only fifteen, I think it's too soon for you to leave home."

"Mom I can handle it, I will be sixteen in seven months, less than a year. I will call every night and I promise I will not do anything to diminish how proud you are of me, don't worry you and Dad did a great job raising me you'll see. Besides I won't be by myself long, Eryka and Monica will join me in two years."

". . . But . . ."

"Mom I did what you told me to do, I worked hard for this because this is what I want and am ready to do. I will be home every holiday, summer break, birthdays, anniversaries and definitely my sister's and brother graduation. We will talk every night just as we have for as long as I can remember, minus the hot chocolate of course. I won't outgrow you Mom and I definitely won't forget you . . . how could I when I miss you so much already?"

"I miss you already too."

"Don't worry I will be fine on my own." Kim always felt so safe in the comfort of her mother's arms, no matter where they were her arms felt like home: warm, safe, secure and guarded from the outside world Cameron showed her exist. Mrs. Jenkins did not want to let go and as Kim's heart beat faster with each passing minute she knew she did not want to let go either. Kim thought to herself, *I want this kind of relationship with my daughter* as she often thought about a family of her own.

Mechelle Davis

"Okay break it up, Daddies need love too."

"All come here Daddy, I need two hearts for all the love I have for Mom and you. I love you Daddy."

"I love you too sweetheart, but think about what I said about going to Harvard, I can arrange it."

"Come on Daddy let's not do this right now. I have made my choice and am very happy, I look forward to going to this college it is everything I need to grow into a successful woman. Please Daddy don't, let's not make my last day with you be an argument about something I have already decided and you can't change."

"Oh hold on young lady I can change it!" Her Dad said with a stern voice as he held her shoulders, at arm's length to look her in the eyes.

"What I mean Daddy is you can't change what I feel is right for me in my heart." Her Dad smiled at her.

"You're right Sweetheart that I cannot change. You are so grown-up well beyond your years. Okay, we won't argue, anything for my baby." Mr. Jenkins said as he bent down to hug Kim and whispered in her ear, "Remember what we talked about."

Kim whispered back with a smile, "I will Daddy, I promise."

As Kim was saying her goodbye's for now to her sister's, Pete—the family's Universal Man—pulled the family car around. Well there is my ride, oh wait I forgot something, I'll be right back!" Quickly running up the stairs to the room the three shared by choice, Kim dug in the closet and lifted the board to retrieve an envelope of papers she made copies of one year earlier, "can't investigate without this." Running out the front door expecting to jump right into Pete's arms as she always have she ran into her brother. "Oh my gosh Cameron I didn't think you were going to make it!"

"Miss you going off to college two years early, never. How did you get so smart?"

"I remember a certain brother threatening to beat me up when I did not get my spelling and times tables correct and then making it fun for me to remember. Or a certain someone waking me up hours before school if he discovered one wrong answer on my homework and my favoritest brother helping me to win the science fair by using a battery to light a bulb that set off a volcano we spent hours

Mechelle Davis

building. Getting teary eyed, Kim confessed, "I am going to miss you so much Cameron, you're the best!"

"No you are"

"No you are"

"No you are"

"No you are"

The family started to laugh Kim and Cameron have done the 'No you are' routine for as long as Kim could remember. Kim loved the closeness she felt with her brother and loved even more that they were able to repair the distance that briefly grew between them before it was too late. As she hugged him and he swung her 101 pound frame around she saw the love her mother had for them in her eyes, on her face, in her smile, in her stand, in her being and Kim loved her even more at that very moment as if it were possible.

Kim demanded that her brother come see her more in college than he had when she was at home and as he responded their Dad interjected.

"Not so much the first year, maybe next year or the year after."

Cameron smiled with hurt in his eyes, "Maybe next year and every weekend to make up for the year or years we are apparently going lose."

Cameron had always felt that their parent's loved Kim more than him and they proved it when they sent him off to boarding school at thirteen. The Jenkins promised him that being a pyromaniac and burning down the kitchen, lighting matches between the four points of Pete's hairy toes, blowing up the backyard, attaching a homemade bomb to a stray cat blowing it up, making a bomb fire with his cousin as the main attraction and setting the neighbor's doghouse on fire with their dog still in it had no bearing on their decision. Cameron had an illness and even in his illness Kim knew he loved her more than anything, he was her twin and extremely protective of her. He knew that there were more of him in the world and he did all he could do to prepare and protect her.

Kim reluctantly let go of her brother, hugged her sister's again and headed toward the limousine. She looked back at her family who were all standing with wet faces to match hers. She went in one last time for a group hug and her Mom whispered in her ear, "I need you to come back this weekend there is something your Dad and I have to tell you and Cameron it's really important." Kim separated her face from her mother's to look into her eyes and she seen the seriousness, the fear and anxiousness her mother was feeling. Kim kissed her Mom and promised she would make it back. Pete called her name, "You're going to miss your flight." Kim peeled herself away from the group only to land in the arms of Pete. He whispered in her ear, "I am so proud of you!" Kim smiled up at him and he too had tears in his eyes. She knew Pete loved her and Kim loved him more than what people would consider normal for whom Eryka called the hired help.

As Kim watched her family through the back of the limousine window she felt alone, surrounded, loved, excited to be on her own anxious to see what New York held in store for her. *"You are the maker of your destination, move in one direction: forward*, the words of her Dad rang in her head as he had always said that to them . . . and he is so right. My destination is Columbia University and I made it happen!" She let out a scream of excitement and Pete peered through the rearview mirror at her and smiled.

Her mother's exactly five foot six, hundred twenty pound frame grew smaller as Pete and she drove down the long driveway leading to the road and heading to the airport. As she closed her eyes to remember the smell of her mother, she wished she had allowed her family to go to the airport with her. She reached for her oversized purse, retrieved her journal and opened it to remind herself that going to the airport alone was the first step to stepping out on her own, leaving her parent's house a child, but returning a woman. She thought to herself, "the next time I see home I will be sixteen." Kim opened her 500 page journal that she titled the top of the page 'Kim's Twelve Steps to Becoming Independent to page 220. She crossed off number one on her list: Go to the airport alone.

Kim looked at her list and thought, *simple and challenging enough I will revise this list as I go, but for right now I think this will do just fine. Daddy you're wrong, I am not too young to go off by myself and I am not making the mistake of my life and in three hours, forty-two minutes I will begin to prove it.*

Mechelle Davis

T he atmosphere was surreal there were greeters, people offering assistance for those who looked lost and confused such as Kim. It was more than Kim expected, definitely what she had hoped for and she was sure that through Columbia University she would prove to herself and her parent's that she had made the right choice. Standing in awe with a smile on her face she felt someone touch her elbow but did not respond because of the business of what was happening around her.

"Girl if you keep standing their looking like Daddy's little freshman, you are definitely drawing a target on your forehead." Kim smiled as she turned expecting to look in the face of the voice but found her chest. The girl laughed hysterically. It reminded Kim of Cameron when he thought he'd done or said something funny and would laugh harder than anyone else at his dull humor and like Cameron; the girl's hard laugh forced Kim to laugh too.

"Hi, I'm Jessica I'm a freshman too. What quarters are you in?"

"L." Kim replied

"Me too."

"Come on, let's walk together."

"You know where it is?" Kim asked

"I know this campus like the back of my hand, my sister graduate next year. She's on the Dean's list and is a part of everything. You'll learn soon enough. I have followed my sister everywhere for as long as I can remember and her friends treat me like a little sister. It was a no brainer that I would want to come to the same University as her. I almost did not make it. I fell in love with some guy who was only worth the 'L' not in love but, loser. I still see him from time to time, but strangely enough the love I thought I could not live without no-longer exists. Humph, who would have thought?" Jessica said with a brief faraway look on her face.

"Rough breakup?" Kim finally was able to get a couple words in.

"Psst, that's an understatement, a rough realization, but that's the past." Successfully evading the details of her breakup that Kim hoped she would not share anyway. Jessica continued, "We live about an hour from here my Mom would not let us move out of state so here we are. It's okay because I love New York and Columbia. I am going into communications. What's your story?"

Kim paused for a moment to make sure the chatterbox had exhausted herself. "I think communications would be perfect for you. As for my story, it's simple; I was ready to spread my wings away from Mom and Dad. I am from a black home, but my Mom and Dad does not act or speak as though they are black, I think they are kind of embarrassed by their roots, which is sad because you can't escape who you are. So I wanted to learn more about what made them so ashamed to be who or what they are and the only way I could learn that was to place myself in the mist of history and the future all at once. I am the twin of the only male in the family; Cameron and I have two sisters: Monica and Eryka, who will join me in two years . . . more or less."

"Kind of sounds like you have parent issues." Jessica said sarcastically bringing embarrassment to Kim.

"No I don't have parent issues; I have great parents."

"Seriously, who are you trying to convince me . . . or yourself?"

Kim grew defensive . . . "Convincing would indicate that I lack either the knowledge or the experience of my parent's. So the answer to your question would be . . . neither! I have great parents, they have their faults as all, I wouldn't trade their faults for world. Faults and all they always have my siblings and my best interest at heart. I was merely stating that I would love to know a little more about my history from an educational point of view."

Ignoring Kim's defense and continuing as if Kim had not spoke a word. "Okay this is our dorm let me see your dorm number, maybe we are roomies." Jessica said excitedly. This was the first time Kim was happy that her Dad used his influence.

Mechelle Davis

Holding tighter to her dorm assignment Kim responded, 'Um, no I have my own room."

"You mean you're not rooming with anyone?"

"No."

"How did you pull that off, freshmen never have their own room?" Jessica asked jealously.

"My Dad wanted me to continue my honors tradition and he knows that the first year is tough with all the enticements, he wanted me to not be dissuaded."

"Your Dad must be loaded, because there are only two things that can change that rule, one, like any other is money and two lots of it! So you're a spoiled rich girl. Now I understand the parent issues."

"Again, I do not have parent issues. My Mom and Dad have been saving for as long as I could remember for my siblings and me to go to college and I had to work for a year to help save, so spoiled yes, rich no."

Removing the campus map from Kim's hand Jessica said, "Well Kim, I am in this direction, the servant's quarters and you your majesty, looking at the map, are here. Just follow this path, see ya around." Jessica said wiggling her fingers in the air, while turning slowing as if she were in a model audition.

"See ya." Kim said, but thought, *hopefully not.*

It had been six months since Kim last seen her family, the phone was no longer a good substitute. Kim spotted Pete half way across the airport terminal he was heading in her direction and just as she did in the past when she laid eyes on him, she ran straight into his arms but there was something different in the way her responded to her this time.

"You're much too mature now to run into my arms that way, what is a man supposed to think?" Kim felt sick and disgusted and removed herself from his grasp with repulsion. Pete attempted to correct his words with unheard humor, but Kim's actions held him to his words. The ride from the terminal was long and quite as Pete's words ran through her mind. She thought back to the times when she was young and he made a similar comment. Pete had barged into her room just as she had positioned the end of her nightgown over her knees. Surprised to see him standing there in complete violation of her privacy he made her feel worse with his stare and as he said, *"you are definitely going to make some man happy one day."* And *the time when he helped her hide Monica and Eryka and he told her he wanted his payment in full.*

Engrossed in thought and wrapped in repulsion Kim did not realize the vehicle had stopped until Pete opened her door and extended his hand saying with historic humor and in a British accent, "my lady." Only this time Kim did not take his hand with a smile nor return the playful accent, instead she helped herself out and walked pass Pete and her bags as quickly as she could. Her mother looking from the window heart sank because she thought that if Kim had become too independent to play with Pete then surely she had outgrown her own mother. Especially since her contacts in the last eight months were not as frequent as Kim promised.

Kim was anxious to see her family she quick-stepped into the house with Pete directly behind her. He sat the bags at the door and Kim responded to him like a servant. "You can take those up to my room and set them outside the door." Kim's parents were mortified at her treatment of Pete and her father came to his defense.

"No Pete nothing has changed, Kim will take her own bags to her room, won't you Kim?" Kim neither gave an ingenuous smile nor response. When she turned to look at Pete to divert her parent's disapproving stare he was gone to retrieve the remainder of her things, and her luggage remained where he placed them. She turned to look at her Dad again and noticed how drastically six months had changed him. He was a lot grayer with a little less hair and he did not look like the giant he had to her all her life. Kim had quickly surmised it was because of all the six foot plus basketball players she had had the pleasure of getting to know.

"We are so glad that you made it home for Christmas we missed you for Thanksgiving, we were beginning to think you didn't love us anymore and now here you are again proving me wrong."

"Oh Mom, a ton of locomotives, a fleet of Lear Jets and an army of ships could never carry away how much I love my family." Mrs. Jenkins smiled and kissed Kim on the forehead, "you are so corny." Kim smiled back and hugged her mother extra long to smell and feel her soft hair, embraced the renewed sense of safety and security and rubbed her face against her pillow soft skin.

Mechelle Davis

Kim took in a deep breath, "Where are Monica and Eryka?"

"They didn't tell you honey, they went to spend Christmas with one of Monica's friend at their parent's cabin. They said they were not sure if you would make it home or not and didn't want to miss the opportunity to go away for the first time without old Mom and Dad."

"So I won't . . . see them . . . before I go back?" Kim was hurt.

"Don't worry honey you will see them New Years." Her Mom said reassuringly.

". . . But you will see meee Cameron said in a sing-song, surprise voice arms stretched out. Kim turned to run into her brother's arm, but the action made Pete's words flash into her remembrance. Instead she smiled hard with a shriek not sure of what to do with her excited emotions.

"Oh, you're too grown-up now to give your big brother a hug? Cameron playfully trotted to Kim, swooped her into his arms and spun her around, kissing her aggressively on her cheek before placing her back on her own two feet. Man sis did I miss you, look how mature you are, can't call you flat chest anymore, can I? Did Mom and Dad spring for those for you?"

"Oh my GOD Cameron no; Stop looking at my chest and if you really must know, GOD sprung for these for me free of charge!" Kim concluded with pride. The girl behind Cameron laughed; her laugh had drawn attention to her because moments earlier she was not noticed, at least not by Kim. Before Cameron could introduce the two Mrs. Jenkins ask in her Mom-like voice, "anybody hungry?!" Cameron and Kim raced to the dinner table as they did when they were younger. Neither of them would lose because they had claimed their permanent positions at the table a long time ago; right next to each other. Kim smiled as she looked around the table at her family and a brief moment of sadness swept over her when she looked at the empty seats belonging to Monica and Eryka. Her smile returned when she noticed her Dad looking across the table at her. She smiled deeper thinking to herself, *"its okay Dad you will always be a giant to me."*

Mrs. Jenkins had prepared a feast, more than the five of them collectively could eat. Dinner was kind of quiet Mr. Jenkins was in some sort of mood. Unusual for him, he is usually jovial, but bossy, demanding; but pleasant. Kim did not understand and learned early on that on the rare occasions he is that way to stay out of his way.

"I'm stuffed," Cameron said happily slightly leaning back and patting his stomach.

"Me too, dinner was exceptional." Kelly, Cameron's lady friend said complimenting Mrs. Jenkins, whom just nodded and softly smiled her thank you's.

"I am glad you enjoyed it now you can earn your keep. Kim said playfully. Grab a plate and follow me." Kim lead her down a hall that lead to the back of the house that opened up into a massive living room, sprawling staircase and fireplace that seemed to control one side of the house, but beauty commanded the room. The young lady paused at the breath taking sight, "it's beautiful." She placed the plates on the counter that connected the living room, family room and kitchen. "Did you design this?" She directed her question to Mrs. Jenkins.

"No, we all did." Ms. Jenkins said with a proud smile. "Kim the staircase that leads to the bedrooms from the front end of the house as well as the back, Cameron the four-step step up, one for each member in the family, that connects all three rooms, the arched doorways and the game table the appears from the middle of the floor with the push of a button. The young lady looked around as Mrs. Jenkins detailed each family member's design contribution, Dad the fireplace and me the kitchen. When Monica and Eryka joined our family; Eryka the overhead beam that looks like a log which conceals the central air, the family pictures she took herself and Monica the controlled-lighting chandelier, furniture, curtains and slip covers to change the design of the room with each season. The intercom connecting the kitchen and dining room and other parts of the house was an idea resulting of the kid's laziness. It was a welcomed feature the yelling back and forth was more noise than I cared to bare." Mrs. Jenkins teased and gently pushed her hip into Kim's. While the young lady continued to enjoy the scenery Kim and her mother continued to clear the table, kitchen counter and wash the dishes, but right before dessert was served in the dining room Mrs. Jenkins called to Kelly.

"Yes Mam," she replied.

Mechelle Davis

"It is the Jenkins family tradition to package the remaining food and take it down to the church and feed the homeless."

Kelly smiled, and added, "My mother works with the homeless all year. She's kind-hearted with a good spirit just like you, Mrs. Jenkins. Is there a particular way that you package the food?"

Kim replied for her mother, "the storage bags with the red strip are for vegetables, Mom says they're more important than meat, the brown bags are of course for meat, the yellow bags are for dairy, and this marker, Kim held up playfully tilting her head, is for writing the dates on them." The three women chattered softly while they packaged the food.

Mrs. Jenkins noticed Kelly eyeing the direction of Cameron and used the opportunity to learn a little more about her troubled son.

"Oh don't worry about dessert Kelly we always eat dessert after we package food for the homeless it allows a little time for food to digest. I think tonight we will do things a little differently we will have dessert in the family room. This will give all of us a chance to get to know you and me a chance to catch up with my beautiful daughter." The statement was met with sincere smiles and silence, but the silence was quickly filled with opportunity.

"How is Cameron doing in school?" Mrs. Jenkins asked Kelly who stood at the kitchen counter writing Dairy November 23, 1998 on two large zip lock bags just before she filled them with deviled eggs. Slightly holding her head down, but looking up at Mrs. Jenkins through her naturally long, but unnatural-looking eyelashes. Kelly smiled, "He's doing fine Mrs. Jenkins, I am sure if there were something adverse that needed to be known he would have shared. The school conducts a lot of parent-student-teacher days to help keeps parent's abreast of how the students are doing. And because Cameron's school and mine socialize we have parent-student-teacher relationship-building days twice a month every two months. I am not sure if Cameron ever told you, but it is in the manual that was given to all parents when we're registered. Anyway, my parent's would love to meet you I think the four of you will get along well."

Mrs. Jenkins smiled, it was apparent Cameron had shared his feeling about the family with her and she support and respect whatever his feelings and decisions are. She subtly avoided betraying Cameron's trust, but extended an invite to bring her family and his together. Mrs. Jenkins and Kim's fondness of Kelly deepened.

Mr. Jenkins asked the same question, but directly to Cameron as the two sat at the dining room table. "How have you been Cameron? How is school?"

"I've been great Dad life is finally returning the smile."

Cameron felt a strong discomfort and sighed, collected himself. The sudden show of emotion alarmed and unbalanced Mr. Jenkins but he gave his son a chance to collect himself and soon after Cameron gathered his thoughts and emotions, he looked at his Dad, "Dad there is something I need to say and I need you to hear me out before you respond." Cameron did not wait for his father's reply he continued quickly before he changed his mind, "Dad I know that there has always been some contention between Mom, you and me and that it was always encouraged by me, I know I was incorrigible, scary and definitely hard to deal with. So much in fact that now, looking back I wouldn't have blamed you if you had me committed. Dad I just want to say I am sorry and thanks for choosing to be my Dad, I appreciate and value everything you and Mom have instilled and done for me especially the way the two of you spoil Kim, she needed, needs you two . . . and so did I." Cameron looked at the tears well up in his Dads eyes, Cameron continued. "I hope that we could put the past behind us and move forward from here. I really want our immediate family: Mom, You and Kim plus our extended family: Pete, Monica and Eryka to have a good relationship. I don't want any of you to be afraid of me or to hate me because of the things I have done and if there was ever a choice for either of you to choose to have me in your lives or not I would want you to choose me. Cameron sighed again and continued. Going away to school has really improved my view on many things, life itself school has forced me to grow up. I just want you to know that I in no way do I resent you or Mom for sending me away in fact I owe both of you my life. I behavior was ubiquitous to say the least, I didn't know what to do and you and Mom were parent enough to know that I needed more than just being showered with love. Because of you and Mom I was taught how to discover who I really am . . . ." Pausing Cameron nodded his head slowly in an appreciative thought . . . . and I learned that I like me, that I am not so bad after all. Thanks Dad."

Cameron walked over to hug his Dad, a flagrant, uncomfortable hug. The first between the two since Cameron turned eight and his behavior became impossible to understand. Mr. Jenkins reciprocated, hugging Cameron as if he wanted to make up for all the years he missed embracing him. Before he released his son from the last hug he would ever have the opportunity to give him, through tears in his voice, he kissed Cameron on the cheek and told him he loved him and meant it.

Mr. Jenkins paused he could not speak another word his emotions got the better of him; a smile came across his face as tears laid tracks down his cheeks, soaking his goatee. This was the first time his son acknowledged his misdoings he was becoming a man and little did Cameron know that alone made his Dad extremely proud. Mr. Jenkins caught his breath enough to finally manage to say, "I am proud of you son." That was the first time in so long that Cameron could remember his Dad saying he loved him and was proud of him and in some strange way they were better, but remained the same; I guess years of habit is hard to break. Mr. Jenkins sat, playing Cameron's words over and over in his head, *"thanks for choosing to be my Dad. Does he know, or was his choice of words a coincidence?"* To break the new uncomfortable feeling between him and his Dad and also give his Dad a chance to completely collect himself, Cameron pushed the 'kitchen intercom' button, keyed in on the ladies conversation and took his chance to join in when he heard Kelly say her parent's went skiing for the holiday.

Cameron pushed the button again to activate the two-way intercom, the beep and Cameron's sudden deep voice startled Kelly. "Mom wanted to go skiing, but Kim just wanted to enjoy the comforts of home, since it had been awhile since she had been home as she promised." Kim spoke gently and playfully in the air. "When was the last time you were home?" Cameron did not respond he turned to his Dad without pushing the button to allow the ladies to hear his question.

"Hey Dad, what would you say to us joining the ladies in the family room?" Rising from the table, the inaudible base in Cameron's voice had rang out from the dining room his voice had changed, he looked older but not hard-life older; a mature kind of older. He had gained some weight; it looked really good on him and when he went home this time he did not come alone. He had a girlfriend: Kelly. She was dark-skinned, shoulder length hair, same height as Mrs. Jenkins, but about 130 pounds with a perfect set of teeth, a real pleasant but bossy personality, friendly, confident and really appeared to be in love with Cameron and herself; the Jenkins family liked her instantly. Kim thought to herself, *'Wow a lot has changed in six months.'*

The three finished packaging the food, but Mrs. Jenkins decided to break tradition and deliver the food to the Church first thing in the morning instead of that night. She went to the massive refrigerator that seemed to be stocked with more than the average grocery store would hold for public purchase and retrieved dessert.

Kim and Mrs. Jenkins instructed Kelly to join Cameron and Mr. Jenkins in the family room stating the two of them would bring in dessert. This was an attempt for Kim and her mother to steal some alone time and for things to be somewhat like they use to be before their family grew and she went off to college.

Directing her question at Mrs. Jenkins Kelly asked, "Are you sure, I am very good at serving I use to be a waitress."

"It's okay honey, go ahead, have a seat, relax, you didn't come all this way to work. Enjoy it while it lasts, I will definitely put you to work the next time you come to visit." Kelly smiled toward Mrs. Jenkins and to herself she took Mrs. Jenkins words as an invitation. Kelly was elated because she wanted to come back and soon. She followed Cameron, who was standing on the threshold of the kitchen and the family room waiting for her, down the four steps. Mr. Jenkins being who he is asked Cameron, "Why would Kelly parents allow her to come so far away from home, with a male friend without a chaperone?"

Kelly responded, "Hi Mr. Jenkins—wiggling her fingers. I'm sitting right here and I can answer that. My parent's attempted to get in contact with you through the school, Cam's and mine, nodding her head in Cameron's direction, but were not successful. Initially Cameron spoke so highly of his family and recommended that my parent's speak to the school about you, and again you and Mrs.

Jenkins were highly spoken of. My parents did not feel the need to speak to you directly because my Dad feels that in first meetings people tend to appear somewhat unauthentic, but the opinion of a collective group of reputable individuals would prove to be more accurate to the content of a person's character or integrity. So after speaking to the school my parents thought you would be the perfect chaperones and felt that I would not be in any danger coming to meet Cam's family without them. I could call my parent's and have them fly me home if they were mistaken."

Mr. Jenkins ignored Kelly's question with another question of his own. "My son attends an all male school. When would your parent's have the opportunity to speak with school officials about my son and his parents?"

"My parent's initially thought the phone would have been a perfect avenue but decided that personal contact would render better response especially because of confidentiality agreements and all. I attend the all girl school two miles from Cam's school. Our schools interact as part of the various components of our curriculum. We learn the proper etiquette in which to sit and speak in the company of a man . . .

". . . or woman," Cameron chimed in.

Kelly smiled deeply to acknowledge Cameron without losing a breath. "We are taught the proper manner in which to enter a room and since we share the world with such lovely creatures as Cameron, who better to learn with, wouldn't you agree? To further answer your question, my parent's and I have a very close family relationship, they visit me quite often and in the interim have built a very healthy relationship with the officials of the school in which I and Cameron reside, respectively. So my parent's respect and trust the officials opinion emphatically and because my parent's trust that I have the ability to do well with all the tools they instilled in me throughout life they trust me. Cameron's mentor was going to accompany him to this Christmas dinner, but thought this would be a perfect time for his parent's to get to know a very important part of his life. Would you have preferred Cameron's mentor Mr. Jenkins?"

Mrs. Jenkins intervened, with a silent smile, she liked this girl she reminded her of herself in her younger days before she decided to give her life to her husband instead of keeping some for herself. "Cameron you did not tell us about a mentor. Who is she? Tell us all about her."

Cameron started with a smile on his face and in is voice, "Mom she's a he and he is pretty cool, he says I am the son he never had. He treats me like an adult, but is firm about my studies and taking the right path in life. I told him about what Dad always says to us about being the maker of our own destiny and he agrees. He also has adopted Dads mantra, 'Move in one direction: forward'. He loves to say that to me especially when I talk about the things that led my parent's to placing me in an all boys' school." Cameron said slightly solemingly contradicting his previous conversation with his Dad.

Mrs. Jenkins gave an uncomfortable sigh while shifting in the chair she claimed in the family room as Cameron continued.

"He is helping me figure a lot of things out; Cameron raised his eyebrow to maintain his secret from his family—it is as if he knows the entire family through pictures, conversations and . . . a far off look showed in Cameron's eyes as he slowly continued . . . he seems to know the family better than I now realize. Looking at his father he continued I like that he pays attention to me, what is important to me is important to him. Through pictures alone he seems to adore Kim. Kim imagined Eryka's face tensing as Cameron continued—seriously how could he not when she is so beautiful? Cameron placed his hand over his heart. I asked him to come with me, but he told me that it would be best to bring Kelly instead because it was time that my family knew that she is a very important part of my life. Besides you all met him about one year ago when you came to see the play, The Lion King I directed for the community center. He became my mentor a short time thereafter. Dad if I am not mistaken he said the two of you briefly worked on a common project."

"Which project? Where?" Mr. Jenkins asked.

Cameron responded "actually he didn't say, I probably would not have remembered anyway."

"Does this saint have a name?" Mr. Jenkins asked jealously when he saw how Cameron's face continued to light up when he talked about him.

"His name is Whill . . . Whill Montessori. He said his mother named him Whill as a form of eternal encourage."

Mechelle Davis

"Encouragement?" Kim questioned.

Cameron kept his attention on his Dad, "Yes encouragement, you know the saying 'Where there is a Whill there is a way." Cameron smiled again and continued to fill the night with stories of his and Whill's adventures, the skills he is learning from him, like: being a man and asserting, but not aggressively asserting himself, going after what he wants and taking no prisoners." Occasionally smiling at the secrets he cleverly held out of some of the stories.

Kelly whispered in Cameron's ear and regrettably for Kim the stories ended. Kim loved hearing her brother talk; about everything and nothing. "The lady is tired" Cameron said with a smile and eagerness in his voice to accommodate her request to retire. Mrs. Jenkins interrupted Cameron's private intentions to share his room with the love of his life.

"Cameron there is fresh linen on the bed in the second guest room I believe that would be enough room to accommodate Kelly and all of her things."

The couple paused but knew it would be futile to contest. Looking at one another, Kelly spoke in a manner that made Cameron smile when she asked, "escort a lady to her room?"

Continuing with a smile, love in his voice and eyes, "Can't think of anything better I would like to do at this moment."

Kim was elated to see her brother smile constantly for the first time in a long time with such light in his eyes. He was the Cam he once was seemingly so many years ago. Mrs. Jenkins walked with Kim arm-in-arm to Kim's room talking about much of nothing. Each missed the other miserably.

"I am so happy you made it home this time, I have missed you so much. It feels good to have you home again."

Kim looked at her mother and smiled. "I have missed you too Mom." Looking around she continued. "You have no idea how good it feels to be home."

Mrs. Jenkins pointlessly adjusted Kim's long hair as she always did when she was nervous or about to get mushy. Mrs. Jenkins looked at Kim as if it were the last time she would see her and asked in a mother's voice of worry.

"Kim honey, Is everything okay?

Mechelle Davis

"Yes Mom, everything is great. Why do you ask?"

"You seemed a little out of sorts today. You seem to have been preoccupied all night, truly perplexed, deeply enthralled in whatever is going on in your head. Is everything going well in school? It isn't too late to come home."

"Everything is going great Mom, don't worry."

"I can't help it. It's one of those job requirements as a mother that increases with age." The two smiled and Mrs. Jenkins continued. "You do know you can still talk to me about anything without judgment and it will stay between you and me?" Kim was severely preoccupied with her thoughts about Pete's behavior that she missed her mother asking her if she loss her purity.

Kim sighed really not knowing what to do. "I know Mom. It's just that I didn't think growing up would be so challenging. As a child everything was black and white, as an adult there is too much grey area and it's difficult to act because so many other people and things are involved. Making the wrong decision when others are involved can hurt a lot of people and if you are wrong you have to live with the outcome. How do you do that without becoming selfish in an effort to save yourself?"

Mrs. Jenkins looking at her daughter knowing she is troubled she wanted to give her the best general advice she could.

"Oh honey, saving yourself is a natural instinct it doesn't make you a bad person, just human and as long as you regard others feelings and well-being as well as your own there is nothing wrong with speaking up. If the people you are trying to protect are the same people you are worried about hurting you really need to speak up you will save a lot of pain and heartache. Not to mention the people involved you are unaware of.

Kim you have always been careful in your decisions and I don't expect whatever decision you come to to be a hasty one. Depending on the situation, decisions are made using 60% of the heart and 39% of the mind, nothing's perfect. You have always been able to balance the percentage out that is one of the many things I love about you and have made you mature well-beyond-your-years. I have faith in you, tap into the faith you have in yourself, think it through, pray about it and make a decision without regret. Whatever you do in life Sweetheart, think it through so that you will do it without regret."

Mechelle Davis

"Thanks Mom." Kim hugged her mother and sniffed at the same time. She missed the way she smelled, even after a long hard day at work.

Mrs. Jenkins looked her daughter in the eyes and rubbed both Kim's arms as if she were warming her up. "You're welcome Sweetie." Pulling Kim to her she hugged her tight.

"I Love You." They both laugh at saying it simultaneously.

"Good night." They shared another laugh "Jenks." Kim said.

"You better believe it." Mrs. Jenkins replied with a smile.

Kim laid awake most of the night thinking about her mother's advice and how she could apply it to what had transpired between she and Pete. His words rang in her head like a church bell and she continuously relived the feeling of disgust she felt when she realized what he said. She remembered the feeling of sadness when her parents thought that she had become a shallow, self-observed and inconsiderate individual. Kim did not know which was worse, Pete or her parent's disparaging view of her. Now the feeling of confusion tidal-waved over her, she was not sure whether to save herself and tell her parent's what happened or do she just ignore what Pete said to save her parent's and hope that he would never put her in that position again.

Kim attempted to marginalize her thoughts; maybe she was reading more into his comment than there was. Sleepiness and the love for her parent's forced her to close her eyes and forget about the entire incident.

Morning came sooner than Kim wanted or was ready for. She heard a knock at her bedroom door, quickly turned over and pulled the covers over her head. Her mother and Kelly poked their heads in the door and Mrs. Jenkins smiled, thought Kim was playing asleep as she did so many times when she was younger and was not ready to get out of bed.

"Want some breakfast?"

"Not particularly, I want to sleep" Kim said in her best childlike, whiney voice.

A cheerful voice said, "I saved you some oatmeal, toast and tea."

Kim quickly removed the covers and turned her torso toward the door. Feeling a little embarrassed, Kim cleared her throat managing to ask, "How is my hair." No one answered, but Mrs. Jenkins stated. "I have tea, coffee-cakes, crumbs cake, bran muffins and hot milk downstairs, hurry up; we'll be waiting for you. I told the Church we were coming with enough food to feed their normal breakfast and lunch customers."

As the door closed Kim heard Kelly and her mother walking down the hall tickled by whatever Kelly had said and for the first time she admitted to herself she was jealous her mother was spending time with someone else. Kim quickly got out of bed, rushed her hygiene and dressed. One hour forty-five minutes later she walked into an empty kitchen, her father catching her attention from the family room. "Good morning sweetheart, you're . . ."

"Good morning Dad, Where is Mom?" Mr. Jenkins heard it in Kim's voice that she knew the answer and was hurt. He put down his newspaper and walked with nothing in mind to the refrigerator. Carefully, but casually placing his words. "Your mother said come on down to the church there was not enough room in the truck to carry the food and . . ."

". . . Me?" Kim finished her Dads sentence unknowingly sharing the hurt in her voice with her face.

Ignoring her question Mr. Jenkins continued retrieving paper from the kitchen counter and handing it to Kim. "Your mother left directions just in case you lose your way. She wants you to bring everything on the bottom shelf of the refrigerator. Need some help loading it in the car?"

"No thanks Dad, I got it." Kim said with paper in hand semi-supporting herself on the kitchen counter. Mr. Jenkins kissed Kim on the forehead and cheek playfully moving her hair from the front of her shoulder to the back.

"You know your mother loves you right and would never intentionally leave you. She's just become more involved with the church since you went off to college, Cam to school and your sister's have established their own lives and group of friends."

"I know she loves me Dad it's okay. I will be alright, don't worry. Okay?"

"Okay, just don't allow your mind to overwork itself. It isn't what you think."

Mechelle Davis

Speaking to herself so her Dad would not hear, "Now that Eryka and Monica are gone I want to spend time with her alone."

Kim picked up the fuchsia and pink paper with the dark printed letters, lines and arrows, dots, and squares that were neatly and meticulously written and drawn across a paper that led to a medium sized square which read, 'CHURCH HERE.' With sadness in her face, hurt in her eyes Kim fought back the tears and her Daddy noticed.

Kim returned her attention to her Dad. "No thanks Dad I got it. While she had his attention she asked, "Why did Mom leave?"

"She said the church needed to get set up in enough time to heat the food and learn if in fact they would have enough to feed all those people." Mr. Jenkins felt Kim's hurt, walked over to her, to hug her and in a failed attempt to make her feel better he said, "You know your mother would not have left you if there were time. She is extremely committed to her community, anal about keeping her word. Honey don't take it personal, your mother did not mean anything by it." Kim smiled to her Dad as if she understood and agreed as he hugged her and kissed her on the top of her head.

"Where is Cameron?" Kim asked

"He's sleeping in, let him sleep we had a really late night." Mr. Jenkins said in his proud voice attempting to hide the excitement that was so apparent on his face and failing miserably to hide the happiness in his voice.

"I can help you load the truck if you need help."

"Thanks Dad, I have it. I just wanted to talk to Cam. I had not seen him in a while."

Kim finished loading the truck with the goodies her mother prepared for the church and waved at her Dad. The drive was shorter than Kim remembered, but the food line almost made her want to continue driving. She pulled around back and was met by her mother; instantly Mrs. Jenkins noticed that Kim was not happy.

"Are you okay honey."

"Sure I'm fine."

"All don't be that way, I told you we had to leave soon. You know I would not have left you if I didn't have too. Come on let's make this a pleasant day the people in here are dealing with a lot more than being left behind.

Kim felt silly as she reached for the end of the roaster that held one of the largest hams she had ever seen and carried it into the Church's kitchen, grunting, "Thanks Mom for understanding."

"Oh honey don't worry about it, I think that it is cute that you are jealous." As always Mrs. Jenkins took extra time to reassure her daughter that she has always and will always come first. "You do know that you are irreplaceable, but you are practically an adult now and you must know that I will spend my time with many other young ladies other than yourself."

Kim smiled shamefully, "I know Mom on both accounts, but I am not use to sharing you with anyone else other than Monica and Eryka. After a while I hated doing that."

"Honey I never knew that!!

"I know. How could I tell you that I was jealous when I bought them home and you told me to be sure, that once the decision was made to whether they stay or not the decision was final?"

"Kim what you are feeling is normal. Is that why you don't come home or call?"

"Yes and no. I felt that way when I was younger. I mean the holidays were not the same after they officially moved in. I had to share you and at first I didn't mind but because they came from homes very different than mine, I had to share you more than I wanted and now these two, two people I brought home were taking over. I was upset . . . hurt, feeling shutout. Now it feels like once I went to college all they receive is praise and me . . . criticism for the school I chose and expressed fear that I will become some sort of loose, young woman."

Mrs. Jenkins smiled and kissed her daughter on the cheek. "Honey I know that you know how to hold yourself, your Dad and I were never worried about that, we just fear for your safety being away and so young, especially with Cam not being around to protect you. As for being shutout, you could never or will ever be shutout, I love you, you are my daughter! I waited a lifetime for you and when you finally came along as perfect as the both of you were and are nothing could replace you. I could not have begged and pleaded for a better daughter than you. You and your siblings mean everything to me." Mrs. Jenkins put the food donations down and wrapped her arms around her daughter. "If I have said it once I have said it twice, you are irreplaceable." Mrs. Jenkins looked at her daughter and smiled to reinforce her statement. "Come on, there are hungry people waiting."

Kim smiled as Mrs. Jenkins turned and disappeared through the back door. Kim followed. As soon as she put the roaster down her mother was shelling out directives to Kim and everyone around her. Mrs. Jenkins was ready and in charge. Kim had never seen her like that and did her best to keep up. She thought to herself, *I don't remember this being this difficult to keep up a year ago I should have helped out more.* Before long Kim found herself on the front line as the people continued to pour in. Standing behind the counter that lined the churches' dining room Kim was overwhelmed and quickly scolded by her mother for standing still. Glancing to her right Kim noticed Kelly smiling and running the line as if she had been this her entire life.

"Can I have some peas?" A voice asked in a friendly and understanding way. Briefly taking a look back at her mother to acknowledge her scolding Kim turned and looked into the face of Helga and froze again.

Standing before her smiling was Helga, or Hannah Brightenson, the girl's mother affectionately named her. There was something different about her. She now has gentleness and somehow her rough edges are smooth. There was not an instant fear of her, but an overwhelming sadness.

"Hi Kim."

"Hi Hel . . . Hannah."

"What's going on, you work her now?"

"No, I am here with my mother helping out. You live here now?"

"Well this isn't exactly a place to live but it is definitely a great place to get a good meal. Don't look so mortified this place is like home to me. Its great here and so are the people, they treat you with respect and dignity no matter what you did or where you come from. Especially Momma Kindness, she is great. Everyone around here loves her to death!" The people in line murmured in agreement.

Mechelle Davis

"Come on keep the line moving you got your food already there are other people back here that are hungry!" A man yelled from the middle-end of the line. Mrs. Jenkins recognized Helga and motioned for Kim to be relieved from serving. Helga moved forward on the customer side of the line and Kim followed from the server side.

"Fix yourself a plate and come eat with me."

"I'm sorry I can't we are not allowed to eat here."

Hannah knew Kim was lying because Mamma Kindness ate with her plenty of times, especially when she needed her to sit with her and talk. Kim recognized that Hannah knew she was lying and shamefully told the truth.

"I would not feel right eating here that one plate of food I eat could cause one person to go hungry. I could not handle that, someone going hungry because of me." Kim's explanation fell on semi-deaf ears. Hannah smiled as Mrs. Jenkins walked by and she reached out to her in a hurry.

"Momma Kindness? Momma Kindness, come here for a second, there is someone I want you to meet." Hannah said in a calm, child-like excited voice.

"Kim this is the lady I was telling you about . . . this is Mrs. Jenkins also know as Mamma Kindness! I love her" Hannah whispered before Ms. Jenkins reached the two.

Kim turned and approaching was her mother. *I knew it!* Kim thought and attempted to turn and walk away but Hannah quickly persuaded her by securing her arm.

Hannah loved seeing Ms. Jenkins come. Mamma Kindness this is Kim we went to school together until I got kicked out for jumping on her. This is the one I told you her brother paid me to beat up and he got away scot free." Kim and Mrs. Jenkins were mortified—for their own reasons-, but held their composure. Kim thought *all these years Eryka's claims were true.*

Hannah turned to Kim, "Your brother saved and ruined my life at the same time or maybe just saved it I don't know, but I do know it is because of him that I am where I am."

"Kimberly this is Momma Kindness, Momma Kindness, this is Kimberly Jenkins."

Mrs. Jenkins refused to mislead Hannah and attempted to tell Hannah in a casual manner.

Mechelle Davis

"What a beautiful name, especially when someone says it with such high regard; it makes me so proud. We like to call her Kim. Hannah, Kim is my daughter she's here from college helping out for the day."

Hannah stood looking as though she was forced to swallow a bowl full of alphabet soup spelling deception. Mrs. Jenkins saw the pain in Hannah's eyes and the change in her demeanor that she had spent the past six months helping her heal. Hannah's heart thumped so hard that she secretly thought there was something wrong with it.

Mrs. Jenkins walked pass Kim, over to Hannah and attempted to put her hand on her shoulder but Hannah pulled away. Mrs. Jenkins knew her work was in vain and wanted to repair things before they were too out of hand. Speaking with hurt in her voice and tears in her eyes Hannah continued, "Mrs. Jenkins I told you so many things, about Kim and Cameron and Monica and Eryka and you're their mother, you deceived me, why didn't you say anything? Mrs. Jenkins' answer me please! Why would you let me go on and on about your family that way and never say a word?"

"Hannah I didn't deceive you, at the very least not intentionally. You seemed to be so lost, you were feeling forgotten and needed someone to talk to, and I wanted to be that someone for you. You had come here with a desperate need for love and I had more than enough to give. You needed me and I needed to be needed, but at the same time the children you described are not the children I know and raised and maybe I knew all along that your schoolmates were my children, but I did not want to accept it, it would have meant that I was and am a bad parent. We never covered all the bases to make me face the truth. Hannah I never lied when I said I thought of and loved you as a daughter. Please don't pull away from me. Come on let's sit and talk." Mrs. Jenkins motioned toward Kim and Hannah, both stood still not moving, not saying a word, each felt betrayed in their own way.

"You're not who I thought you were either. I told you how my mother and father abandoned and betrayed me, mentally abused me that my Dad killed himself, very private things and you were lying to me all the time. You abused your children the same way by denying them. You are just like my parent's . . . no worse, at the least they were upfront about being miserable, lying, abusive people!

Mechelle Davis

You hid yours behind a smile, kind words, wisdom, a listening ear, wanting to help people, this church—throwing her hands in the air briefly looking around—and your Mary Poppins suit. I should have never trust you, your kids got it honestly! Thank GOD I am not your daughter." Hannah briefly looked at Kim, "Because if being your daughter earns you the hurt that I see in Kim's eyes right now, I'll pass.

Kim looked at her mother, "You hid us from her? You kept Cam and my existence quiet for a stranger. You denied us the right to have a position in your life for a stranger?! Wow a mother's love!" Kim stared at her mother in disbelief she did not recognize the woman who stood before her. "Really Mom? You and Dad scolded me, made me feel less than who you raised me to be when you thought that I treated Pete unkindly. You never investigated why I treated him that way you nor Dad ever asked! So it's okay to make your children feel less than, but not a stranger? You are a real piece of work!" Exhausted from the pain that being hurt brings Kim turned to walk away but paused turning to her mother, "You're a real piece of work!"

"Kim wait it wasn't like that, let me explain, but first no matter how you are feeling you will never talk to me like that again!" Mrs. Jenkins paused staring at Kim and Kim at her; Kim distanced herself. Sighing Mrs. Jenkins continue, "You and Hannah are misunderstanding." Kim turned to look at her mother.

"Wow Mom she isn't here and you're acknowledging her."

Mrs. Jenkins stepped toward Kim to console her and Kim resisted her touch.

"You're right Mom, I don't understand." Kim looked around the room at the gawking people. "I won't hold you up it look like you have a lot of people to save."

Kim hurried from the church in tears, shyly glancing over her shoulders hoping her mother would be in pursuit. More hurt that she was not, Kim decided to return to school early, things were becoming too much.

She pulled into the entrance of the driveway and paused looking at her childhood home she cried even harder. She heard a horn encouraging her to move forward, looking in her review mirror she waited a moment longer to collect herself and drove forward; she didn't want to worry her father. Kim drove the long driveway, pulled into a parking spot, and cleaned her face, unknowingly to her, her father pulled up beside her. She pushed the button to let the window down, waited as her father positioned himself on the outside of his car.

"Hey Dad."

"Hey Sweetie, is something wrong with the truck?"

"No it's fine." How did the volunteering go?" Mr. Jenkins asked as he walked around to the driver's side of the truck.

"It was a real eye-opener; you'd be amazed at the things you learn in church!" Holding back the tears her Dad noticed. He kissed her on the forehead. "You're still upset with your mother for leaving you this morning?"

"No Dad, I learned this afternoon that there are a lot worse things than being left behind."

"You definitely have that right. I am glad you and your mother talked."

"Me too Dad . . . me too. I learned so much about her."

"Dad, is Cameron around? Have you seen him?"

"No honey I haven't. Do you have anything in the truck that you need help taking in the house?"

"No Dad I left all the baggage and *unwanted* extras at the church." She said as her Dad opened her door and she exited the truck closing the door behind her.

Mr. Jenkins walked next to Kim with his arms wrapped around her, she needed that.

"Come on in, Daddy's got a surprise for you." Kim looked up at her Dad with a smile hoping that whatever the surprise is her mood would not cause her to disappoint him.

Just before Kim and her Dad entered the house she heard screams that startled her, looked up to see Monica running full speed ahead in her direction. Prepared for the collision the two hugged like two long lost childhood friends. Monica being Monica could see past all of Kim's smiles.

"What's the matter Kim?"

"Nothing Monica, I didn't realize how much I missed you two until now. I didn't think I would get to see you before I left. Mom told me you two went away for the holiday."

Mechelle Davis

"We did, but we couldn't let you get away without seeing you. We have two whole days to put old times back into effect." Monica said in a Welcome Back Carter sort of way. Kim smiled playfully swinging at her and purposely missing. "You are still silly."

". . . and you are too serious, loosen up!" Monica said shaking Kim who ignored her comment by focusing her attention on Eryka and Pete in the distance.

Kim felt coldness from Eryka before she spoke, "Hey Eryka." Eryka responded coldly as she walked by Kim with her arms folded.

"Hail to the Queen!" Monica said with her harms in the air and bowing as Eryka walked by heading toward the woods.

"What's up with her?"

"Don't pay her any attention, she's been difficult for a while, she wanted to stay, I wanted to come home to see you and you know Mom and Dad's rules. Both said mockingly, 'you leave together you come back together.' She isn't too happy about us being home early, she'll get over it. So what do you want to get into today?" It broke Kim's heart to tell Monica she was leaving early without a complete explanation.

"You're leaving early!? When? Why?"

"Now and it's a long story too hurtful to talk about at the moment and hopefully not worth talking about later. I am so sorry that you cut your vacation short for me, but I have to go," Kim said almost in tears as she disappeared into the house and quick-walked the seemingly half mile to her bedroom with Monica in hot pursuit.

"I knew something was wrong, what's upsetting you to the point of tears?"

Kim knew Monica would not let up so she decided to share what Pete had said to her. Please don't tell Eryka, you know for years she has felt there is something not right about him."

"And she was right, have been all these years! Kim she has a right to know so she can protect herself, you know what she has been through."

"I know, but I could be wrong."

"You're not wrong and you know it otherwise you wouldn't be this upset if you thought you were remotely wrong."

Mechelle Davis

"Let's keep this to ourselves for now, Okay? Just stay on the look-out."

"I'm sorry Kim; I know how you adored him."

"Thanks Monica, I love you so much!" She hugged her sister.

"I love you too."

"You know what hurt most Monica?"

"What's that?"

"That Mom and Dad did not give me the benefit of the doubt when it came to how I was responding to him after what he said. They automatically thought the worse of me. I'm not some Pre-Madonna, never have been. I can't believe they would think that I would change so drastically in a matter of months."

Monica allowed Kim to vent because she could understand how their parent's would see things the way they did with Kim cancelling coming home and not keeping her word.

"Kim you know no matter what Mom and Dad love you first, maybe you should have told them what Pete said."

Kim briefly thought back to the Church. "No, I think I made the right decision by keeping it to myself." Their conversation ended as Kim closed her last suitcase and reached for her duffle bag. The two exited the room, headed for the small elevator and loaded it with Kim's luggage.

"I'll meet you downstairs. All of this and us would be past capacity."

"Okay." Kim replied and pushed the down arrow. Monica stopped the door from closing.

"Kim?" She looked up serving as a response.

"I would have given you the benefit of the doubt?"

"I know Monica, thanks."

"What are sister's for?" The two smiled at one another and Monica allowed the door to close.

The two chatted like old times as they unloaded the elevator and walked the long hallway leading to the kitchen. Pete was in the kitchen retrieving water from the refrigerator.

"You're leaving Kimmey?" Pete asked as he headed for her luggage. Kim turned to Pete with a cold hurt stare, "It's Kim, I'm too old for Kimmey and you don't need to help with my luggage Monica and I have it."

Mechelle Davis

"It's no problem I just prepared the car for outings."

"How could it be a problem, it is what you are being paid for? Besides I'm taking the truck you can arrange to have it picked up from the airport later." Pete did not like the coldness in Kim's voice and the ice on Monica's eyelashes.

"Kim let me talk to you before you leave I believe there was some sort of misunderstanding between the two of us."

"Wow it is amazing that before college I was considered intelligent and after entering my comprehension skills decreased. I understood your intentions, what I don't understand is why you are still here! I don't need your help Pete, you are dismissed!"

Pete stood frozen and fearful for a barrage of reasons he had a lot to lose if what he said to Kim and her feelings about him as a result were made known to her parent's. How would he explain to his wife he was fired from working for the people that mutually looked at one another as family and why?

Kim and Monica loaded the family truck with Pete looking on, and said their good-byes.

"Tell Dad, Eryka and Cam good-bye for me. Oh yeah, Cam has his girlfriend here, you will really like her?"

Monica stepped back, spread her feet, flicked the side of her nose with her thumb, and positioned her arms and fingers as if she were about to pull out a gun from a holster. "I will or else we will run her out of town like we did his other loser girlfriends!" Kim entered the truck, began to back out and playfully said through an open window, "Monica you have been watching way too many western movies with Dad." The two shared a brief laugh.

Monica called back. "Kim you didn't mention Mom!"

"We said our good-byes. Make sure you come visit me and I promise to do better with being in touch with you and Eryka. Love you."

"Love you too." Monica said as the two waived and Eryka looked on from the woods.

Unloading the truck by herself was more than a notion, but Kim was proud that she did as she pulled the cart though the airport and up to the ticket counter.

"Please let me be able to get a ticket, please let me be able to get a ticket." She prayed to herself.

Mechelle Davis

"Hi, may I help you?"

"Yes I need a one way first class ticket to New York."

Surprised that she was able to get a ticket last minute she paid for the overpriced ticket and ran to beat the ten minute she had left to board. She boarded, put her duffle bag in the overhead compartment, seated, buckled herself in, retrieved her diary from her large shoulder bag and wrote:

I think I know why it's so easy for my mother to deny me but it doesn't stop the hurt, she's the only mother I know. I am deeply hurt and can barely contain my emotions. I've forgiven her already because I know she has her reasons and whatever they are I am sure were never to slight Cam and me, but to be denied in any form for whatever reason hurts and even if her intentions were good it doesn't hurt any less. This weekend was not what I had planned or hoped for; the family I once knew is no more. Changes like that I needed in small doses and are too drastic for me to return any time soon. In time I am sure I will feel differently, but right now I can't imagine how or when. I feel emotionally abandoned. I can't believe she hid Cameron and my existence. Mom and Dad still did not have the talk with Cameron and me. Maybe the conversation she wanted between the four of us is the reason she could deny us by omission so easily. I wonder if Dad feels that same way Mom does. GOD I pray that he doesn't.

I have decided to put what Pete said to me in the past. I am devastated that he would look at me that way and disgusted that he expressed it. Eryka was right about him, he isn't right and I know that if he hid that part of him for so long that there are other hidden personalities and major secrets that we don't know about. Pete just isn't Pete anymore he is Pete with a secret. Thinking back on the way he looked at me, the expression on his face I almost didn't recognize him. I forgive him, but I will definitely proceed with caution.

Cameron came home with a new girlfriend, I love her. I know Monica and Eryka will love her too. Well at least Monica will. She has a subtly-loud confidence about her and the way she respectfully stands up to Mom and Dad is priceless. She and Cameron seem to really be happy together, I think she is good for him; some light with the dark is just what he needs.

Mechelle Davis

Tried to talk to Eryka, but there is something more different about her than it was before I left for college; her resentment of me has me worried. What happened to my family?! I need to pull it together I can't expect things to stay the same. Kim thought for a moment before she wrote again. But I can expect for change not to be this extensive.

Monica checked in with the guard, signed the book, put her things into the locker and stuffed the key in her front pocket. She stood at the door of room 212, she took a deep breath and went in. "Hello Nurse Jordan."

"Hello Monica. How are you?"

"Well."

"Good. Try not to stay long this time, she is really upset today. We may have to increase her dosage."

"What happened? What upset her?"

"She's still blaming herself. She get's like this every time Eryka comes to visit."

"Eryka's been here?"

"Yes, yesterday right after you left. She's pretty calm compared."

"Listen, from this moment forward I don't want Eryka here. She is no longer allowed to visit my sister. How do I make that official?"

"You just did, I will talk to her psychiatrist."

"Thanks Nurse Jordan."

"No problem. Your brother's death and then your parent's have been too much for her to handle. I understand why Kim is here, she could very easily be me. She doesn't need any more stress and I want to make sure that none goes her way."

I won't stay long it looks like whatever you just gave her is working. I want to visit before she goes to sleep."

"I'll go talk to her Doctor about your directions."

"Hey Kim, Can I sit next to you?"

Mechelle Davis

"Sure." Kim said patting the space next to her on the twin size bed. "I'm not sleepy." Kim took the pill from her mouth and showed it to Monica. "Don't worry; I'm going to take it just not right now. They help me sleep through the night. Without it I would be inside my head all the time."

"How are you?"

"Good. Thanks for having Nurse Jordan keep Eryka away for a little while. I didn't have the heart to ask her not to come back." There was silence for a moment. "In group today they said talking about the past sometimes help you see your future a lot clearer, I believe that. I was sitting here earlier doing my homework, trying to keep up and I was thinking about how I got here. Do you remember that Christmas I came home and left early?"

"Yes. What about it?"

"Cameron was murdered before the following Christmas and Mom, Dad shortly after and now I am here. Much can happen in three years."

"Yeah Kim it can and did, but you are still alive and you have to go on, you have to push through this and I know you can do it."

"I can and I will I am just going to need some time. I was thinking about that day you and Eryka's first day at college. I was so happy, things were going well considering. My relationship with Mom seemingly fixed itself, in fact we grew closer and I attributed that to the family losing Cameron especially in such a horrible way. I thought the death of a sibling would have brought Eryka and me closer, but instead it put a greater distance between us and then I needed everyone to help me deal with his death and that didn't help. So I threw myself deeper into my schoolwork and concentrated more on family. I never really grieved losing him; I somehow convinced myself that he was still away at school doing his own thing.

Then I saw a new appreciation of me from Dad and I could hear that his concerns were no longer just my college choice, but me being so far away from home. I just wished our conversations were not always the same. "The college you attend carries a lot of weight in corporate American." It was those times that I missed Cameron the most. Hearing his deep voice would make me feel protected, secure in the person I am, decisions I've made and reassured even from miles away. I was grateful that Dad had passed on such an excellent attribute that I found solace in. The same solace I use to feel talking to Dad. I use to love hearing Dad's voice then it became a sound I dreaded.

Kim became a little jealous as she reflected over all the time that her sister's were in the house and she never once heard her Mom or Dad complain about Eryka and Monica who both failed their freshman and sophomore year. Kim's minute anger was solely toward her Dad because she knew her Mom was disappointed with Eryka and Monica and she expressed it in more ways than verbal. Despite what Monica and Eryka had been through both had an inborn resounding propensity to hold on to the passion they have toward school, some challenges were expected, but Mrs. Jenkins made no excuses for them and would not let them make any for themselves. She punished them for failing, but was silently happy because the house was still filled with 'young laughter' as she called it, but Kim's Dad said or did nothing.

Mrs. Jenkins, Monica and Eryka had built a stronger relationship in Kim's absence and Kim was evermore jealous. The two had developed the same passion for shoes as Ms. Jenkins. Monica had the fetish when she was younger but Ms. Jenkins helped her develop it. The three would sit and have long talks at night just the way Mrs. Jenkins and Kim use to and it truly bothered Kim, though she never expressed it to any of her siblings.

Shortly after Kim went off to college the girls moved into their own rooms and Monica and Mrs. Jenkins redecorated Monica's bedroom together, Monica accepted all of Ms. Jenkins ideas and 'Momma Jenkins' loved her for that. Mrs. Jenkins even showed Monica how to sew and design cloths telling her that it was much cheaper and more rewarding to wear your own name on your backside than someone else's. Monica took her advice to heart.

Kim laid across her bed, opened her diary and flipped back to September, 1994 reviewed her list and with a smile retraced her checked off goals and the one she seemed to have a darker trace than any was number 1. Prove Daddy wrong. She smiled briefly as she thought about how well her first year went. Kim reviewed her list again: graduate school one year early, Kim decided to go ahead and check it off. Just before she placed a checkmark in the self-made box

Mechelle Davis

she heard her mother's voice, *"never mark something accomplished unless you have actually accomplished it it brings about a bad look, and it's never good to be presumptuous!"* Kim loved and respected her mother, but was convinced she knew herself better and Mr. and Mrs. Jenkins would be coming to see her walk in two years, she checked the box anyway.

September 22, 1995 my sister's will be joining me in three days, one year early with the help of summer school and extra credit, to begin their college experience and I can't wait, for more reasons than one, mostly because they are getting too close to my mother. I know that I should not be jealous, but I cannot help it. They are positioned in her life just like me and everyone is replaceable. I mean I did step aside a little so that each of them would find their place in our home and they did just what I hoped. While I was home I was able to maintain more of Mom's love but now I am gone, it seems as if I've been replaced. I resent them for failing and spending more time with our parent's than me and I also hate that I was so willing to share her. Anyway I still miss my sisters and can't wait until they are here. We all have grown so much I hope in that growth we have not grown too far apart.

September 25, 1995. Three days had passed quickly and I love my sister's being on campus with me, it would be like old times. The three of us walked the campus and I introduced them to new friends for hours, reintroduced them to hot spots, not-so-hot spots and of course the great guys and the guys to stay away from.

Eryka was into acting so I knew she would be excited to see how they remodeled the drama hall, but Eryka seemed unimpressed. I felt it right off that there was something about me Eryka no longer liked and the vibe were greater than it was the last time I was home. I felt, then caught a few of the hatful glances from Eryka and the responses to my invites to parties and into conversations came off as if Eryka resented me for something. Between glares I would catch the look from Eryka that read, 'I know something about you that you don't know I know.'

Monica already knew what I was noticing, there is a *secret* Eryka just as there is a *secret* Pete and is a *secret Cameron and* I wondered if Mom and Dad knew Eryka, the Eryka I see . . . the Eryka she really is?

Mechelle Davis

Teasingly Monica asked, "Hey Kim, did Eryka tell you about her secret boyfriend?"

"No, spill it," I said playfully to Eryka attempting to recapture the closeness we once had.

"If that was something I wanted to share with you I would have done it without the encouragement of Monica," Eryka replied snidely.

"Wow, somebody is having a bad day. Are you tired?" I asked.

"No, just sick of people being in my business" she replied as she walked ahead. Neither I nor Monica acknowledged her behavior and continued on with the tour and making plans for that night. It was something about Eryka that felt hopeless, sad, and envious; Monica and I felt sorry for her and hoped that she would come to us when she was ready. I am confident that she will because we have always talked about everything. Kim flipped the page.

I whispered to Monica, "This is definitely not the sister I had two years, three days ago. We looked at Eryka in confusion we didn't have a clue as to why she had changed so drastically, even her appearance become dark. We decided to give Eryka her space and leave the door open for whenever she was really ready to talk.

Monica whispered, "She has been this way for some time now Kim, forget her. Remember what Mom and Dad told us the only actions we can control are our own and the outcome of the actions all depend on how conscious we are about what we are doing?"

"Yes. But . . ."

"There is no butt's Kim, Eryka is fully aware of what she is doing. Because from it all, you can see that she is sorry for whatever she's doing, but is not willing to stop. Whatever it is is more important to her. Let it go, she's made her choice!"

I could not help it; Eryka's behavior and attitude toward me really worried me. Thinking back to the few times I went home for the special occasions how distant Eryka was to me and at times cruel. I want to help my sister but I need to pin-point the start of her behavior and thought of two points; Cameron's new girlfriend and then his death.

Kim slowly turned through several of the pages.

Mechelle Davis

J ust before Kim's 17th birthday her parents died unexpectantly
leaving millions. Kim decided to donate it all telling herself
that she would donate her entire inheritance to prove to herself
that she could make it on her own accord. But when she took a
moment to be honest she knew her donation would be because she
felt guilty for not calling her parent's as she promised now they're
gone and she will never have the opportunity.

Kim wrote 'Broken Promises' at the top of page 1196 of her
diary as Eryka words resonated in her head she looked at her dorm
door as that awful day played in her mind's eye. Kim heard the floor
in front of her door squeak and looked at the door just before it
swung open. Monica and Eryka barged in, "Did you call Mom and
Dad and wish them happy anniversary?"

"Did either of you?"

"Yes we did and they said you are not answering your phone.
Kim you really need to call them something could be wrong, but
Eryka's concerns fell on deaf ears. Kim thought as she cut an eye
at Eryka, *now you want to be half human and show concern,* but
continuously said, "I will its finals and I have a lot of studying to
do. Plus I am really not in the mood to hear Dad ball me out for
attending predominately black college. Wait, don't say it, I know
that they support us in everything we do, but this time Dad is
wrong. It has been years and he still won't let up. I love it here,
I mean the work is challenging, it is a well known college, it is
dead center of everything and the company I have my eye on is
here. To add whip cream to the—the girls joined in—HOT MILK
my sister's—are here. He won't acknowledge any of that and I

am tired of not being good enough, I am beginning to feel like Cameron did."

"We love you Kim, Monica said and you know Dad does too he just wants what's best for you."

"Yeah, his best, I have found my own best and I love it!"

"Fine you love your own best Eryka said snidely, what's new? Call Mom and Dad today, right now even, so they can stop calling me. I am so sick of people acting as if I am your dam keeper! Get off your self-righteous horse and make the dam call!" Eryka slammed the door as she stormed out.

"Wow, what's with her?"

"Whenever Mom and Dad could not get in touch with you, even now, they drove us crazy. She has a right to be annoyed, but not that angry."

"Sorry, I didn't know, okay look, it is five o'clock, I will call them once I finish studying these last two chapters, which will be about eight o'clock I promise, now go away and leave me alone, the sooner I finish studying the sooner I can call them." Kim was good at keeping her promises so Monica agreed and left.

Hours ticked by as Kim watched the clock in efforts to maintain her promise. *"Dang an hour has passed already; I still have a long way to go. I should call them now this way I could get it over with."* She dreaded the phone call and the conversation that she knew would ensue. As she read on all the words began to look the same. She put her right thumb over her right eye, her right index finger over her left and by the time she finished rubbing and looked up again it was three a.m. and the knock at her dorm door startled her completely awake. Angry that she had broken her promise, Kim got up and groggily opened the door, never asking who it is. There stood her dorm master and Eryka. Kim's heart pounded she knew why they were standing in her dorm doorway, she had the same feeling when her parent's stood at her door to break the news to her about Cameron, but her mind wanted, needed confirmation of the news she already knew. They stepped in out of the hall and Eryka did not speak a word, when she tried bone chilling sobs came out. With tears already rolling down her face Kim caught Eryka as she collapsed.

"Mrs. Brewer, what's wrong," Kim asked? Already knowing the answer her instincts warned her of.

Mechelle Davis

"It's your parents."

"My parents, are they here?" Kim asked pointlessly looking past Ms. Brewer.

"No sweetie they're not."

"Are they all right?" Kim continued to ask questions to prolong the news, to keep her normal college life a little while longer.

Mrs. Brewer responded, "No sweetie they are not. Your parent's were killed in a house fire. The fire swept through so quickly they didn't have a chance, the fire marshal and the coroners said they did not suffer they died in their sleep." The title "coroner" rang in Kim's head as the dorm master continued to give her the details. Mrs. Brewer continued.

"They had been celebrating someth . . ."

Kim cut her off, "their fortieth anniversary."

"What?" Mrs. Brewer asked.

"They were celebrating their fortieth wedding anniversary; I could have gone home yesterday and I chose not to." Kim unconsciously released Eryka and sat down on her bed, to try and gain her composure; Eryka sat beside her, put her arms around her and said, "at least we got a chance to talk to them one last time." Kimberly burst into tears, depression, guilt, and remorse, hit her all at once. Eryka did not give it a second thought that Kim had not responded to her statement. Kim looked at Eryka through eyes that looked like a person who had just lost their whole world and had gone insane as a result, Kim asked, "Where is Monica?"

As suddenly as Kim began to cry she stopped. She cried a silent cry, tears running a steady stream down her face, mind racing, her body heaving as she suppressed the cries that would inevitably lead to screams of agony. She paced shaking her hands uncontrollably, rambling.

"I'm all alone, my parent's, my brother, this is all my fault, Kim mumbled to herself, I should have gone home, I should have called, I could have sent flowers, I could have . . ." before she could continue mumbling Mrs. Brewer secured her by the shoulders and gently shook her. Kim was visibly unstable on her feet and she slowly focused her eyes on Mrs. Brewers face.

"I need to be alone; I want to be by myself . . . . I need to be by myself." As Mrs. Brewer objected Kim glanced at her books lying in the middle of her floor. Mrs. Brewer misread her concerns and continued, "It is the end of the semester and I will work something out with the instructors to keep you one track, don't worry about finals you and your sister's take some time off.

"Thanks," Mrs. Brewer, Eryka said as Kim dazed into space. Mrs. Brewer left and on her way out she told her assistant, "she doesn't look well, we will have to keep an eye on her." "Call the schools psychologist and have her speak to the Jenkins girls right away."

"It's three thirty in the morning, the assistant stated.

"I have a watch thank you. I don't care what time it is, wake her up and get her over here!" Mrs. Brewer replied sternly.

"Eryka I need some time alone." Kim continued to plead using the words that mattered most in the world to her right then. "I need to be alone."

"Kim you don't need to be alone right now, would you please let me be here for you? You have always been there for me please don't push me away when you need me most."

"You were right."

"What?" Eryka asked through a trembling mouth.

"You were right when you said to call Mom and Dad because something bad was going to happen."

"Kim I never said something bad . . . that isn't important right now what is important is that you talked to them and was able to hear their voice one last time."

Those words deepened her dagger of guilt and Kim's emotions turned on Eryka. "How do I know you didn't kill my parent's or at least had something to do with it? You have always been jealous of my parent's and my relationship since day one!"

"Kim you know that is not true, Mom and Dad have been parents' to me since my mother willingly gave up her parental rights, they became my foster parent's and I changed my last name. How could you say that? How could you accuse me of having something to do with their death, come on now that's as ridiculous as it sounds?"

"Monica told me how you had been disappearing, making them worry and disrespecting them, hiding my pictures and GOD knows what else. Your actions show there was and is something there that isn't right. You have not been a good daughter or sister and it showed in all your actions. Now you want to stand here and pretend like you care!"

"Kim, stop before you say something you or I cannot take back."

"Yes your right," Kim said. "Stop, turn around and get out, you and your evil ways had something to do with their death, you, I and everyone knows it. Intuition my ass, you make things happen!"

Eryka stood starring in disbelief of Kim's out of character behavior and the many truths that hid in between her words. Her heart pounding wondering if the things she just said were out of anger or if she knew what she had been doing.

"Kim you are sounding silly." The two girls sat quietly for a moment unsure of how to respond to Kim's emotional outburst. Eryka broke the silence.

"I will make the reservations for the first plane home."

"Don't bother, Monica and I will handle it we will fly home together, unless you see death in that!" Kim asked sarcastically. With tears streaming down her face for the lost of her surrogate parent's and apparent loss of one of her sister's, Eryka turned and left. She admitted to herself that all of what Kim said, though out of anger was true. *What else does she know? What else could she possible know?"*

Kim burst into tears again her body weak from the many emotions she was feeling and she collapsed on the floor of her dorm room.

On the way out Eryka ran into Monica and Jessica, sneaking back in from an off campus party. Knowing that Kim could and should not handle the news on her own, Eryka told Monica the horrible news of losing their parent's.

Midday had come quickly, the three girls returned to Kim's dorm room. Kim was awakened by the sound of Monica's voice, looking into both her sister's faces, Kim looked up at Eryka and began to speak, but Eryka cut her off, "it's okay, I understand. I made reservations for all of us on the one o'clock flight out."

"Us?" Kim asked

"Yeah, I am going too, so if I see something bad is going to happen we're all going down . . . together." Kim smiled and Monica sighed, "That's not funny, Eryka, man you are morbid! You can't say things like that just before we get on a plane! Kim and Eryka smiled at Monica.

Monica repeated in fear and frustration. "Seriously, you can't!"

"Come on get up our flight leaves soon," Eryka said to Kim. As the two stood up there was a knock at the door. Neither noticed the creek. Jessica opened the door.

"Yes?"

"Hello, is this the room of Kimberly Jenkins?"

"Yes, how can we help you?" Monica interjected.

"May I come in?" Jessica stepped aside.

"Hi, my name is Dr. Kowen,—hand out—stretched—I am the schools psychologist are you Kim?"

"No, I'm not that's Kim." Nodding her head in Kim's direction, Monica never accepted her hand.

"Hello Dr. Kowen, I'm Kimberly Jenkins is there something I can do for you?"

"No, but I was hoping that there is something I could do for you. The Dean thought that you might need someone to talk to. I am really sorry about your losses, turning her eyes toward Monica and Eryka as to include them in her wishes of condolences.

"Thank you, but I have my sister's and friends to talk to."

"Family and friends are a great tool or source of comfort to get through grief, but I would love to help you professionally. Sometimes the magnitude of such a great loss isn't realized, but it manifests in the things a person does and they or the family may not see it because you all will be grieving together. Are you sure you don't want to talk not even for a little while?"

"Yes, I am sure. Thank you."

"Well I am here if you or your sister's want to talk later. I will be here for the remainder of the afternoon here is my card, feel free to call me if you change your mind; my cell number is on the back for easy contact. This invitation includes Monica and Eryka too. Please neither of you hesitate to call me if you need anything." Dr. Kowen turned and began to walk out the door "Call me if you need anything." She turned and repeated before leaving.

"Thank you Dr. Kowen, but our flight leaves in a little while. Thanks for coming. Kim replied politely with a puzzled look on her face."

"Oh you're welcome."

"Dr. Kowen?"

"Yes?"

"Have we met before?'

"I don't think so sweetie, you are a little young to associate with my realm of friends, but anything is possible."

Dr. Kowen had to admit to herself there was something definitely special about Kim that drew her to her it was apparent that Kim felt the same connection. Dr. Kowen had an overwhelming urge to run to Kim and pull her into her arms, but professionalism held her back.

Running down the terminal; bags in hand, Monica struggling with her book bag on wheels that she was using for luggage, Kim running but in slow motion. *Something isn't right with her it's more than losing Mom and Dad, maybe she should have talked to Dr. Kowen. I will encourage her when we get back,* thought Eryka. They weren't too far from the gate, when the Flight Attendant started closing the curtain. Monica yelled, "Wait we're coming!" The Flight Attendant looked, thwarted her gaze from Monica and proceeded with closing the curtain. Monica grabbed everyone's ticket, ran faster and through the curtain almost running the attendant down. Looking at her displeasingly she said, "You have three more, thank you for waiting." The attendant smiled, looked at the tickets and took them out of Monica's hand just as Kim and Eryka finally made it through the curtains. Eryka looked at Monica and asked, "Is everything all right?"

"Yes, the attendant is just about to show us to our seats, in FIRST class." The attendant looked at the tickets again," right this way."

Eryka tugged on Monica's arm, "You know you cannot be acting a fool on the plane. What did you say to her? I am not going to jail with you!"

"Nothing, I promise, I didn't say anything."

The words 'I promise' triggered something in Kim and she began to cry. All three looked at Kim because her tears seemed out of the blue. Eryka placed her arms around her and escorted her onto the plane. The attendant questioned if she were all right. In unison Eryka and Monica said, "She's fine; just show us to our seats." As

Mechelle Davis

Kim cried Monica thought I *am definitely going calling Dr. Kowen to meet with Kim first thing when we get back.*

Eryka arranged for the family personal limousine to pick them up. When they arrived in Texas six hours later and walked into the terminal Kim recognized the driver immediately it was Pete. Kim relied on Pete heavily to get through the death of Cam. She had long ago forgiven him and was elated to see him, but from a distance she could tell there was something very different about him, almost like a stranger. With his body language he may as well been holding a sign that read: JENKINS? His eyes were red as if he had been crying all night as he approached Kim and put his arms around her she reciprocated and sobbed, moments later he invited her sister's in for a group-hug. Pete was surprised to find Eryka's arms wrapped around him. The remainder of their patch-work family headed for the limousine. The three girls took their usual place in the back.

"To the hospital," Pete asked?

"No." Surprised Pete looked at Kim through the review mirror.

"To the house!"

"Are you sure Miss. Are you sure you're ready to see that now?"

Miss? Kim thought.

"Yes, Kim said assertively semi-responding to him as if he were an employee as he had responded to her as his employer, "To the house." She returned to the blank daze she had on the plane. As they drove the two-hour drive seemed like twenty-minutes. To Pete it wasn't long enough, he had been to their home the night before and he could not hold his composure while driving up the once pretty green forest-like entrance that led to the Jenkins home, the home that held so many good memories, are now charred, black and gray. All the beauty and color that was once there is now gone, to them forever. The swing the four of them use to play on as a child was scorched from the intensity of the heat, but still partially hanging from the tree. Before the limousine could stop Kim opened the door with tears streaming down the four of their faces.

The sadness in the air was so poignant it was paralyzing, Kim gathered herself enough to move past the threshold of the limousine door. She stepped out and the burned tree branch cracked under her foot. As she looked down, sound reminded her of five Christmas's ago, Kim shared her memory out loud.

"Remember that one Christmas Mom and Dad decided that we would not go away for the holiday? I was so glad we didn't it made us closer as a family. Dad went outside to bring in more firewood, picked up a branch and with much discouragement from Mom and me; he put the branch into the fireplace saying that it would give off a wonderful smell of the outside and hours later when he went to reload the fireplace the branch cracked, flung itself out of the fire, onto Mamma's favorite sweater burning a huge hole in it. Dad was running around looking for something to put the fire out but everything he reached for was another of Momma's favorite things. Finally he threw the sweater on the floor rolled it up to smother the fire when it was out we were all standing in disbelief. Dad said, "Mmmmm, smells like chicken!" We all laughed as Mom ran to his side and kissed Dad as a reward for being a hero. "Mmmmm, taste like chicken." She said.

Kim stood in front of what was left of their parent's home with a small smile on her face, but still a steady flow of tears made tracks down her cheeks. Monica's touch ended Kim's momentary reminiscing.

"Are you all right Kim, can you do this?"

"Yes . . . Yes . . . I can, I need to." As Kim stepped forward Monica continued to get out of the car while Eryka proceeded to exit from the available door. Rushing to Kim's side, Eryka attempted to embolden her to do 'this' another day because it really was not necessary. Kim insisted she needed to do 'this' today something inside said she needed to. Stepping forward she walked over to the shell of a house and pushed the front door open instead of walking through what use to be a wall.

"*What about the rest of the house, Daddy?*" She remembered asking when he and Pete were putting up the door.

"*This door is much heavier and flame retardant.*"

"*Daddy, how can a door be retarded?*" *Dad gave Mom the look and she called me to her and we headed for the kitchen.* It felt weird entering into a door that was rarely used. When Kim stepped in she immediately noticed her mother's necklace. Her heart dropped and for a moment she could not breathe because she knew her mother loved that particular necklace and would have never taken it off. It was a gift from the great Mrs. Jenkins collection of jewelry when she was nine. Kim walked over to the charred banister and as she picked up the necklace the banister fell. Her sisters rushing to her side with concern, "Kim are you okay?"

"Yeah, I am fine," she said in almost a whisper. Unsuccessfully thinking to herself, she lipped her thoughts and her barrage of questions as she took a few more steps forward. *"I wonder how this got here. Why didn't the police see this? Why did the fire department put this there and not in Mom's property? How did it get off my mother's neck?"* Some questions clearly confirmed her suspicions as fear began to settle in and questions continued to fill her head. *"This was no accident, someone killed my parent's, but who and why?"* She looked back at her sister's and decided to keep her discovery a secret at least for now. She gently folded the necklace in her handkerchief and placed it in her pocket. *"I wonder if they suffered, if they seen it coming? What were their last words? Why didn't they try to get out?"* Looking over at Pete, *"and why does Pete keep calling me Miss. Jenkins?"*

T he sound of Kim brother's voice kept ringing in Whill's head.

"My sister would never date you, you are not her type and you are old enough to be her father. You're a sick man Whill my sister would see right through you she's a smart girl."

"You're saying your sister is too good for me?"

"I didn't say that, but come to think of it . . . yeah!"

"You don't think that she could ever love me?"

"No, honestly Whill, I don't. I mean don't get me wrong you're a good-looking guy you would be perfect for my Mom if she weren't married." Quinn did not enjoy being told that he could not have something nor did he like being made fun of and he definitely did not like being called old. It was at that moment Quinn devised a plan. He turned to Cameron, "I can get your sister to love me in spite of our age difference."

"Come on Whill, give it a rest. You have been looking at my sister now for years, since she was in the eighth grade, probably longer. I know there are some things you are not telling me. If you were too afraid to approach her then you're too afraid now; especially since she has grown into the fine woman that she is. You would have to do something really dramatic to get her attention, she doesn't even know that you exist and you have plenty of her favorite pass time . . . money."

You don't know your sister as well as you think, her favorite pass time is reading, visiting the art museum, being a mouth piece for demure students and volunteering at one of the top law firms in New York: Cadwalader, Wickersham & Taft."

Mechelle Davis

Cameron grew defensive, "Are you stalking my sister? She's off limits, you need to back off you're treading on dangerous ground with Kim. Give it a rest she will never want you and even if she did I would never approve!"

"Well, I'll tell you what, if I can't have her, I will have everyone around her in any way I choose, this includes your parents." Cameron's smile went off his face quickly and he ceased shining his machete.

"What do you mean? Whill I swear that if you hurt my sister or my parent's I will kill you, shred you to pieces!" The deepness of Cameron's voice grew louder and Will glanced at his room door as a sign to down.

"Who said you would be around to see?"

"I will be the only one of us around my sister. Stay away from her!"

Whill took a deep breath. "You said I needed to do something drastic to catch her attention, well . . . okay."

Before Cameron could say anything or adjust himself, in one fell swoop Whill took Cameron's favored machete from his hands and struck him across the mouth, cutting through muscles and bone, his jaw immediately fell to his chest. The look of it shocked Whill; even he had never seen such tragedy. Realizing that most of his face was gone Cameron attempted to scream, but his mentor struck him again across the stomach and instantly his ugly insides spilled the floor. Blood was everywhere and Cameron looked at Whill with a surprised look of horror that Whill deeply enjoyed. Gurgling on the blood that filled his throat Whill stood for a moment and watched Cameron slowly drown. He walked over to him, pushed the machete through the remainder of his lower extremity and pulled the machete up until his body fell north and south of his bedroom.

"Now who tore whom to pieces?" Quinn asked as he stepped over the mangled body heading toward the door and paused just before exiting. Never looking back he said, "as your Dad always say move in one direction: forward, but you never did listen. Onward and upward, I have a love to that needs my emotional support."

Whill wiped the excess blood from the machete on one of Cameron's shirt's hanging in the closet, replaced the machete into its sheath, tucked it under his arm and left.

Mechelle Davis

"W ow," Mr. and Mrs. Jenkins your son's death was really horrible yet fascinating as he told of the last night of their only son's death with desperate fascination in his eyes, appreciation for the experience in his voice and a smile on his face.

"Can you believe that was nearly two years ago? Time flies when you're having fun doesn't it? Are you two . . . having fun?" Quinn grabbed Mr. and Mrs. Jenkins head and moved them individually up and down.

"You see I want to thank you for neglecting your son because if you had not then I would have never seen Kim. Okay I'm lying, you can thank my brother for that I really hate him." The Jenkins looked at Whill with puzzlement in their eyes.

"You don't know, do you? . . . Pete, yep good OLE Peter Dennovotti is my brother." He put his face close to Mrs. Jenkins's, "Look you really don't have to look closely to see the strong resemblance. Whill continued as he bucked his eyes and slowly moved his face in a circular motion to mockingly give Mrs. Jenkins a good look and opportunity to recognize the resemblance. "Fam. mi.ly is what we are." Whill said as the hugged himself and shook his body, but he threw that away, I am sure that he did not tell you all about it, did he? Aw and you won't have another chance to ask him about it, this is an awful predicament he put you in. I won't tell you either, you don't have that much time, besides you already have enough on your mind and I don't want to burn any bridges between my brother and you two. "Get it, BURN BRIDGES? Laughing hysterically, awwwww forget it you two have no sense of humor."

Mechelle Davis

Picking up Kim's picture from the nightstand, "Isn't she beautiful, beautiful inside out? I really must commend you two on the wonderful job you two have done with her. Or should I? Maybe she is who she is genetically and you two have nothing to do with it. Does she know? Cameron did. He knew you were not his parent's . . . that you Daddy did not love him. I mean how could he not know when Daddy here so passionately said that he hated and was afraid of him? Dear old Dad here praised Kim and assassinated the mere thought of his own son. Then you two agree to send him off to a boarding school far enough away that he could not come back. You two did a hell of a job making him feel unloved, and Kim oooh, one more year of you Dad I believe she would have put herself in boarding school. Don't worry all that is behind you now and I promise I will take good care of her. Now Mom, I know that you would want Kim to have this necklace Cameron told me how important it is to you so, here let me help you take it off. Dad I don't need anything from you unfortunately your son preceded you in death. I don't think he would have valued anything from you anyway. I am really sorry that I have to do this, but some things are truly necessary when pursuing love and happiness and your deaths is one of them. I think that it's great that you all had planned to spend her birthday with her she is really going to need to know that you still loved her and need me to get through these difficult times. I really would have loved you two as in-laws."

Leaving Mr. and Mrs. Jenkins tied up on the bed—"don't go away"—Whill went to the shed and pulled out the ladder. When he returned he returned through the window that he would exit. Whill injected Tetrodotoxin in Mrs. Jenkins arm and almost instantly she became stiff. Completely aware of what's going on around her, but could not move. He did the same to Mr. Jenkins then laid the gun on the table.

"You two will be in this paralyzed state for an hour I am sorry you will feel everything. Now I need some time before they find out what really happened. So I am going to have to make this your fault, but first let me remove these ropes. I have a feeling that neither of you will be uncooperative. We don't want any questions of how you two got tied up."

Mechelle Davis

He pulled Mr. Jenkins mouth open, slid down a tube and filled his belly with liquor and the same to Mrs. Jenkins, pouring a good portion onto the bed. Whill burned the house in sections, putting the fire out and starting it again. The last room he set fire to was Kim parent's bedroom, which quickly engulfed the remainder of the house. They lay helpless as they burned alive helpless to help themselves or their daughter.

As Whill exited the window he said, "Sorry for the intrusion, happy anniversary!"

While Kim walked through the shell of the house it was as if everything had burned, but at the same time maintained its shape. Kim's childhood home felt as though it had a story to tell and when Kim seen her mother's necklace hanging from the banister she knew that it had and she would find out what. She walked over to the fireplace and the sofa was charred, outlines of the pillows to the sofa were still there and so was what appeared to be her mother's sweater she kept on the sofa. Kim's heart dropped and instantly she got a headache as she always did when she became frightened. She quickly searched the room and nothing. She looked up and the only room upstairs that still had somewhat of a floor was her parent's room. Speaking out in a loud whisper to herself, "How do I get up there?" She remembered the shed and quickly ran to retrieve the ladder.

"Ms. Jenkins I would not advise you to do that it is extremely dangerous, please let me go after what you are looking for. What is it Miss that you are after?" Kim ignored Pete's questions and offers of help or was she ignoring the person that kept calling her Miss. Jenkins?

"Please Ms. Jenkins you could be seriously injured allow me." With his pleas Monica and Eryka ran to his side and joined him, just at that moment Kim desperately crawled through her parent's window. Carefully planting her feet on the floor as it creaked, but Kim did not pay attention she quickly scanned the room. She noticed that the room was a mess it appeared to be this way before the fire-mental note: *my mother's room was never in disarray.* She noticed her mother's bathroom door open and steadied her small frame to head in that direction. As she walked it was as if she could hear her mother's voice and the many conversations they had while sitting or lying across the once beautiful bed. Once again tears began to fall, "I am so sorry Mom I wish that there . . ." The floor started to give way under her feet just as she made it to the bathroom, looking around, part of the bathroom floor wasn't there. Frozen for a moment Kim was brought to her senses with the sound of Eryka's voice, sounding like her mother.

"Kimberly Ann Marie Jenkins, you get your butt out of that house right now, you are being completely selfish to have us worry about you like this. There is nothing left to the house, you have to know the danger you are putting yourself in and for what? What on earth are you looking for?" Kim ignored her questions and demands but made her way back to the window her sister's secured the ladder to steady it as Kim climbed down. She yelled down before she made her way to the bottom, "Now I know why I seriously dislike my name, Mom always called me by my full name when I did something to displease her. Eryka, you are not Mom, please do not call me by my full name." Ignoring her request, they all hugged with a sigh of relief that she made it out safe. Monica looked Kim in the face.

"Kim what the hell is wrong with you, don't ever scare us like that, what were you doing up there?"

Walking toward the limousine as if she had seen a ghost, "someone killed our parent's." Kim said as she glared at Pete.

What!" Monica asked.

"We'll talk about it in the car, let me gather my thoughts." Kim seated herself in the middle seat and Monica and Eryka seated together to her left, positions they had claimed the first day the three climbed into the limousine together. Monica pushed for answers.

"Okay, the fireman said that the fire started in Mom and Dad's bedroom, right?"

"Right," Eryka and Monica said in harmony?

"Then why is it that their room is so intact more so than the rest of the house?"

"That is a good question Kim, but that does not mean that someone killed our parent's. They were good people and everyone who ever met them loved them who would want them dead?"

Mechelle Davis

"Oh come on with the clichés' of endearment Monica, I appreciate what you are saying but think about it—Sitting at the edge of her seat but requested privacy before she began. Monica let up the privacy glass—" The fireman said that Mom and Dad never had a chance to get out that they were heavily intoxicated. Our parent's didn't drink anything, but non-alcoholic beverages because Dad was a recovering alcoholic. Remember? You two remember when Dad fell off Mom threatened to leave him and he went through recovery again and while he was gone Mom replaced everything with non-alcoholic beverages and we stopped having dinners at the house because Mom did not want to temp Dad?"

"Yeah we remember." The two said in harmony looking at the other comically frustrated for choosing the same words.

"So our parent's did not drink. What about it?" Eryka asked.

"When I went in the house it was as if the house were trying to tell me something." Monica and Eryka looked at each other and then at Kim who caught the look and ignored it. Desperate Kim went back on the personal agreement she had with herself and showed her sisters her proof.

"What is the one thing Mom never took off no matter what the situation?"

"Her necklace, she adored it." Monica said.

"Right," Kim responded with excitement. Reaching into her pocket—against her better judgment—she pulled out her mother's necklace. Both girls were flabbergasted. "Where did you get that?" Eryka reached for it then tried to reason. "Maybe it fell off her neck." Kim held the necklace up.

"It was hanging on the banister when I walked in. If they were too drunk to get out of bed and lay there and burn to death, then what was it she would have been doing to allow the necklace to fall off, land hanging on the banister? Not only that, if the necklace did fall off then who clasped it back together and hung it on the banister?" Kim took a deep breath ". . . and why didn't the firemen see it there before they left? This means that whoever killed our parent's had taken the necklace before they killed them, and came back after the fire and placed the necklace on the banister for us to find because they knew that we would be here to say our good-byes." The girls remained quiet and Eryka hung her head. "One more thing, what was it that Mom always kept at the house, we all curled under it when we were younger, and she just gave it to me last year for my birthday?"

"The quilt." Monica said, "You loved that quilt."

"Right! The sofa is remarkably identifiable everything that Mom left on it was there . . ."

Monica interjected . . . "except the quilt."

"Right! Kim said. I went upstairs to see if she took it in her room with her, but it was not there. Whoever placed this necklace on the banister has Mom's blanket." She looked at her sister's, "Whoever it is want something from us so badly that they were willing to kill our parent's to get it, but who and why kill Mom and Dad?" The question pained Eryka more than she would admit aloud.

The memorial was sad Kim and her sister's laid their parent's to rest beautifully. It was a memorial fit for a King and Queen, Kim spared no expenses. She had her parent's cremated just as she had heard them request many, many times before and she was grateful because there was nothing left for an open casket after the fire. Kim sat in her seat dazed unaffected by the show of affection that strangers, family and friends alike showed. Because their deaths were publicized there were hundreds of people at the memorial and unbelievingly people were concerned about Kim's and her sister's finances until the reading of the will took place. In total Kim was given $262,000 enclosed in envelopes and cards of condolences.

As Kim sat and listened to her mother's favorite song by Ms. Mahalia Jackson; How I Got Over, being sung so beautifully she could not help but remember when she was six. Her father hadn't come home from a drinking binge after she and her Mom sat up all night waiting for him. Even though her Mom had to be at her office job at 7 a.m. and Kim at school at 8, they still sat and waited. They drank hot chocolate with marshmallows and whip cream together. Kim's always cooled because she could tell when her Mom was afraid, she would rock her and stroke her hair—Kim loved when she done that—until Kim fell asleep in her arms and the soulful voice of Mahalia Jackson playing over and over one song after another. Kim always knew when there was something troubling her mother because no matter how many times before that she would listen to Mahalia she would listen to her many, many times more.

Mechelle Davis

A strikingly handsome man suddenly and gently took Kim's hand, in the middle of the song and offered his condolences briefly interrupted Kim's reminiscing and simulated rocking. He exited from her sight as quickly as he appeared leaving a rather thick envelope in her hand and a small box in her lap. The envelope was beautifully embroidered and sealed with what looked like candle wax and some type of carved object pressed into the wax. Red with two black strings delicately placed around the envelope with a single daisy in the center. Red and black: her mother father's favorite colors and a daisy in the center of the envelope: her mother and her favorite flower. Taken aback by the beauty and intimacy of the envelope only she would enjoy, Kim looked up quickly searching the crowd for the stranger, but he was gone. Kim quickly and carefully opened the envelope to find wax paper, outlined in gold; a daisy in the center, written in gold was the quote,

"IN EACH OF US, TWO NATIONS ARE AT WAR—THE GOOD AND THE EVIL."—Dr. Henry Jekyll Which nation will you ultimately take alliance with?

What does this mean? Kim thought, quickly searching the crowd with the same results as the first; returning her attention to the envelope and the beautifully decorated box Kim did not realize the Eulogizer calling her name until Monica and Eryka removed themselves from her side? Looking up at her sister's she admired the strength they displayed though they were as torn inside as she was, she loved her sister's and now have a greater appreciation for them.

Monica spoke first; she looked down at Kim, tears in her eyes and equally in her voice. "You know it is only once in a lifetime that you find a family that is your family in every sense of the word except DNA like I have . . . we have, found in Kim, Cameron, Mom and Dad. The three letters of DNA have been replaced with my heart, soul and spirit. They opened their doors to Eryka and me without hesitation and treated us just as they treated Kim and our late brother Cameron with love, affection, kindness and understanding that we as children, teenagers and young adults needed to grow into women and men.

Our parent's have inadvertently taught us that DNA is something that society has used for many years to connect us to one another when it is really how you feel, treat and love one another that make you family. GOD could not have placed better angels in my life and it is because of them that I am who I am today and will be tomorrow and years to come. This family—my family—has remarkably impacted my life and so many of yours I am sure, and if for nothing else I know that GOD has held a spot in heaven for them just as you will always hold a spot in your hearts."

Eryka chimed in, hands and voice trembling as her eyes searched the crowd for nothing in particular. "I believe that GOD places each and every one of us on this earth for a period of time, but before he does he trains us in heaven. Some of us pay attention to that training when we respond to our gut feelings or the inborn kindness and generosity we display without a moment's thought. The way we give our last, love, trust and understanding without expecting anything in return. Just the way Mom and Dad did. GOD only loaned us his best angels for a short while and though it may hurt that they are no longer in our lives he needs them to come home for refreshers training before he places them in someone else lives to touch and make a difference just as they have in all of ours. I truly believe that if GOD would be so kind and unselfish to share people like this with us, if only for a while, then we too should be just as unselfish to let them go, but use what they have taught us to touch someone else's life just the way they have touched ours and no matter how difficult the challenges we face, the heartbreak we endure or the choices we me make we need to forgive ourselves first, opening the door for others to forgive us. Dad taught us an expression, 'Move in One Direction: forward. I never knew the importance of that until now and the many areas of my life . . . our lives it could be applied. We lost great people—Eryka continued looking down at Kim—and Mom and Dad would not want that to stop us and whatever we did not have the opportunity to say while they were alive they knew and I am sure they forgave. So in the words of our Dad, 'Move in One Direction; Monica chimed in and Kim mouthed the words through dazed tears . . . Forward."

Monica kissed her hands and placed them on the urn. "Goodbye, I will forever miss you." Turning to the urn, Eryka kisses her hand and places them on the urn, "I love you Mom and Dad, thank you for a job well done."

Mechelle Davis

A woman approach Monica and Eryka as they returned to their seat. She retrieved Kim's hand and spoke to the three of them. "I am a really close friend of your Mom and Dad, but I was really close you're your Mom. There are few people who are blessed enough to find their soul mate, the one when God created you he created your partner and ordered your steps so that you and he would meet. My friends have lived a long and productive life they have experienced materialized hope, dreams happiness and most of all love." The woman looked at the three girls—now sitting—listening to the woman and she continue," your mother use to say to me all the time and these are her words because she said it so often from the heart." *God could not have blessed me with no-greater gift than my fabulous four. Each having their own personalities and strengths makes them remarkable in their own way. I can't imagine life without them, each of them is truly a gift from God and I thank him every day for each of them.* The woman finished Mrs. Jenkins words with a tearful offer. "If any of you need me for anything call me." She handed the girls her card. Kim starred at the card in her lap as Monica and Eryka smiled their appreciation. As the woman walked away, Kim caught a glimpse of the side of her face.

It seemed to Kim that people must have spoken kind and endearing words about her parent's forever, but she did not hear a word they said her thoughts were on the envelope, box, quote and her mother's necklace.

"What does this mean? Does it have some type of connection to my parent's death, should I go to the police?" Echoing in her head Kim heard Monica calling her name. When she looked up and looked around everyone was gone except a few people standing around talking.

"Come on Ms. Jenkins, let's go." Pete wrapped his arms around her, with tears in his eyes and stroking her face he said, "I am sorry, so sorry, I should not have left them alone." Kim hugged and consoled him reassuring him that her parent's death was not his fault, but when she looked into his eyes they bore the guilt of a man who had part in the demise of someone he loved dearly. Kim brushed it off because she knew that Pete had always been over protective of her and her family and the guilt she knew he felt displayed an implied

Mechelle Davis

admission she knew was false. He took great strides to make sure Kim and her sister's were safe acting more like a bodyguard than a part of the family. Pete took Kim and her sister's back to the hotel and neither Kim nor her sister's heard from him again until one day when . . .

K im and her sister's returned to school nearly twelve weeks after the death of their parent's and it seemed as though everyone knew of their tragedy. When Kim reached her dorm room the visits were endless, she just wanted everyone to go away, leave her alone she had hoped the extended stay at home would have leveled the shock of her parent's death. Visually, Kim looked wonderful, rested and content, but on the inside she was falling to pieces. She blamed the death of her parent's on herself.

"If only I had called them, they would still be alive. I would have been on the phone arguing with Dad about what college I should have attended." She thought about what the coroner had said several months prior, *"I estimate the time of death between 5:30 and 7:30 p.m. The damage to the remains is extensive. Right now I can't tell if they died from smoke inhalation or of the fire itself, but whatever came first, it appears they did not suffer they were heavily intoxicated. I will complete a more in-depth autopsy by the end of day: 7p.m, but it will take several months to receive the results of the toxicology report. The results that I will provide will be on things I can determine right now, but their blood alcohol level, or if they were inhabited by any kind of narcotics will take some time."* The day seemed to have taken forever to end and all Kim could think about was the unofficial autopsy report. Finally 7:45 p.m. and the call still had not come. The day ended as it began, rough, mentally noisy and full of anticipation. 12 Saturday mornings had come, 12 Saturday afternoons had gone and then nights. 9:45 p.m., the thirteenth Saturday the phone rang.

"Ms. Jenkins?"

Mechelle Davis

"Yes."

"This is Dr. Mordoron with the Houston morgue. My apologies for the delay and time of the call, but I have conducted a complete and thorough autopsy on your parent's; again my condolences. Your parent's death has been ruled as a homicide, I found trace mixtures of Rohypnol and a dose of Tetrodotoxin in the tissues of your mother's hand when she closed her hands it allowed for a small piece of tissue to be tested. I sent samples to toxicology to reinforce my suspicions of something unseen.

"What is Tetrodotoxin and Rohypnol?"

"Tetrodotoxin and Rohypnol are predatory drugs, which intensifies with the use of alcohol and your parent had a strong scent of alcohol. These drugs rendered your parent's paralyzed, aware of their surroundings but unable to fend for themselves, simply intoxicated they would have never laid there. I believe the closing of your mother's hand was a natural reflex to the pain. You said your parent's did not drink so the smell of alcohol raised questions. I am sorry, but your parent's felt the fire; their deaths were horribly painful. I wish I could have better news, but I don't." Kim sobbed as she received the news from the examiner her worst fears were realized, her parents were murdered and suffered horribly just like her brother. She felt she had no choice but to take their deaths personally, a simple phone call would have saved their lives.

Continuing to torment herself Kim thought, *My Dad suffered twice, he died not being proud of me, wanting me to attend the right college and all I did was disappoint him. How can I live with that?! How am I going to forgive myself when I know that a simple phone call would have saved their lives?"* She sat on the edge of her dorm bed and cried incessantly. *"If I could not please my Dad when he was alive, I can please him now that he's gone. The only way I could do that is to leave and go to the college he wanted me to in his honor.* Kim continued to battle with herself, *now what would that prove. If I could be firm in my decision when he was alive I definitely can be firm in my decision now that he's gone, he would have wanted that. I miss them so much, I feel lost without them.* Kim looked at the pictures of her parent's; her parent's together, them by themselves, and then pictures of her immediate family. She missed them all so much; the life she had, seemed to have been so long ago that it almost feels like a recent but distant dream. Morning came far too fast.

There was a knock Kim looked at the door, but made no efforts to answer it. She heard rattling accompanied by the jingling of keys. Before she could get to the door it was already open. Her sister's walked in, words in motion.

"Thanks Stacey."

"No problem. Is she in there?"

"Yes. Come on Kim, we have to go turn in our assignments before two and pick up the rest of them by three. We have a lot of ground to cover and not much time to do it in. Why do you have your door locked, anyway?"

The sound of Monica's voice made Kim want to tell what she had just found out, but she thought better of it. She felt there would be no point because they seemed to have moved on.

"I Just wanted some alone time. Kim got up, walked to the door and twisted the lock leaving the deadbolt sticking out. Stacey is in violation of the use of her pass key. I will have to remind her of that.

"Let's get a move on it!" Eryka continued!

Monica stood looking puzzled at Kim's actions Eryka never noticed. Kim did not respond, she went to the bathroom instead to get herself together, but the flush of her caramel complexion was a dead giveaway of the pain that she hid so well with her hair and a smile.

"Kim, are you all right?" Monica called behind her in short hot pursuit.

"Yeah, I'm fine, I am almost ready, give me a sec."

"Kim, turn around and look at me. Monica said in an almost demanding tone, you are not fine, you've been crying! Escorting her to her bed, come on sit down."

Apparently dazed Kim slowly said, "It is amazing how one decision good, bad or indifferent can alter your life's past, present and future. The last time I was happily in this room I was so worried about studying for finals that I never . . ."

"You never what," Eryka asked?

". . . I never."

"You never what?" Eryka insisted.

Mechelle Davis

"Finals . . . I never took, that's what! The last time I talked to Dad there was disappointment in his voice about my college choice. Since I came here I never got a chance to hear his voice without disappointment. I never got or will ever get to hear happiness in his voice, how did you put it Eryka? 'Once last time' before he died, I never got to say 'I love you', Mom and Dad because I meant it and not out of habit. All those times before I wasted arguing with Dad about what college to attend I could have used it showing him how much I love and appreciate him. I missed the last chance I would ever have to say anything of importance, but of no importance, of meaning, but of no meaning, all to study for a final that I never took."

"Kim you almost sound as though you never ca . . ."

Kim deliberately cut Eryka off and continued, "Mom and Dad, our parent's are gone, Cameron; our brother is gone, sobbing heavily and I am all alone."

Eryka looked down and her watch and Monica elbowed her in her thigh for her bold disinterest in her sister's suffering. Kim noticed it too.

"It's okay Monica; Eryka's right, life must go on. They were only her parent's while they were alive now that they are dead I guess they served their purpose. Come on, let's go." Kim said wiping her tears, grabbing her book bag and heading for the door.

"You don't want shower first at least wash your face?" Monica asked.

Eryka did not give Kim the opportunity to answer. "Oh come on Kim, you know that isn't true or fair." Kim opened the door, walked out never speaking a word. Monica closed the door behind them, in a low voice, with her words on the back of Eryka's neck, "looks that way to me too!" Eryka paused in the hallway attempting to plead her case when the three were met by the dean.

"Hello ladies."
"Hello Dean Williams."
"Kim, I was just coming to see you, speak with you to touch bases, ladies I need to speak with Kim alone for a second if you don't mind. Go ahead, she will catch up later."

Monica turned to Kim, "Are you going to be okay. If not, this is a good time to ask the Dean for a little more time. You have been through a lot Kim."

"Thanks Monica, the same as you, but I just might do that." Monica hugged her sister and turn to walk away only to find that Eryka had already moved on. Monica's body was in the direction of Kim, but her destination was in another. As she temporarily surrendered her concern for Kim she ran to catch up with Eryka.

"So Kim, I just want to learn how you are doing."

"I'm not at all okay Dean; I received the final autopsy report last night. Kim started to sob, someone killed my parent's, burned them alive. Who and why would do such a thing?" The Dean held Kim as she cried uncontrollably. "It's as if I lost them all over again but in the worst way this time. Dean what do I do, how do I . . . will I ever get back to normal? Kim paused, I think the only way that I will is to find the person or persons who killed my parent's. I think I might need a little more time."

"I understand I am so sorry" was all the Dean had to offer. "Come by my office later and we will see what we can do."

Monica caught up with Eryka, what is wrong with you, why are you acting so cold to Kim, I know if I see it she has to see it too?" Abruptly Eryka stopped and turned to Monica.

Mechelle Davis

"Don't you get it, she killed the only real parents' I ever knew, you ever knew, the only man that has ever really treated me like a father and wanted nothing from me in return, she has always been selfish like that, it is always, has always been all about Kim!" Breaking down like Monica had never seen Eryka do. Monica stood and listened as everyone on the grounds watched her tantrum. "What would it have hurt for her to stop and call Mom and Dad? What would it have hurt to go home for their anniversary? What would it have hurt for her to take a break? Oh I remember what was it? I really don't want to hear Dad's mouth about going to a predominantly black college. Monica It is always, always all about her, this whole mess is all because of her and I am sick of it!"

"How? What whole mess Eryka? Mom and Dad dying or are you talking about something else?" The girls never got the opportunity to complete their conversation before Kim caught up and immediately Eryka tried to justify her behavior.

"Kim it was not that I am not interested in how you are feeling, you have to realize that we all lost our parent's and it seems that as usual all the focus is on you. I know that they were not my biological parent's but they weren't . . . we'll they were the closest people to parent's I had ever come to, even before my mother gave up her parental rights when I was twelve. Look I know that it will take a lot and it will be a long time before you're ever able to accept that Cameron, Mom and Dad are gone, but Kim they are gone not you. Whatever happened, or didn't happen, between the three of you that night cannot be changed. You cannot undo it and you have to know that their death is not your fault. It would kill them to know that you believe such a thing."

Kim continued to walk and Monica listened. Eryka took Kim by the arm to cease her steps. "Look we will be there for you no matter what, but we can only be there if you let us. We love you Kim and I think that once we see the attorney and finalize some things that your healing process can really begin, because you would have passed that stage of your grieving process. Whatever or however many stages you go through, it will be a lot easier if we went through them together. Kim please let us in . . . please." Eryka said with tears in her eyes as she shook her sister's arm. Kim tears came easily, this was the Eryka she had known and loved, the Eryka before all the secrecy . . . jealousy . . . anger. The Eryka they all knew and loved, but still a very different Eryka. The real Eryka turned actress. "We're family, not by blood but by choice which is even better, not many people get to choose their family. We chose you and you and our family let us in . . . without hesitation. We're family, let us be that for you we are all we have left.

Kim turned to look at Eryka and Monica, "I am so sorry that I shut you two out, I know that I am not the only one that loss, but . . ."

". . . But you still feel all alone?"

"Yes like . . ."

". . . like no one else understands?"

"Yes, but . . ."

". . . but we do, more than you know."

"Stop cutting me off Monica!" Kim demanded frustrated.

"I'm sorry, but I am finishing your sentences to show you you are not alone and I understand more than you know. Kim I lost two sets of parents, you lost one. I know what you are going through so if ever you need someone to talk to you can talk to me."

"I know that you two are my family and have been for a long time, but neither of you have family by choice, I have no one, when we graduate we are all going our separate ways and I was able to somewhat handle that because I still had Mom, Dad and Cameron. Then I just felt alone, now I am alone and jealous of you two for having someone if you choose. I hate whatever or whoever took our family from us and I know that people are saying that it should be easier for me because Mom and Dad left me loaded, but that money will not fill all the emptiness I feel inside. There's a black hole in me and everything I do to try to feel better keeps being pulled into it." Kim suddenly stopped when she seen the concern in her sister's eyes, wiped her tears, hugged her sister's, "I am glad you two weren't pulled in."

The three finally shared a laughed, "NEVER!" Monica contended. We will never be sucked in and will always be here for you no matter where we move to, come on we have to go our time is running out. The three walked with their arms linked Kim in the middle, crossing their own right leg over the other left just as they did when they were children.

Mechelle Davis

"Kim?" Eryka called in a soft guarded tone.

"Yeah?" With a little more fictitious cheer and hope in her voice.

"You can choose not to be alone too."

"What do you mean?"

"I mean that Mom and Dad didn't tell you but . . ." Monica shot Eryka a dirty look.

"Mom and Dad didn't tell me what?" Eryka paused for a long time before she continued, "they didn't tell you that when they became our foster parents you would never be alone, we will always be here for you?"

"Eryka sometimes you can be so corny." Kim replied, but she knew there was more to what Eryka actually said and she could feel the new info would not have been good anyway. Monica knew it too, so each readily let it go.

Monica looked over at Eryka she knew that Eryka knew something and though she did not tell it now it would come out at a time that she will use it for her benefit and at the expense of Kim, Monica's dislike for Eryka deepened.

"What did the Dean say Kim?"

"Just checking in, but I took your advice Monica. I need it."

"I can't believe it is Friday already Kim thought, it's going to feel great to get out of this dorm room for a while." Kim had locked herself in the attention was too much. She decided to go to the library to stay on top of her studies, thinking, "*I cannot fall behind, I have come too far, I graduate in less than six months.*" She pulled out her agenda and began studying one of the chapters from her accounting book when she was approached by a fellow student giving his condolences for the death of her parent's.

"I'm sorry about your parent's I can't imagine what that must feel like so I won't pretend. I hope I am not bothering you, I wanted to say something after class, but your gone minutes before the class end; May I sit down?"

"Sur . . ." Before Kim could complete his invite he proceeded to take a seat.

"We have been classmates for some time now and you have never looked in my direction . . . no one's direction in fact after the tragedy. With a sheepish smile on his face and a voice so deep that commanded attention, he continued with Kim's full attention . . . a smile on his face and hope in his eyes. Putting his hands up in surrender fashion, its okay; no I don't take it personally . . . . I have paid attention. Since I know that you are not dating anyone, I was wondering if we could go out to a movie and dinner. It will help you relax for at least a little while; how about it?"

Kim smiled and wanted to accept his invite, but felt that she did not deserve to have fun since her parents couldn't.

"So you're saying I'm uptight?"

"No my lady, just securely packed. You seem to be beating yourself up, suffocating yourself with something you can't change. Whatever happened or didn't happen you can't change it. You're cheating yourself out of life and you're placing all of your parent's hard work in the category of 'in vain." Kim smiled she knew he was right but she could not help herself.

"So if not dinner and a movie, how about ice cream, a long walk, and great conversation, I am a great listener?!"

"I'd love to, but I am behind in my studies and I really need to catch up, thanks anyway, maybe some other time."

Rising from his self invited seat, he slid the chair back under the table. "Okay, I just want you to know that I am going to keep trying." Both smiled. Kim thought to herself, *"I hope so."*

It seemed after that the approaches were endless. *"This is why I stayed in my room. It has been six months and four days since my parent's death, how long will these people give their regards? I will never get any work done here I may as well go back to my room."* On the way out of the library, it seemed as though everyone stopped what he or she was doing to watch her walk out. She wondered to herself, *"were they expecting me to look different? Its okay people I didn't let you down, I feel different, and therefore I am definitely different."*

Kim sat in her dorm room, once again tormenting herself with the fact that she never called her parent's. *"If I had called them would they still be alive? Where did so much liquor come from? Who took Mom's necklace off and where is the quilt? Maybe she took the necklace off to give to me just in case I decided to go back for their anniversary, but I explained to them that I would not make it back for their anniversary, weeks before. Why did the house burn in such a strange way? If the fire started in the bedroom, then why did the bedroom burn the leas? Even if they were drunk, I don't think that they would have been so drunk to have lain in their bed and burned to death. Eryka's right this entire tragedy is my fault. I am alone because of my own selfish behavior; my parents are dead because of me. My brother died alone because I was too wrapped up in my own affairs. Maybe he was trying to tell me something that he was in danger and I was too self-consumed to listen. When and why did I become this way? So what Dad was going to complain about me attending his less favorite college."* Right now Kim longed to hear him complain, to hear him lecture her on how the name of the college you attend have a great impact on what place you take in the world or even how far you go.

Kim sat silently for a moment "I did not deserve any of that inheritance. I don't deserve to live happily ever after on their sweat and hard work. Kim's swollen eyes looked up at her clock, it read Sunday, November 14th 3:30 a.m. six hours had passed and she had not noticed. Five hours before she had to get up to make their 11 a.m. flight. She lay down to get some sleep before she and her sister's met with the family attorney at 5:00 that evening. The family attorney flew them to his New York office on Sunday so they would not miss anymore school. I will listen to what he has to say, but I will have him make the arrangements to donate everything to The United Negro College Fund, my Dad always donated to them. I will donate my inheritance in the memory of my parent's. 'Title it 'The Jenkins College Fund."

Kim, Monica and Eryka walked into the office of Johnson, Jones, and Sykes P.C. at 5:45 p.m., they took their seat among the four individuals waiting to see whomever they were there to see. Monica and Eryka were excited for Kim, but at the same time could not help but think about the only way to have received this inheritance is through the death of their parent's.

A tall man confidently walked into the room. "Good morning Ms. Jenkins." Recognizing Kim from the endless pictures her parent's had shown him. Kim looked up into the face of Mark Johnson the attorney handling her family's estate. He was extremely attractive even for a man of his age.

It is Ms. Jenkins right?"

"Yes but that's mostly my mother I like to go by Kim." She said softly and with an unspoken confidence, as she stood, but even in that quiet confidence her attorney seen the core of her was unbalanced. He approached her with his hand outstretched, her body accepted, but her eyes and her presence never connected to him or the moment.

"You have grown into a very fine young woman; I am sorry to learn about your parent's, you three have my deepest condolences. They were remarkable people and loved you ladies very much." He said as his eyes scanned the three of them to acknowledge them and reinforce his statement.

"Thank you" Kim said. Mark looked at his notes and photos before speaking again. "Ms. Bronson. Ms. Hargrove?" Hand out-stretched, "It is a pleasure to finally meet all of you." Their pictures were equally shown by the proud parents.

"Miss Jenkins . . . Kim, is Ms. Bronson and Ms. Hargrove aware of why they are here?"

"No I did not tell them, they believe they are her for support." Kim replied.

"Then this should be a welcomed surprise for them. Will you ladies follow me?" Monica and Eryka looked at one another while Kim walked ahead.

Making small talk attorney Johnson said, "I will try to move this along as expeditiously as possible, I know you ladies have a flight to catch." Kim did not respond and his years of experience told him that this young woman, though very attractive and noticeably intelligent, was in a lot of trouble.

"How is school going?" The attorney asked Kim to further confirm his suspicions.

Monica and Eryka answered for her. "Good"

"We are all . . . well not all of us, Monica said looking at Eryka, are on the dean's list."

"Excellent, maybe you will come work for me when you graduate."

"No, I am studying Chemical Engineering, Eryka Psychology; and Kim is going into law."

"Excellent choices," he said as he looked at Monica. "What prompted you to choose Chemical Engineering?"

"The challenge and the money Monica said smiling, mostly the money."

"Having a little difficulty with finances?"

"Wow am I!" Mom and Dad said I need to learn how to budget, I love to shop, and I have a passion for fashion."

"Obviously," He said with a fatherly smile. "Maybe not after today," He continued. Eryka and Monica looked at each other and then at Kim who offered no explanation.

"Okay, shall we get started here, the attorney asked? How about we all move from the couch to sit at that table, there are a lot of papers that will need to be signed? Let's say we start with—looking through the four folders that he had his secretary place on the table—Eryka

Bronson and then Monica Hargrove?" Monica flirtatiously put her hand up and waved her fingers.

Eryka leaned over, "You are such a slut he could be your father." The attorney raised his eyebrow to acknowledge that he heard Eryka's comment.

"You must be Eryka?"

"Established." She said sarcastically.

"You're the mother of the group."

"No I wouldn't say that."

"Well Mr. and Mrs. Jenkins did, they respected you a great deal for that." All the while small talk was taking place Kim stared into space, closing her eyes periodically to hold back the tears.

"Ms. Jenkins? Ms. Jenkins?" Her attorney called and finally she looked at him. "Are you all right?" Her sister's turned their attention to her.

"Yes. I'm just thinking, us being here means they're really gone and won't be back. I can no longer go home and crawl up in my mother's bed or catch my Dad staring at me with so much love in his eyes. The absence of a folder with Cam's name on it means I will never be able to talk to my brot . . . I'm okay; go ahead I'm listening." Silence filled the room not from Kim's statement but for the concern of her well-being.

"Okay Ms. Hargrove, Mr. and Mrs. Jenkins wanted to say a few words to you. The note here says . . . would you like to read it?"

"No go ahead, please?"

"Okay," the attorney said with a smile.

"We have enjoyed you as an addition to our family. Your bright spirit and smile has added extra value, excitement and spice to our lives, to our heart and home and for these reasons and so many more we looked at you as our daughter even before you became our daughter. As our daughter we wanted to make your life a little easier after we are gone. We have made preparations to ensure that you start your generations to come off with love, success and prosperity. We love you.

"Mr. and Mrs. Jenkins left you an inheritance of $4M in addition they want me to make sure that all your student loans are paid. Mrs. Jenkins happily left you the black and white mink shawl that you

Mechelle Davis

have adored for the past three years, in addition to her handsome shoe and purse collection. I remember when she spoke about her collection of shoes she reminisced very fondly, just before you entered into high school you were always in her closet playing in her shoes she said you have always had a passion for fashion. In addition to the mink, they wanted you to have $150, 000 when you leave here today. Spend it wisely they said. They love you." Monica smiled.

Ms. Hargrove there is something else. Your case is a little different. Mr. and Mrs. Jenkins states that you took your parent's to court when you were around the age of 11 to be emancipated, you were placed in their care as their foster child."

"Yes that is true, Eryka and me."

"Okay," the attorney said noticeably irritated by Monica's inclusion of Eryka. "Your biological parent's understood how you felt, agreed that they were not emotionally capable of taking care of you and wanted to share some of the expenses that were incurred by Mr. and Mrs. Jenkins. Your biological parents have made some provisions for you to receive a lump sum of money on the conditions that you complete college. In addition, they wanted you to know that they moved to Japan. The Jenkins kept in contact with them over the years just in case you wanted to see them after they were gone. They expressed to me that you were adamant about keeping them out of your life and wanted to respect your wishes. They also wanted to make it easy for you after you were older and found it in your heart to forgive, find and/or contact your parent's." Attorney Johnson slid Monica, her parent's address and phone number. "Your parent's have written you a letter and requested that you read it in private enclosed you will find a post-date check for the expected date of graduation. Well Ms. Hargrove it appears that you are a very rich woman. I wish you happiness in your new found wealth."

"Getting right to the point, Ms. Bronson the Jenkins also made substantial provisions for you, but before I get to that Mr. and Mrs. Jenkins wrote you a letter." He slid Eryka her letter, Eryka looked at the letter and then him the stare between the two were almost battle like.

"Shall I read it?" The attorney asked.

"Please!" Eryka said with a nod and gesture of her hand.

Mechelle Davis

Dear Eryka,

You too have brought so much joy into our lives. You display strength and courage that is well beyond your years and our daughter's are so lucky to have you as a sister. You have always displayed qualities that we hoped Kimberly and Monica would pick up in combination of their own. You have been a spectacular addition to our lives and we know you will be a great success in whatever you do

We view you as the family person, from that observation we know that you will have children so we have purchased two trust funds in the amount of $1M each for your future children. At this Moment Mr. Johnson should be handing you a diamond watch left to you by your mother. Also your biological mother have taken care of your entire student loan and expenses so you are free and clear of the responsibility of paying back your student loans. Upon graduation your biological mother has placed in a trust fund for you the amount of $50,000 in addition to the compiled interest that took place on the account. Your mother wanted you to know that the scratch offs finally paid off and that she know and understand no amount of money will ever undo what she has done, but she hopes that one day you will be able to forgive her and accept her back into your life."

Mr. Johnson slid Eryka her mother's complete contact information.

"Mr. and Mrs. Jenkins left you $4M the sum of which you will receive after graduation. The $150,000 from your biological mother you will receive today."

"Now Ms. Bronson, Ms. Hargrove, I am willing to help you manage your inheritance or at least provide you with numbers of some reputable Financial Advisors so that you may invest your funds wisely. You two may think about it while I speak with Ms. Jenkins." With the flick of a button, his family pictured separated displaying a flat screened television. The two women were briefly confused. Kim was still sitting in her chair in her own world. It appeared that she did not hear how well her mother and father had taken care of her sister's and that they had the opportunity to see

Mechelle Davis

their bio parent's, she was still in a place all her own internally marinating in her own grief. With much effort her attorney was able to get her attention.

"Ms. Jenkins, do you mind if Ms. Bronson and Ms. Hargrove sit in on the reading of the will?" Ms. Jenkins your parent's has a video message for you. Do you mind if your sisters sit in?"

"I don't care, sure, play the video."

"Your parent's stated that if for any reason you are having visible difficulty with their death then you are to be placed under care until which time you are determined to be of sound mind and body."

Eryka interjected, "We have that covered she's fine. I will brief you on it later."

"Okay. First and foremost, your parent's have a life insurance policy placed on both of them some time ago. As you know if their death is accidental or not caused by self-infliction it doubles. The life insurance policy is worth $2.5 million, which means it doubles to $5 million each, totaling $10 million." Kim shrugged her shoulders. "As you know your parent's estate is worth well over $225 million."

"No I did not know that." Kim replied and Monica and Eryka gasped.

"They led me to believe we weren't rich, that we were the average family. They made me work to pay for my first year of college!" Kim looked confused, hurt and angry. Monica was grateful at least she showed some kind of emotion aside from the blank stare.

The attorney continued, "This does not include the homes and office building recently purchased and the new construction company your Dad started eight months ago, which is doing exceptionally well. I will have to get back with you as to the dollar amount. Because of the death of your brother your inheritance is nearly 100% with an estimated value of around $650 million." Kim sat completely unaffected. Monica and Eryka could not believe their ears, their parents were rich beyond anyone dreams and all they were left was a couple of million dollars!

"Ms. Jenkins, your mother and father left you this video letter"—at that moment he gained Kim's complete attention—and it plays like this:" With a push of a button from his remote, Kim was starring in the face of her parent's.

Mechelle Davis

Our Dearest Kimberly;

You and Cameron, Kim smiles at the mention of Cameron, have been nothing but a joy to us since you entered our lives. It seems as soon as we brought the two of you home our lives has been extremely joyous, you two have added value that no amount of money or material things can come close to, there is absolutely no comparison. The amount of love we have for you is immeasurable, thank you for being our daughter and loving us unconditionally as we have loved you. We want you to be strong, draw strength from your sister's and don't push them away we can see that they love you. Having Monica and Eryka in your life makes our leaving a lot easier. We know that you will not be alone. You have made our life whole, rich, complete and worth living and we know that the fulfillment that you have placed in our life within a matter of time you will one day establish in your own.

We have always been so proud of you, your determination, will, intelligence, spirit and ability to think things through and make the right decision. You exude the strength we'd hoped you have when you stood strongly in any decision you made. Know that your Dad and I are proud of you and if it seemed as though we were not, it was only to keep you strong. From the bottom of our hearts to the depths of our spirits, we love you immeasurably.

Kim sat in her chair visibly trembling, sobbing without sound and though her sister's could see all the loneliness she was feeling they could also see the failed valiant attempts to contain her tears. The attorney stopped the tape and everyone allowed her the moment she definitely needed before they went to her side to console her. Ten minutes had passed then attorney continued to play the tape.

Your father and I need to tell you something that we wished we could have told you sooner, but we were afraid of losing you.

Kim cried harder as she watched her mother begin to cry from whatever was painstaking for her to say. Eryka sat with a smirk on her face that the attorney did not understand but Monica did. Monica knew that whatever their parents were about to say Eryka already knew what it was, but what she didn't know was Kim did too.

Mechelle Davis

You and your brother has been our biggest success and I want to thank your biological parent's for giving us the opportunity to live a life filled with the two of you.

Monica gasped and asked in a whisper, "The Jenkins is not Kim's bios? As she looked around the room she seemed to be the only one surprised. She turned back to the video message.

I was not able to have children because at eighteen I had ovarian cancer causing me to have a hysterectomy, but that did not stop me from wanting children. When your Dad and I settled down we had no alternative, but to adopt. We wanted so desperately to have a boy and a girl young enough not to remember their natural parent's and to take on our beliefs and practices. Ten years had passed and just when I thought it wasn't meant to be I got an e-mailed picture of the two of you; perfect in every way.

Your mother was only fourteen at the time and her mother would not allow her to keep you two. Your father, very wealthy, was not allowed to care for you either, which only meant the two of you were born to be with us. Please forgive us for not telling you sooner. Mr. Johnson should be handing you a yellow envelope with your original birth certificate and a little history on your biological parent's and family. So if you choose to search them out you have a starting point. Unfortunately I was not able to keep in contact with your parent's after you and Cam turned four along the way we lost direct contact. I hope that you take the opportunity to search them out, their choice to put you and your brother up for adoption was not their own. Kim thought to herself, I knew it but it is definitely different to hear it especially now. Cameron's feelings were right, we are adopted. I wish I had told him when I found out for sure and went with him to ask Mom and Dad it would have made things in his life so much easier to have known that. It would have explained a lot.

The tape continued, *"I want to give you something that I have never showed you, I wanted to wait until you were married and give it to you as something old. Your natural father gave this to your mother and she requested that I give it to you only on your wedding day. I put it in a safe deposit box and gave a key to our attorney just in case I was not able to make it.* Kim's mother reached to her side and picked up a large pink-Kim's favorite color-velvet box

Mechelle Davis

simultaneously with her attorney. He slid the box over to Kim and she heard her mother say, *"Let's open it together."* Kim turned her attention back to the monitor. "Ready? 1-2-3, open." Kim nearly hit the floor there beautifully laid were a pair of stunning diamond earrings, necklace and bracelet. Kim's father continued and the sound of his voice moved her to tears. *"Sweet heart you have always been my princess, my little girl, my angle and at times I were angry with you for doing what you could not help; grow up. I missed you even before you were gone. I want to give you this just in case I am not here when you're knight and shining armor comes along to take my princess away in his arms.* Mr. Jenkins bent down to pull a large black box from under his seat. When Kim turned to Mr. Johnson the box sat in front of her. *"Let's open it together princess, 1-2-3."*

In all its beauty against and sunken into red velvet laid a tiara made of diamonds. The three girls could not breathe and from the expression on her mother's face on the video she knew nothing of it.

We all want you to have a part of our history, now your history and when you are married please allow your sister's to help you put your tiara and jewelry on as something old and something new. Kimberly we want you to know that if we had it to do all over again we would keep you as our little girl a little while longer, over time, you grew up much sooner than we were ready to let go. We want you to know that we are so proud of you, always have been. All your life you have made wise adult and adult like decisions. Mr. Jenkins' voice trembling, tears in his eyes and equally in his voice: *I know that we, well I, were on you about your college choice, but that was only because we-I—wanted you to learn as much about your heritage as you possibly could though us and not some revised textbook. As a child, you were deeply into the African culture and I did not—do not want you to ever lose that interest it is a big part of who you are. You made a wonderful college choice and I am proud of you doing so and hold a greater pride that you held to what you believed even in what appeared to be strong opposition. I can leave knowing that whatever comes your way in life you will be strong enough to withstand it. Stay the strong, independent, intelligent, beautiful—inside and out-person that you are. Thank you for adding joy and value to our lives with all our love thank you for being our*

Mechelle Davis

daughter. Her mother added "With all the oxygen in the world we love you so much." Her father added: . . . *and always, always . . .* The three girls said it as their father did . . . *Move in one direction: forward. Love you.*

Attorney Johnson had never seen such a bond, even in the absence of three members of a patchwork family and he admired the Jenkins even more. The love they had for each other made him want to take their children under his wing.

No longer able to hold it in, Kim let out sobs that would soften the blackest of hearts. Her sisters rushed to her side. Once she gained her composure she said, "The only thing I want is this necklace, tiara and my parent's house, donate everything else to the United Negro College Fund A.S.A.P.—including this $262,000 given to me at my parent's funeral—I will sign the necessary papers today."

Monica was stunned that Kim and Cameron were adopted and even more stunned that Kim said to donate her parent's estate. She spoke in shock, "Kim are you crazy? There is nothing left to the house!"

"Ms. Jenkins, are you aware of what you are giving up?" Mark asked.

"Yes I am. I have thought about it and I am certain."

"Your parent's asked that I oversee your estate for one year after their death, from the day of the reading of the will, to ensure that you do not do anything irrational and Ms. Jenkins I feel that giving away your entire inheritance is a bit irrational. I think that you should reconsider. I cannot, not in good conscious and overseeing your estate, do such a thing. I will place a freeze on your account for a total of one year and if you still feel the way you do today we can do as you wish." I will make certain you are financially stable and your education is taken care of.

Kim did not put up a fight, debate or anything, she was definitely out of it and Monica and Eryka did not realize she was so bad off. They thought the Attorney Johnson was making a wise decision.

"Ladies I need you to read over these papers and sign where the X's are if there is anything you do not understand please do not sign until I explain it to you. Ms. Jenkins may I speak with you for a moment?"

Mechelle Davis

Kim slowly rose from the chair and joined her attorney in the added private room attached to his office. He closed the door.

"Ms. Jenkins are you alright?"

Kim slowly shook her head yes, tears still streaming down her face like a rain storm.

"You appear to have lost yourself. Is there anything that I can do to help?"

Kim babbled. "No. No one can help me. My brother's, my parent's death is my fault." Kim said as she stared into nothing. "I did not visit my brother as I said I would and if I had he would not have died that weekend. I was trying to teach him a lesson about not being the person I wanted him to be and now he's gone. Did you know he could not have an open casket? My mother and father blamed themselves and I let them know that his death was my fault. Just as our parents death is my fault. I was so concerned about my Dad lecturing me about not attending his college choice that I did not want to go to the house to listen to him complain nor did I call them to wish them a happy anniversary. I broke tradition and a promise all in one night my punishment is my parent's death."

"Ms. Jenkins, don't you think that is a little extreme? Who would punish you for not going home?"

"God, GOD knows. He knew that I have been selfish all of my life and he is punishing me for it, he took my entire family away from me to make me appreciate something."

"Something like what, Ms. Jenkins?"

She mechanically turned to her attorney and said, "Good ole L.I.F.E., this is my wakeup call not to take anything for granted. That is one of the reasons that I must donate my entire inheritance. The students who will benefit are people who have to work to get that money or assistance to go to college I know they will appreciate it." Looking away, "not like me who took everything for granted."

"Ms. Jenkins I was extremely close to your parent's and selfish and unappreciative is not the impression I got of you nor is it the way that your parent's described you. The manner in which you brought those two girls into your home to share everything you had. I remember one story of favor your parent's shared with me about when you were in junior high. Shortly after your parent's told you they knew you were hiding the girls out in your room Monica was playing in your mother's full length Lynx fur coat, ripped the bottom and hung it back in the closet without a word. Your mother viewed the 'Cam-corder' they hid throughout the house for your brother to learn that Monica was being dishonest. You had been saving for some time to buy yourself a dirt bike your parent's didn't want you to have, but agreed that if you saved up 60% of the money they would indeed give you the remainder. You did, you worked around the house, baby sat, cleaned the yard, whatever you had to do to get that dirt bike and you gave the money to your Mother to have her coat repaired so that your sister's could stay. Do you remember that?"

"No."

The Attorney Johnson moved intensely closer. "Kim that is not the act of a selfish person, you do not remember it, even more proof that you are not selfish. What about when it was time to go to college and your parent's said that they only had enough money for you to go, you were willing to sell your family pearls and Japanese hairpins so that it would help your sister's go to college. Or even the time you went home for the holidays and there was a misunderstanding between, you, your mother and Hannah. You were so hurt that you went back to school early. Even in that hurt you found it in yourself, found the time to go back to Houston without telling your parent's, found Hannah and helped her get on her feet. You gave her words of hope and encouragement and helped her believe in herself again. You even helped her reconnect with her Mother and Stepfather. I know all this because Hannah's parent's told your parent's what you did and thanked them for having and raising such a remarkable person. You never looked for recognition. You've changed people lives and never looked for recognition."

Kim stood unmoved by the attorney, who sighed at the young woman that appeared polar opposite of the girl his clients so proudly spoke of. "You are not in slightest a selfish and unappreciative person, but you are a lot confused. You need a vacation, I will set it up for you, maybe when you come back you will feel a lot better."

"My parents have already set up a vacation for me, all expenses paid. They were like that you know? Always doing anything they could to make me happy. Why couldn't I do the same?" She looked at her attorney, Mr. Johnson you could use all the attorney reasoning

Mechelle Davis

you want; I too am almost an attorney, so I recognize it. I really appreciate what you are trying to do, but one year from now or ten years from now my decision is final I would like to donate my entire inheritance to The United Negro College Fund in the name of my Mom and Dad-Evelyn and Richard Jenkins. Now to get you to understand how serious I am I will put it this way. As long as you are handling my affairs I employ you and as your employer I tell you what I want not the other way around. Now what you will do is start the proceedings to do exactly what I have told you, this matter is not up for discussion or debate. The next time I speak to you you would have told me how much help that money will do for the college fund of choice, are we understanding each other?"

"Not quite Ms. Jenkins. Until the terms of this Will are fully carried out I am still employed by your parent's, not you. My dilettante days are long behind me and my experience allows me to see a woman in trouble. Your parent's anticipated that whenever or however they died that you would take their death pretty hard. They anticipated that you being the person you are you would personalize their death. So as a clause to your inheritance a portion of your inheritance would be released only to your college to pay for all tuition cost, present and future. All funds thereafter are to be put in escrow for one year if I deem it necessary because of your mental instability. This is a Last Will in testament, which as "almost" an attorney yourself know that it is enforceable by law, unless you contest it and I cannot see you doing that. Now Ms. Jenkins, I do deem it necessary that I enforce this clause not only because it is the wish of your parent's, but as your attorney it is my job to have your best interest at heart. If you completely understand what I have just said to you and do not have and further questions then yes I believe that we do understand one another. Do you have any further questions?"

Kim disregarded his question and exited the room to the chatter of her sister's planning how to spend their newfound inheritance.

Kim heard Monica say, "How about the trips Mom and Dad gave us?"

"Mr. Johnson my parents gave me a trip along with Eryka and Monica. When school ends next year I want my trip to be given to the high school student who received the highest S.A.T. score and who will also receive assistance from United Negro College Fund."

Mechelle Davis

The attorney did not respond because he placed the trip under the one year clause.

"Okay ladies if you do not have any questions about what you have signed or anything at all, this would conclude our meeting. "Ms. Jenkins, would you wait outside while I talk to your sisters?" Kim did not respond she just exited the office without a word to anyone.

Once Kim closed the door he instructed her sister's to take good care of her. "She has taken their death really hard and believes that your parent's and your brother's death is her fault."

"I'm not sure when she started feeling that way, but you're right she does and I did nothing to instigate those feelings. Maybe she feels that way because it is the truth, women's intuition, maybe?" Eryka responded dripping with sarcasm displaying a smirk.

"I don't think that she started feeling that way until our parent's died and someone gave her a little nudge"—cutting an eye at Eryka. It's as if she is going over her whole life and all the unfortunate or displeasing things she's taking blame for them. She is not looking at all the good in her life. I don't understand and don't know how to get through to her.

"Your sister is in the danger zone and as her attorney, financial guardian I have to take action. I believe Ms. Jenkins is suicidal she has internalized your parent's death and she wants to give away everything, true signs that she is contemplating suicide."

"I see that too," Eryka interjected. The attorney looked at Eryka, but did not respond. "Don't worry you will be paid for your services they will be taken care of within the week!"

"Eryka, what are you saying, Kim would never kill herself!"

"I would thank you in advance Ms. Bronson, but Mr. and Mrs. Jenkins took care of the bill long before their passing; I was "taken care" of years ago. But thank you for your unwelcomed concern. Now that I have paid you some attention let's place the attention back to who really matters." Turning to Monica, he continue, "at the very least I have to have her evaluated to be confident that she is not a personal threat to herself and able to come out of this zone she is in."

Sounding offended, Eryka sharply cut Mr. Johnson off, "as I previously stated at the start of this meeting we have that covered. I contacted the school psychologist, who came to see Kim shortly after learning of our parent's death. She will be waiting for us when we return to campus." Monica turned and walked, but not out of the office but a short distance away sharing Eryka's feelings of irritation.

"Ms. Hargrove," the attorney called Monica's name. "Is there something that you would like to say or ask?"

"No Eryka responded sharply!"

But Monica shared her concerns in a whisper to Eryka, "How do we help her, what if this psychiatrist can't help her, what do we do then? I can't lose her; I cannot imagine life without her. She is my best friend, my sister, and my confidant; if she were a man she would be the perfect husband," Monica cried as she whispered her concerns to Eryka.

Acknowledging that he overheard Monica's concerns the attorney continued, "I can see where you would be concerned, perhaps your University could be of some assistance, but I believe your school deals with grief counseling on a smaller scale Ms. Jenkins needs a psychologist who has dealt with grief of such magnitude; she may need to be medicated and I do not believe that your school is equipped to do that. With that being said this is the course of action that I will take to ensure that she is safe now and later. I will place a one year hold on Ms. Jenkins estate to uphold the clause in her inheritance, I will allow her to see the school psychiatrist, who you Ms. Hargrove will call me back with her name and contact number. In two weeks I will follow up with the psychiatrist and if Ms. Jenkins has not improved, I am sorry I will have her hospitalized for her own safety. So for Kim's sake let us hope that the school psychiatrist can penetrate that dome of grief, self-hatred and pity she has covered herself with. I have another meeting in a few that I need to prepare for, thank you Ms. Hargrove for listening and being there for her she really needs someone that is truly in her corner right now. I can completely understand the origination of her feelings of loneliness. I am glad she has you, looking at Monica and cutting an eye at Eryka. Have a good day and I will be in touch in two weeks."

No one said a word on the plane ride back to school and the drive from the airport was extremely quiet. Monica spoke first.

"Kim when we talked yesterday you said that you were going to let us in that we were going to get through this together. Then we find out from a total stranger that you still blame yourself for the death of our parent's and Cam. What happened between yesterday and today?"

Frustrated, "I am fine ladies honestly. I can't change how I feel in a matter of a day especially if what I feel is genuine," cutting an eye in the review mirror at Eryka. "I heard the three of you talking about me as if I am some kind of nut job. I just need some time without the constant reminders. We all grieve in our own way, but with each new day there is something new. Did either of you know that Cameron and I are adopted?" Both girls looked at Kim sympathetically.

"No Kim I did not know."

Eryka never responded.

"I knew" Kim said. "I found out two weeks before I left for college. I went in Mom's room, as I did every morning to get on the treadmill. I sat on her bed to put on my gym shoes and there was a piece of paper sticking from under the bed. I bent down to pick it up without the intentions of reading it, but I couldn't help it. The paper was thick and folded in three, like a letter. I opened it and immediately recognized it was a birth certificate, with my name on it along with some other papers. Mom had always said that she couldn't find Cameron and my birth certificates and I believed her. I read the birth certificate and it said that I was born in Boca Routon Florida. My mother, fourteen at the time of my birth name is Denise Marie Kowen and my father, 18 at the time of my birth name is Liam Bryan Dennehee, dual live birth, girl, Cam's read, dual live birth boy. I ran to the office and made copies and put the paper back under the bed. I did not believe it, I didn't think that Mom would ever lie to us, so I somewhat put it out of my mind. I took copies to school with me planning to do some research before I went to Mom and Dad with what I found. I really did not want to know that would have meant my whole life was a lie. Cam felt it and he had a right to know, but I did not have the heart to tell him with him already feeling like an outsider. I don't know how much worse that would have made things for him personally or between him and our parent's. He died feeling incomplete and alone and I let him die that way."

Eryka smirked briefly thinking back to when she planted the birth certificate at the foot of the bed for Kim to find.

Mechelle Davis

"So you have known for quite some time that you are adopted?"

"Yes and I believe that is the talk Mom and Dad wanted to have with Cam and me."

"Oh my goodness Kim this is a lot to take in right now, maybe we should go somewhere, relax and forget about school, these people . . . Mom and Dad and Cameron. Let's go shopping."

"Look Ericka, I can't move on as easily as you, I lost my family twice, neither by choice. Then I find out that Mom and Dad are not truly Mom and Dad. I am dealing with a lot. I am fine, but I really need to be by myself right now."

"No Kim you are not fine, you were out of it in the office and it was no act. You were gone girl; what is going on, talk to us?!"

"Monica, what's going on is obvious, I guess I am going to need a little more time than I thought. Yesterday I went to the library and people kept approaching me giving me their condolences as if our parent's just died. It has been over four months, how long will I be reminded that I am orphaned? I know that they did not mean any harm and it is not that that bothers me; it was the way they were looking at me when I walked out, as if I was supposed to look different in some way now that I lost both of my parent's. I just don't need to be reminded, I need to be left alone."

Eryka interrupted. "It's like you said Kim they did not mean anything by it. They don't know what to say or to do. They continue to give you their condolences because you have basically locked yourself in your room since Mom and Dad died and yesterday was the first time they really had a chance to express themselves to you."

"Don't misunderstand me, I am not upset with them, it just made some feelings resurface that I thought I was finally able to suppress."

Monica joined the conversation, "look Kim, I won't try to psyche you by saying you shouldn't be suppressing feelings anyway you need to find a way to deal and heal. Once you do that you will feel a lot better."

Quickly ending the conversation, Eryka asked, "Are you riding with Monica and me I want to go spend some of the money I got today?"

Mechelle Davis

"Riding with you? What money, Kim asked?"

Eryka and Monica looked at each other. "Maybe you should go lie down for a while," Eryka continued, but first can we borrow your car?"

"Sure, go ahead."

"What? Monica screeched. Kim you never let anybody drive your car." Monica held Kim's hand for a moment while Kim starred off into nothing.

"Kim you are the only true family I have, no conditions, no guidelines, no set ups or sneak surprises and I really don't want to put any more pressure on you than needed, but you have to get some help, I need you and right now you need me. I am here, unconditionally and with no guidelines. I love you and you really need to know that you are not alone." The two starred at each other with tears in their eyes before Monica turned and opened the car door.

Before Kim closed the door she said with a sadness that darkened the brightest day, "I learned that there are more important things in life than the material." The door scarcely closed Eryka began to drive off. Monica wanted Eryka to wait until Kim entered the dorm, their normal safety measurement, but Eryka sped off. Monica yelled at Eryka, "You are taking advantage of her."

"No I am not it is always about her. We have our own money now; we don't have to kiss up to her."

"Kiss up to her Monica yelled we never had to kiss up to her. She has never asked or implied that we needed or need to."

"Whatever, we are loaded on our own accord. Forget her for now!" Monica looked at Eryka in a whole new light and her mistrust of her deepened, she thought. *How long has she been PLAYING Kim's sister? Better yet, how long has she been playing my sister?*

It was as if Eryka were reading Monica's thoughts and she attempted to redeem herself, "All these years we thought, our parent's did not care, they did and they provided for us. We thought we knew the Jenkins, but they were strangers to us, hell they were strangers to Kim and Cam!"

"They are 'The Jenkins' now, uh Eryka? It isn't Mom and Dad that are the strangers it's you! It's as if you hung around for the big pay off, they were Mom and Dad before they made you a millionaire, but now that they have made you a millionaire, they are 'The Jenkins!'" Eryka knew that Monica was angry because she did something she never does, repeat herself. "We made it clear to Mom and Dad that we did not want anything to do with our parents that is a choice we made, not them! They respected and loved us enough to adhere to our request, but loved us enough to not only provide for us but keep in touch with our parent's in case when we got holder we forgave them. They always let us make our own decision, pointing out the consequences, they loved us it was you that didn't love them. I don't want to talk to you about this anymore Eryka let's get this shopping thing done. My sister needs me."

The few hours of shopping passed quickly, but not quick enough. Monica was angry with Eryka and was determined to let her know how angry. The day was still young Eryka planned to blow a lot more of her new found wealth before she did something wise with it, but Monica cut that short when she demanded for her to take her back to check on Kim; all the way back to the dorm they argued and the more Eryka spoke the more distant Monica began to feel from her.

"Monica why are you so loyal to her, we were sister's first?!"

"Eryka I don't believe what I am hearing from you and the more I hear you talk the more I realize that maybe we were never sisters."

"Then what were we?"

"I don't know, because now I am realizing that I never knew you at all, how did you hide yourself for so long from: me, Kim, Cameron, Mom and Dad? Who are you, can you tell me? No wait, I think I have a really clear picture of who you really are."

"Who am I Monica, tell me who I am, I would really like to know who you think I am?"

"You are spoiled, selfish, jealous-hearted, hateful, unappreciative, sneaky BITCH who was only in this because you saw a way out of the disgustingly pathetic thing you called a life. They opened their homes and their hearts to you; Cameron his heart and bed, and all along you have been sticking splinters every chance you got. There is darkness in you Eryka, a space that probably at one time used to be a soul and you use people to get what you want and then you throw them away. But you did not have to be that way to the family, we loved you without cause or pause and you used all of us . . . including

Mechelle Davis

me for whatever reason and now you are throwing us away. None of us were your mother; Angela and you hurt each of us and by hurting them you hurt me. These people have been the best family I have ever had. I prayed for a family like the Jenkins and GOD gave me much more. How can I turn away from a love like that?" The more Monica talked the more she began to realize something extremely terrifying about Eryka and as she said the words it was as if someone had punched her in her mid-section; "you had something to do with their deaths, didn't you?!!!! Screaming, Didn't you?!!!"

Eryka did not answer and as the car came to a halt Monica angrily got out leaving her packages behind. What is this girl capable of, I don't trust her and I need no one else to trust her too. Eryka was losing the one person she truly considered family because of Kim, again because of Kim. The short walk from the parking lot to the dorm revealed a lot about Monica's and Eryka relationship and Monica had to know or at least had to hear it out of Eryka's mouth in her own words. She stopped abruptly, "what is wrong with you, why are you acting so cold to Kim, I know if I see it she has to see it too, what has she ever done to you but loved you? It is almost as if you hate her!

Eryka replied sharply, "Don't you get it, she killed the only parent's I ever knew, you ever knew."

"I knew that that is why she feels that way you put it in her head, didn't you?" Eryka ignored Monica's question and continued as if she had been waiting to speak her mind for a long time.

"She has always been selfish like that, it is always, has always been all about Kim." Eryka breaking down like Monica had seen only once before. Monica stood unsympathetically and listened as everyone on the grounds watched her tantrum. "What would it have hurt for her to stop and call Mom and Dad? One call would have stopped everything."

Monica interrupted, "She did call them! Stopped what?"

"No Monica, she did not! Even if she did, what would it have hurt to go home for their anniversary? What would it have hurt for her to take a break? Sarcastically Eryka said, "Oh I remember, what was it, 'I really don't want to hear Dad's mouth about going to an all black college.' Monica it is always, always all about her and I am sick of it!" By the time Eryka finished there was a crowd that she

Mechelle Davis

hadn't noticed moments before and her t-shirt was so saturated from tears that the warm sun could not dry fast enough. Monica looked at Eryka.

"First of all Eryka if you knew that something was going to happen to Mom and Dad, why didn't you call or go home? Secondly Kim is not selfish she practically gave us her parent's and never threw it up in our faces. When we did not have a place to go because my Dad was an abusive alcoholic and your Mom sold you off to the highest or lowest bidder whenever possible; before she told her parents, she snuck us in her bedroom. She gave us her dinner and her bed and slept on her bedroom floor to give us a place to lay our heads. She even recruited Cameron and Pete to help hide and protect us and when we went to court over and over again she missed so many days of school to be there for us that Mom and Dad made her go to summer school with us.

Do you remember how she went to Pete for us and begged him to get us back into school, keep our secret and as a trade off she had to clean the stables for two weeks, one week for each of us. Did either of us offer to help or help her at all, no?! Still she never complained, never asked for help nor did we hear about it when it was over. When we went to school, she took her clothes money and split it between us, bought us clothes and told mother and father that she lost her money on the way to the mall. Do you remember what they did to Kim's selfish ass? They made her wear old clothes, last year clothes for four months while we walked around in new clothes that her money bought. Do you also remember that we never offered her to wear any of our new clothes nor did she ask? Do you remember that? Do you remember when the truth finally came out that we did not have a place to go that her parent's asked her what did she want to do, reminding her that if the two of us stayed then she would receive less of everything? Kim's words were, 'that's okay, these are my sister's and I don't mind sharing because that's what sister's do.' More importantly, do you remember when we started college neither of us did not have biological parents to ask for money to start off at college. Do you also remember we were supposed to work the last two summers of high school to pay for the first year? When Mom and Dad learned that we did not and we thought that we were not going to start college when we graduated. Do you remember

Mechelle Davis

what she said, what she tried to do? Let me remind you! She said, "Mom can we sell the pearls and Japanese hairpin that grandma left to you to get them started? They are going to be passed down to me anyway." She was willing to give up I don't know how many generations of history to put us in college so that we could have just a good of life as her. You say she killed the only parent's you ever knew . . . I ever knew. Eryka she gave us the only parents we ever knew. Our parent's are still alive out there somewhere; we can find our parent's and reconcile, but her parents the only one's she ever knew are gone . . . Forever! Set aside that she is adopted, the Jenkins were her parents. She gave up so much for us when she did not have to, now you're standing here blaming her for Mom and Dad's death as if she doesn't feel bad enough. You're standing here and calling her selfish because you lost parents that she gave to us. You tell me who the selfish one really is?!"

Eryka looked at Monica with new tears of reason in her eyes. Monica looked at Eryka angrily and walked away, but before she got out of Eryka's hearing range she said, "I will never tell Kim about this, I love my sister too much to hurt her like you just hurt me. Oh, by the way, look around you have a crowd, you finally got what you wanted . . . It's all about YOU!"

In a feeble attempt to redeem herself Eryka replied, "She can find her parent's too." Monica continued to Kim's dorm without Eryka. Eryka stood looking embarrassed because Monica did have a point. When Eryka looked around everyone was still staring shaking his or her head. Kim was well-known and liked on campus and anyone with eyes could see she was suffering. She participated in everything and put her all in what she touched and for them to hear Eryka speak so poorly of her put a bitter taste in a lot of people mouths. It was at least two years before Eryka dug herself out of the hole she put herself in and even then, especially with Kim's mental status continually declining and people found out the previsions Kim's parents made for her she was ostracized by nearly everyone. Her friends were no-longer her friends. Eryka felt alone and Kim noticed the large distance between the two when she visited Eryka, but did not understand why the distance was there.

Kim wanted so desperately for the person she has looked up to for the past eight years to love and accept her. The distance between the two was becoming more than Kim could bear and she had to know what she had done to make Eryka become so distant to her. So cold and shut off without any remorse or sympathy.

I t had been two weeks since the reading of the will and Kim was determined to not need the time off she previously requested. Upon returning to the dorm from an uneventful trip to the library, Kim's dorm mate said as she walked by, "There is a package at your door, it was dropped off earlier today, and it came express with balloons."

"Who is it from, Kim asked?"

"It doesn't say, just says: 'To Someone Very Special.' Not that I read your card or anything."

"Umm hum," Kim said attempting to appear her normal self. Feeling a little better from the brief interaction, Kim quick stepped to her door because she still loved receiving presents. She picked up the package—not noticing that the balloons were missing—and it was quite heavy. She shook the box. Referring to the door another dorm mate yelled excitedly from behind her. "Just open it already!"

Kim turned and smiled. Opening her door she entered to find her room filled with flowers, cards of sympathy and balloons, lots of balloons. When she turned around the entire dorm was standing at her door. Jessica spoke with a smile on her face.

"The dorm master let us in, hope you don't mind, we are all really sorry to hear about your parent's, let us know if there is anything that we can do to help you through this. You have been such a good friend to all of us. Even if you weren't a good friend, you are an awesome person and we love you." Kim started to cry along with her dorm mates as they all gave her a group hug.

"Thanks you guys I really needed this."

Mechelle Davis

"We know you had a long day today, Monica told us so we will let you get settled in. Let us know what's in that package it is wrapped to eloquently."

"Okay, I will. Thanks Jessica. Thanks again everyone."

"Oh and Kim."

Kim turned her attention to Jessica, serving as a response.

"I know you do not need to be constantly reminded about your parent's death, so this will be the last time you will be reminded by us. Whatever we can do to help you heal, let us know."

Kim smiled and lipped a "thank you." Jessica lipped back, "you're welcome," blew Kim a kiss and gently closed her door. Kim turned around and thought to herself; *now what the hell am I going to do with all these flowers and balloons?*

Kim was actually feeling better for a brief moment. She cleared a space on her bed and slowly began to open the package. The first thing she saw was a picture of a baby. Its sex never crossed her mind. She flipped the picture over and there was nothing. No writing, no signature . . . nothing. Written under the picture was a card with the same beautiful detailing as the box, the card read:

'LAYER ONE.' As Kim looked intensely at the picture she slowly sat the picture down on the bed she continued to look at it wondering whose baby it is. It's an ugly little thing she laughed to herself. As she unfolded the tissue paper for the second layer she found a pair of handcuffs, a broken high hill, a birthday hat, two champagne classes and a card that read: 'LAYER TWO.'

As she unraveled the third layer, her heart began to pound, she immediate recognized her mother's apron, but it was wrapped in bricks. Initially she did not understand until she seen all members of her family and her initial's engraved in the brick that they carved when the addition to the house was complete; Kim began to cry. Under the apron was a card that read:

LAYER THREE, READY FOR FOUR?' She smelled the apron the scent of her mother was still faintly on it with a hint of smoke and men cologne, she instantly thought it was her Dad's. Kim sobbed as she held it close to her face. Rocking slowly she unwrapped the last layer, it was her mother's blanket, wrapped around her brother's favorite sword, through the dried blood she could make out the engraving 'Jenk Man.' Kim began to scream as she slid off the bed

Mechelle Davis

and fell to her knees. "Why?" was all she could say as the door filled with concerned friends?

"Go get the dean!" one of the girls cried right into the face of Monica, as she held on to Kim—and Kim to the blanket—rocking her.

"Who would do such a thing, why? Kim kept asking" It took the dean and Monica hours to calm Kim down. While her dorm mate's did not understand what was going on Monica did as soon as she saw the blanket. Kim's look of emptiness, fear and defeat all showed on her face and filled her being as she fell into a deep depression.

Kim's breakdown caused the dean of student's to contact the family attorney. He immediately admitted Kim into a hospital, but not a mental institution. He did not want such a scar on her history feeling she should not be punished for losing both of her parent's and her brother. While hospitalized Kim continued on with her studies—it took her nearly six months to do more than just enough to maintain her grades—her attorney communicated extensively with the school and for the first time Kim was grateful of her parent's success. Even with her wealth her grades suffered but not enough for her to drop out. Her attorney, Eryka, Monica, Jessica and Dr. Kowen visited on regular bases. Her recovery went well with the help of her Prozac and valium. Kim, by choice, stayed in care for well into her senior year of college, she felt safe there. Her mail was inspected before it reached her and her calls were screened—an arrangement set in place by Dr. Kowen. After a while she managed to get herself back on the Dean's list.

Kim was forced to leave the hospital shortly before one year of treatment, not by the hospital, but the school because of the unorthodox way that she was attending class. Kim returned to the dorm, to the same group of friends who were not aware of her hospitalization. They were told she took a break from school. It was easily believable because they had seen the state she was in and thought that she needed more than a break. She was her old self and she actually felt a lot better than she did nearly three years ago, when she loss Cam, she was even able to talk about her parent's without feeling guilty or crying.

One year and a half had passed since the death of Mr. and Mrs. Jenkins, three since Cameron's. Kim's sister's first three years of college were hell, helping Kim to cope, and coping themselves, but their sister-ship appeared to grow stronger than ever before because of it. In their last year Monica, Kim and Eryka enjoyed the college life together. Kim resumed all her normal activities it was as if she never left, everyone was happy to have her back.

Kim joined Eryka on her morning runs. Something Eryka discovered as a stress reliever while Kim was in the hospital. They both were very beautiful women even dressed in sweats, gym shoes, a T-shirt and their hair pulled back into a ponytail.

"Can you believe that Monica will be 21 in a month, man Eryka we have gone through so much and have grown even more in such a short period of time, haven't we?"

"Yeah, who would have thought that our young lives were blissful because our adult lives would be hell?"

"Oh come on Eryka we still have had it good, think about it, the only thing that has ever happened to us tragic is that we lost our parents and brother. I am not discounting the tragedies of Monica and your childhood."

"Don't forget that you lost your mind and you graduate behind your personal schedule."

w"Anyway what are you getting Monica for her birthday?"

"I don't know Kim, I really haven't decided. She has been looking at some jewelry at that popular jewelry store in town."

"You're about to spend that much money?"

"I talked to the owner, you know he got the hot's for me."

"Eryka you think that everyone has a thing for you."

"He does, and I think I can get it at a discount. If not, she's into fashion I will just find her an outfit I am sure no one else has."

"Where?"

"Jessica, your dorm mate-she and Monica have become really close—is going to Paris the end of next week I will have her pick up something. What are you going to get her Kim?"

"I don't even know you know my money is funny now."

"It didn't have to be, I still cannot believe that you gave away all that money."

"You know Eryka you do not have to bring that up again. If I am not mistaken you walked away pretty well off."

"Well it wasn't completely due to your parent's" Eryka retorted sharply. Catching Kim's expression she continued.

"Okay Kim I am sorry, are you all right?"

"Look it isn't like I will have another break down because you mentioned me giving up of my inheritance and Mom and Dad, you are not that powerful. I don't feel—as I didn't then—that I deserve to live off of their money, besides Mr. Johnson paid the remainder of my tuition and for law school, room and board, he refused to not pay that and of course the school was not going to give it back. I just have to work for the extras"

"But why Kim, it just doesn't make any sense; we all know that Mom and Dad's death is not your fault?"

"It doesn't matter why I just don't feel like I deserve any of their money. Don't get me wrong it isn't like I am broke, I still have all that money Mom and Dad and their friends gave me over the years for B-day's, Graduation. I banked that money and the money Mom and Dad paid me for working at the office, and don't forget that Mom and Dad made me work the last two years of high school to pay for the first year of college and since they paid my college tuition, I still have that money. So I am doing well on my own accord, I just can't splurge . . . go on a shopping spree like I did when Mom and Dad were here."

"Touché Kim."

Slightly smiling Kim continued, "All I am saying is I just need to spend carefully until I start working full-time. I give myself a few years after graduation and I will be wealthy, not as wealthy, but wealthy just like my parents were rich. Come on we have been jogging for nearly an hour we have to get back and change, Monica might be at the movies waiting for us."

"What's on the agenda for the night?"

"Eryka you have a serious case of CRS, laughing you Can't Remember Shit! Remember last weekend we all agreed that we would get a movie and start a girl's night, where the three of us spend time together without any of our outside friends. We rented a hotel remember so that we could talk and spend time together without any interruptions. You didn't show up nor did you call and our feelings were hurt."

"Dang Kim if we are not careful people will think that we are dating." Both burst into laughter.

"Shut up girl that is sick." Eryka was sincere but made her statement in a joking tone. "Plus I am really not into spending time with you like that. I'm serious, I'm not, so don't get use to this and don't count on me always being there when you and or Monica call." Kim was stunned by her words and disregard for her feelings, but not completely. Eryka had changed, but long before Kim's breakdown, long before she went off to college without her and Monica, long before Cameron died and definitely long before she lost her parent's. Kim did not try to gain complete understanding of what she thought Eryka was saying she accepted her comment and continued on; Kim's actions or lack thereof surprised herself and Eryka.

O n the way to pick out movies, Monica asked, "Did either of you hear about Nina?"

"Nina? Who is Nina?" Eryka asked using her makeup mirror to look in the backseat at Monica.

"Nina the girl who was almost kicked out of school last year for having sex with the janitor on the back stairs."

"Almost?" Eryka questioned.

"Yeah, he was older than her and the school was afraid that her parent's would take legal actions against the school."

"How, she's above consenting age?" Eryka asked a question in statement tone.

"Yeah, but he is a part of staff. No fraternizing, remember?" Monica reminded Eryka.

"So, teachers and students fraternize all the time. It's normal; she just got caught up., unfortunate for him!"

"Eryka you have an off way, way off way of thi . . . !"

Kim interrupted, "I remember that, Kim said, she should have been kicked out for her bad taste in men. The guy was old enough to be her grandfather, ewh." Eryka and Kim started to laugh.

"That's not funny and he was not old enough to be her grandfather. She died yesterday." Monica said solemnly.

"What?" Kim questioned in surprise.

"She was pregnant, I don't know by whom though."

"She probably didn't either." Eryka said sarcastically.

"Didn't What?" Kim asked.

"Didn't know by whom she was pregnant," Eryka replied. Monica ignored her comment.

Mechelle Davis

"She tried to get an abortion without telling her parent's and went to some off brand clinic and died as a result of the abortion. They tore something *down there* that caused her to bleed to death in minutes."

"Oh my goodness, Monica why did you let us go on about her like that?"

"Us? Kim asked veering in the rearview mirror at Eryka. Don't take me to hell with you."

"Monica turned her nose up, I tried to tell you but you know how you like to go on about people imperfections." Monica said with venom in her voice.

"I do not, Eryka replied hurt!"

"Yes you do, but that another topic and a whole other story." Monica directs her eyes toward Kim only and continued. "Her funeral is this coming Saturday do you want to go with me?"

"You don't even know her Monica!" Eryka said.

"We hung out a couple of times through mutual friends."

"Males or females?"

"Look Eryka, I know where you're going with this, "birds of a feather flock together. If that were true then I would be a jealous, judgmental, uptight, pretentious, furtive, hateful, stuck up bitch like you!" Shocked by Monica's comment the entire car went silent.

"So Monica does that mean you don't think highly of me?"

Kim partially laughed at Eryka's quip, but attempted to break the tension. "Sooo does anyone have an idea of the movie we are going to see or get, Kim asked?"

Video, Monica and Eryka said in unknowing unison.

"Monica?" Kim called looking in the rearview mirror.

Monica freed her eyes from burning a hole in the back of Eryka's head and replied, "yeah Kim?"

"I will go to the funeral with you, what time does it start and where will it be?

"I will come by your room at 8:30 a.m. and we will go from there."

"You do know that I can get the details of the funeral from anyone?"

"Then you do that Eryka!" Monica said snidely.

Mechelle Davis

They finally arrived at the video store and Eryka purposely walked along side of Monica.

"I wasn't aware that we started the bitch game; you don't want to go there with me."

"What?! Who said it is a game? Anyway, what are you going to do, judge me to death? Monica paused to gain Eryka's full attention and whispered so that Kim could not fully hear the comment, "Make no mistake about it Eryka, I'm not Kim!" Monica was fearful of Eryka, she knew what she was capable of, but she also knew better to show fear.

Before Eryka could reply Kim intervened again. The intensity in their stance told her that the tension between the two was greater than she wanted to comprehend. "Come on ladies we have been doing so well, all this time we have accepted each other's faults and flaws do not start making a big deal out of our shortcomings and making threats to one another. I know as sister's we will bicker, but you two are about to take it to a whole new level that will definitely ruin our sister-ship."

"Are you sure that it is a sister-ship that we have or is it a pretend-ship?"

"What do you mean by that Monica? Kim asked.

"I don't know ask Eryka I am sure she can clear it up for you."

Kim knew Monica too well to know that she would not just idly make such a statement for no reason, she learned or discovered something about Eryka: but whatever it was Kim did not want to know. Not now that is.

"Whatever it means, I won't touch it. I know that we usually do our own thing on Friday night, but come on let us be at least cordial to one another then we can do our own thing on Saturday. Okay ladies?"

"Okay."

"Okay."

The three of them pretending to be as close as any true sister's could be, but they knew they were different, their relationship was different and they were drifting apart, there was no denying it. Kim reminded her sisters of the pact they made shortly after the girls joined Kim in college and immediately after the first campus girl died trying to have an abortion without the knowledge of her parents. They agreed that nothing was worth risking the life of each other and no matter what to always be there for one another. They agreed that if either of them got pregnant they would keep the baby and the three of them would raise it together never telling the child who their real mother is.

Kim said, "We will never have to worry about getting pregnant because our agreement never to have sex until we are married and/or have a solid career, supersedes this pact doesn't it?" They all looked at each other, smiled and Kim asked, "right?!"

Eryka replied, "Of course it does"

Monica said, "Without a doubt."

"We made a purity pack with Dad remember? One he so graciously reminded me of the day I left for college, continuing while she had the floor. "Look ya'll I know my troubles made us all fall behind, fall and drift apart I just want to say thanks for hanging in there with me." In an effort to keep things from getting serious or mushy "Can you two believe less than six month we will graduate together?" Monica interrupted because she knew where Kim was going with the conversation and she was not quite ready to listen to it again . . . . and it has been a long time coming, Kim said accepting the change of conversation.

"Seriously Monica we didn't think you were going to make it." Eryka added. They all laughed and Kim jokingly said, "We still have less than six months to get through. All you thought about was partying, boys and clothes."

Irritated Monica replied, "And you and your breakdown!" Kim looked hurt by Monica's comment, but made no reply she just looked to the floor until it seemed that Eryka came to her defense. When in all actuality Eryka really took the opening to pay Monica back for calling her a bitch.

"I bet she's not a virgin anymore, mumbled Eryka.

Offended, "shit your psychic, you tell us."

"Why do you have to get offended, I am only playing with you?" Breaking the circle they were sitting in.

"It's not that Eryka because I know how you are, but every time I turn around I learn that you and Kim have shared conversations or moments that didn't include me. Now I find out that the two of you are sitting around thinking that I broke our purity pact. Thanks for believing in me!"

Kim got up and hugged Monica. "You know that we believe in you and we do not and have not sat around talking about you. Monica rolled her eyes, "yeah right!"

"Kim's right, we don't sit around and talk about you, but you do look a little thick around the middle!" Monica became really quiet. Kim noticed it too and told Eryka to stop teasing her she was hurting her feelings. But that was not the reason for Monica's silence, she thought that she was pregnant, but if she's taking on the appearance she know she is pregnant. Ending the night suddenly, Monica left the room in her PJ's using the excuse that she forgot she had something to do and exited the room before her sisters could ask any questions.

Eryka yelled out the door behind her, "Are you coming back? If so could you bring me some pickles and ice cream?" By the time Kim reached the door Monica was stepping onto the elevator and then she stepped back off.

"Tell Eryka she left something in my kitchen trash!" Monica threw the package on the floor and Kim went to retrieve it. As she picked it up she could not believe what she was reading.

Kim reentered the room, "Great going Eryka, why would you do that?!"

"I guess that means the night is over?"

"You think?! Kim asked sarcastically. "You claim Monica broke our purity pact, but the way you have been acting I would swear someone is tearing that tail up. You have been smelling yourself for some time now even before Mom and Dad died. Eryka if you are not interested in being a part of us walk away don't try to destroy the only thing Monica and I consider family . . . . us. You asked for sometime separate from us, request granted Your Majesty." Kim said as she walked toward to hotel room door. "By the way Monica said you left your purity stick at her dorm!" Kim slammed the pregnancy test on the dresser, walked out the door leaving Eryka alone with her words, demons and her purity stick.

The next morning Monica went to an off campus doctor, three hours away from the school to eliminate the chance that she might run into someone she know or someone who knows the same people she knows. She learned she was indeed pregnant, about five months. Monica exclaimed to herself aloud.

"Shit not again, what am I supposed to do?! How can the same thing happen to me twice? Oh GOD, what are you trying to tell me? Where do I go from here?"

The doctor left Monica alone to gather herself after asking a battery of questions. Realizing that Monica really needed the time he left and instructed her to open the door when she needed assistance. She lay on the table perplexed on how to handle the situation and hide it from her sisters.

Closing her eyes she thought, *what am I going to do? How am I going to get through this? The first time I had Mom and Dad, they found the adopting parent's and everything, now that they are gone, what do I do now? Do I keep it?* She asked as she cried and thought to herself aloud? Monica closed her eyes and thought about the first time pregnancy happened to her? She tried to remember similarities in her behavior; she remembered it as though it were yesterday. *"Why does this keep happening to me?"*

She closed her eyes tight to squeeze away the tears escaping them before, during and after the memories of the first time flooded her mind. His words kept ringing in her head; *I've been waiting for you. I've been waiting for you.*

"Hurry up Eryka, everyone will be here in 45 minutes," Kim said!

"I don't feel well."

"What do you mean? You think you're coming down with something."

"No, it's Monica."

Kim, looking concerned, stopped ruffling through the bag of decoration and quickly walked over to Eryka.

"What do you see?"

"I keep telling you that I do not see anything, but the feelings are so strong that it is just like I can see what is happening."

"Well what do you feel?"

"**I** feel that it is really bad. There is a lot of pain and blood, I can almost smell the violence Kim I am scared." "Maybe we should call her."

"I did that already, her phone just rang, but I will try again." Kim took out her cell phone and began to dial the number.

"When did you get that? Let me see it."

"I got it earlier today hold on its ringing!" "She's not answering."

"Maybe she's not there. Try again in a minute."

"Did you tell Jessica and Robin what time to have her here?"

"Yes I did. Kim we both have done all we can to make this a great party for Monica and it will be. Give them time, they will have her here."

"Okay, but we need to keep trying to reach her if your feelings have you doubled-over like that. I am worried about her now Eryka, it is not like her to disappear and not have contacted one of us by now, that only makes me afraid that your feelings are correct." Eryka became a little offended by Kim's singe of doubt, but it wasn't doubt that she was feeling it was her way of putting aside the truth by taking the reality invoker and mixing it with hope.

"She will turn up don't worry." Eryka tried to comfort Kim.

The two continued decorating the cafeteria it was beautiful, Monica had a fascination with Cinderella, daisies, roses and Kim came up with a design that made the theme non overbearing and not at all childish. She had thought of everything from where each person would hide, where her most special people would stand, to how to start and end the party. She had drinks—non alcoholic because they were on campus and some were underage. She even had the temperature in the cafeteria set just right according to the number of people she invited. Kim and Eryka were excited and hoped that Monica would be too.

Looking at her sister Kim smiles, this was the first time in a long time that she acted like the Eryka she once was. Kim loved her sister and admired her more that even she knew. Eryka caught Kim staring at her and asked . . .

"What did you get Monica for her birthday?

"You know that diamond pendant that she's been eyeing for the past six months, the one I told you about?"

"Yeah, well she can eye it on her neck from her reflection."

"You didn't!"

"Yep, I got it for her it was on sale and the jeweler helped me pick out a pair of earrings and a really nice bracelet."

"What did you get her?"

"Kleenex compared to what you got her that's what I get for getting her a last minute gift."

"Oh come on, whatever you got her I am sure she would love it."

"I got her a cell phone with all the amenities, that new Blackberry she wanted; now I have to upgrade my gift."

"She will love it you know how she likes to run her mouth!"

"Not compared to that set you got her." Sadden and irritated Eryka said, "Kim I was not aware that we were competing on who would get Monica the best gift."

"We're not Eryka; I just wanted to get her something nice too."

"Kim I think you know you did, otherwise you would not have bought her that phone."

"Yeah, but I . . ."

"Look Kim, all of our lives, at least as long as we have known each other, you have always bought us nice gifts and took care of us. Hell we met with you taking care of me. Not once do I remember either of us competing with each other because we know that that would tear us apart. Please, please, let us not let this gift thing become the start of a barrage of things that will tear us apart."

"I'm sorry Eryka, you're right, I won't. But only if you promise me one thing"

Mechelle Davis

"What's that?"

That you would stop pointing out how we met and what Mom, Dad, and me done for you and Monica we did not do anything that one family member would have done for another.

"Okay?"

"Okay!"

"Anyway, I remember you taking care of me when we met by beating down Helga."

Kim that seems like ages ago, I never seen her again after that day, I wonder what happened to her."

"I am sure she landed on her feet." Kim thought for a second with a smile on her face. "You know what Eryka?"

"What Kim?"

"I love you" and Kim hugged her.

"I love you too!" Hugging Kim in return surprised by the sudden show of affection.

"Hey, can I join in?" Cameron asked from a distance. Kim turned, ran into her brother's arms and hugged him like she hadn't seen him in years.

"Wow, maybe I should stay away for three more months."

"What are you talking about three more months; I have not seen you in ten months, three days, seven hours, 57 minutes, looking at her watch and 26 seconds." Kim laughed at her own humor and excitement of seeing her brother.

"Whoa, whoa, whoa, little stalker sister!" Cameron playfully replied. Kim returned the sentiment with a soft punch to the right shoulder.

"What are you doing here big brother?"

"Eryka called me two weeks ago, she said that the two of you were giving Monica a surprise birthday party and she thought that it would be a nice surprise for the both of you."

Kim shot a 'Thank you' look at Eryka and replied, "Indeed it is. "How are you? How are things in that dog forsaken school?"

"Please don't even ask. I finally met someone that I could relate to."

Surprise Kim asked, "Really, who is she?"

"He's not a she; he's a he." Kim looked at Cameron puzzled, but he purposely ignored her look.

Mechelle Davis

"What happened to Joyce Lynn, the two of you are never getting back together?"

"Getting back together, when did they break up?" Eryka inquired but her direction question was ignored but answer in the mist of Cameron's response to Kim.

"No, because Mom and Dad requested that the school put the strictest of strict rules on me she could not handle the curfews or the check "ins" so she checked out. No matter what I did they had to know about it. She said she needed someone whose Mom and Dad were not running their life from 15000 miles away. She already has someone else."

"Aw, Cam I'm sorry, I will never leave you no matter how hard of a time Mom and Dad gives you."

"Me? Have they left you alone yet?!"

"No, Dad is still upset with me for coming here. Isn't that the strangest thing considering grandma did the same thing?"

"You know Dad; he's the king of strange."

Now it seems as though he has recruited Mom. She is beginning to give me a hard time too, she said that I might have been a more rounded and grounded person if I had listened to Dad. It's funny, because I thought that diversity rounded you. Anyway, now she is giving me a hard time about being by myself and not having a boyfriend, yada, yada, yada. I love them, but they make me feel as though with all the decisions I've made not one of them is right. It's as if they don't trust us."

"Trust you, why would they you are such a big disappointment." Cameron said laughing, tickling and pulling Kim's ponytail, as he always did for as long as she could remember. Cameron continued, "Enough about Mom and Dad and their controlling ways."

"Okay, so tell me about this guy what kind of friend is he?"

Looking down at Kim Cameron asked, "What do you mean?"

Looking up at Cameron Kim asked, "Is he the kind of friend that will take advantage of you because you are feeling alone? You know the kind of friend that injects slime into bubble gum and tell you that it's the goo that comes in flavored gum. Or is he the kind of friend that we all need?" Kim hugged a passing by dorm mates, and then continued. "Ooor is he that kind of friend?" Raising her eyebrows and hugging herself.

Mechelle Davis

"I cannot believe that you would ask me that Lil sis."

"Oh come on big brother, I am not little Lil sis anymore, college has schooled me on an array of things, including special kind of relationships." Smiling he walked closer to her and kissed her on the forehead. Kim loved when he did that.

"My have you grown, grown into sounding just like Mom and Dad, as if I can't make a good judgment call when it comes to choosing my friends." "To answer your question, "No, he is not the kind of friend that we all need, but he is definitely the kind of friend that I need. I respect his opinions and advice and when you meet him I expect you to be cordial to him."

"You sound like he is your booooyyyy friend."

"Shut up Kim, don't be such a little sister!"

"Well is he? You still have not made that clear." Kim's question really caught Eryka's attention because it was a question that she wanted . . . needed to know too. Thinking to herself if he is gay maybe that is what's so different about him, but where did the quiet sinister part come from, the part that I am attracted to. He has always been boisterously cocky, he doesn't feel like the man I am used to. He seems passive, submissive, a little less confident yet more dangerous.

"No he's my mentor, the mentor I told everyone about. I kind of feel about him like I did about Joyce time four. I am not sure if I feel this way about him because I have been alone for so long or if it is because it—looking at his sister's out of the corner of his eye hoping they knew what he is trying to say without saying it—has been lying dormant in me and he bought it out. It's just another thing Mom and Dad has to add to their laundry list of disappointments of me."

"Does your friend know that you feel this way about him?"

"No, I would never tell him that. He . . . he is not like me."

"You mean tall with beautiful eyes, a great smile, fantastic body and a wonderful personality?"

"Thanks sis, I mean he's all man he really loves women." Eryka sighed with relief. "But I feel like he leads me on. You know just enough to keep me interested, but not enough to cross the line?"

"Where did you meet him? Kim continued to grill Cameron"

"I had been sneaking out of school for a while so one night I went to one of the local bars, not being twenty-one and all I thought

I had to sneak in and found a way to get in without being noticed. After a few weeks they noticed me, I became a regular and it was easy after that. Until one day I was sitting in the corner by myself smoking a cigarette."

"You smoke now?" Kim asked with surprise, disgust and disappointment.

"Sometimes."

"Anyway, the bartender came to me and asked if I would sit at a table because some couple wanted my booth and since I was alone, I should not mind sitting at a table. I told the bartender that I was not moving and that they could go find their own booth. Not in that manner, but you know what I mean."

"Good for you."

"Then the bartender asked for my ID and when I would not give it to him he asked me to leave. When I told him "no" he got loud. Then Whill came over and said, "Do you always have to be early to everything? If you arrived late sometimes you wouldn't look so desperate and these homosexuals would not harass you."

"You were in a gay bar?"

"No it was straight. Anyway, I looked up at him and he smiled down at me. He told the Bartender to, "Go away, and bring him a beer." Will waving his hands at the guy as if he were inconsequential; a Nat flying around his head.

"I will have the waitress bring you one over I don't serve drinks aside from at the bar."

"No, you will bring me a beer personally because if you can serve harassment from behind the bar you can serve beer. Now go get my beer actually bring two, one for my friend here. That was the first time that I have seen him outside of the realm of mentor, we have been friends every since. Of course Mom and does not like him, but he says don't worry about it he will change their minds because where there's a Whill there's a way." The three siblings laughed at the play on words.

"Mom and Dad met him already?"

"Yes and no. They talked extensively over the phone Whill's schedule would not allow them to meet. I kind of glad you know how critical Mom and Dad can be about the people we bring around. Of course they do not like him very much. Mom said there was something wrong and eerie about him so strong that it is in his voice. According to them there is something wrong about and with everyone I meet—female or male. They hated my choice in friends, in anything, when I lived at home and they hate them now. I don't think they will ever cut me a break and I am sick of waiting for their approval."

Eryka smiled in the background, standing to the side was becoming more and more comfortable but uncomfortable with the vibe that she is receiving from Cameron. She and her mother have always shared the same feelings about almost everything and this wasn't any different. Eryka was scared for herself, her parent's, sisters and anyone that came across Cameron's path. He was definitely not the brother she had grown up with, but how do she tell Kim what she is feeling? Or should she? Hell she was quite different herself with her own horrible secrets. Unfortunately secrets she and Cameron had in common, but only she knew about. She didn't like the secrets she held, but she enjoyed what she did to get them. Cameron's voice faded into her hearing.

"I told him about my three beautiful sisters and he can't wait to meet all of you especially you Kim he thinks you're gorgeous, he says he's in love, but I've already told you that." Eryka's anger deepened as she caught and repaired the expression on her face before either of her siblings did.

"You said couldn't, is he here? Where is he, Kim asked?"

Eryka secretly begin to search the crowd too with anxious anticipation.

"On our way over here about an hour ago he ran into an old friend and she told him about some party of the century. He said he was going to check it out and meet the two of you later. I think that is where Monica is. I don't think that she's coming, Kimmie."

"Of course she is," Eryka said finally feeling comfortable enough to join in Cameron and Kim's conversation without feeling as if she stepped in out of place.

There is something different about Cameron than there was a few months ago. Something changed in him dramatically and it scared Eryka stiff. It was like she had an unknown epiphany of some sort. Her body knew what it was, but her brain, soul would not let her accept or see it clearly. It felt like that something that is on the tip of your thoughts but you can't quite figure it out. Eryka attempted to shake the feeling, but she could not get the feeling to go away and she could not stop thinking about it . . . trying to put her finger on it she half starred at Cameron.

She thought to herself, I have to get it together before they catch on and start asking questions. I won't lie because I don't want to and what will I lie about? Eryka quickly recovered, "Come on you two, enough bonding and catching up let's get the rest of this stuff together this place will fill up soon, you helping Cam?"

Looking at his watch, "I have something to do first."

"What could you possibly have to do?" Kim asked

"I'll be back soon I have to take something off lock." He smiled to himself, but a hint of sadness and guilt crept in that disappeared as soon as he heard his sister's voice.

"What does that mean?" Kim asked.

Cameron shouted words over his shoulder loud enough for them to land in the ears of everyone in the room. "It means I will always protect you first!"

It was Friday, the end of a long week and Monica was thinking about going to the biggest party of the year with Jessica and Robin, but tonight was her 21st B-day, so she just knew her sister's had something planned for her she refused to believe they had forgotten, especially Kim. She looked at the clock and her time was disappearing fast. Kim had not called so Monica thought Kim had to be playing with her. She decided she should go ahead and start getting ready because she or Eryka will be calling soon. Everyone usually start leaving the dorm between 8:30 and 9:30 she didn't have time to shower to perfection. "A quick one will do."

Refreshed Monica pulled from the closet the outfit she had bought nearly two weeks ago when she and Kim were out shopping. She helped Kim buy a cell phone that day, but not herself it was out of the budget she had set for herself. So was the outfit but this is for her birthday she decided to splurge and secretly wished she had worked during the summer as she promised her parent's. She reasoned *"I know Mom and Dad will give me some serious cash for my B-Day and would want me to be the best dressed in the room. Who am I to disappoint.* "I will take the dress, the shoes, and all the accessories."

Mechelle Davis

"I thought you were on a tight budget?"

"I am but, not one Birthday has gone by without Mom and Dad giving us cash. I will budget my B-Day money."

"Which is in two weeks, right?" Monica looked puzzled not certain if Kim's question was a slip of the tongue or if she was serious. "It is on the same date as it has been for the past 20 years."

"What day does it fall on this year: Friday, Saturday or Sunday?"

Monica did not respond she turned her back pretending to look at more dresses. Kim smiled at her. Monica never let on to Kim that she was hurt that Kim appeared to have forgotten her birthday. Monica thought, this is so typical of who Eryka have become, but not Kim.

Kim said, "We better hurry up the store is about to close and I want to hurry up and get back to the dorm to study for this outrageous exam Professor Ritchie conjured up for us on Monday." Kim dropped Monica off in the brand new Lexus her Daddy had bought and had delivered two months prior for her birthday; August 31st. Before Monica could get out of the car, she began to cry. "I can't believe they forgot my birthday." Walking toward her dorm Kim sat there to make sure she got in safely. Monica did not turn around as she usually did when Kim blew her horn to say goodbye. She just threw her hand in the air. When she got in her dorm room, she hung her outfit, still in the garment bag, and then placed her shoes in the closet.

Monica decided not to wait on her sister's she picked up her phone to call Robin and Jessica. Jessica did not answer her phone, she knew that at this time it is either because she has illegally snuck her boyfriend in or her boyfriend has illegally snuck her in. She hung up and called Robin. Robin answered on the first ring.

"Robin, are you and Jessica still going to that party tonight?"

"Yeah, you decided to go?"

"Yeah . . ."

"I knew you would"

"What time can you pick me up?

"I have to pick up Jessica and her friend Beverly and I will be at your dorm about 10:30, Monica please, please be ready."

"I will."

"Really Monica every time we come to pick you up you're never ready and are always trying to change your mind."

"I will be ready, I promise, and I won't change my mind this time!"

"Good we really want you to go. We planned a surprise for you. I have to go Derrick is at my door?"

"Okay."

"Monica." Robin yelled into the phone.

"Uh?"

"What changed your mind? Why did you decide to go?"

"I don't know, looking for excitement I guess."

"Yeah okay."

"For real," Monica said.

"Okay, let me let him in before I have to hear his mouth."

"Okay", before Monica could say by Robin was gone.

Monica laid the outfit on the bed and put the shoes in front of it and smiled with satisfaction. Just at that instant she got an uneasy feeling, but took it as being tired. *10:30 I have time to re-shower, that should help this sickening feeling.* She pinned her hair with a clamp, undressed, and brushed her teeth while letting the shower warm. It took a little longer because almost everyone in the dorm was getting ready to go to this party. She took a warm shower, briefly enjoying the warm water on her face. She paused for a moment thinking that she heard the phone ring at the very moment it stopped. After her shower she blow-dried the small portions of her hair that had gotten wet, rubbed light oil through her hair and curled it in big bulky curls. "Wow that looks better than it does when I take my time." She was just about ready when Jessica and Robin knocked on the door. That uneasy feeling did not go away, it intensified with each knock. Walking to the door, pulling her dress down thinking to herself—neither of them called-she reached for the doorknob, pulled the door open and turned to walk deeper into her room, Jessica and Robin stepped in.

Jessica smiled, "Let's go girl you're holding us up, let's go!"

"I really don't feel like going. I can't get anything to go right. My hair doesn't look right and my outfit is off."

"No it isn't it looks just as good on you now as it did I'm sure when you tried it on in the store."

Mechelle Davis

"Thanks Robin, but it's not just that it something else. I don't think I should go; I am going to stay in. I will pass."

"No you won't" Jessica said. "We have been waiting on this party for over two months, you called me at the last minute and asked me to pick you up and you assured me that you were going you had two hours to change your mind. Besides that, not only did you finally get off academic probation, we are about to start the best 12 week internship program with Genentech in less than two weeks and it's your birthday, we have a whole lot to celebrate. Now let's go!"

"Just to clear the air, you are about to start the best internship program in six weeks not me"

". . . and whose fault is that?" Jessica asked mockingly.

"Whatever comes you will have fun I promise."

"Don't force her to go Robin said. She doesn't have to go if she doesn't want too, leave her alone she's doing right, my mother has always told me to follow my first mind and that's what she should do." Monica turned around and smiled.

"Oh I get it Jessica said, it's your two so-called sister's, isn't it?' They forgot your birthday, didn't they?" Monica did not answer.

"Forget them they are too controlling over your life anyway. Kim is a great person, but a miserable friend and sister to you. She is always defending Eryka and Eryka definitely does not mean her any good, it's like Kim is pawning after a person who doesn't give a flying chicken about her!"

"A flying chicken?!" Monica and Robin asked and laughed in unison.

"Whatever, you two know what I mean, Eryka don't care and Kim is different since Eryka came. Jessica rebutted that is why we are better friend than Kim and I. Look I am not trying to be insensitive, but you have to start living your life, not Kim's, if you don't it will pass you by, now put your shoes back on and let's go partaaaay!" Jessica said in a sing-song manner while waving her arms and shaking her hips then with a smile on her face walked over and kissed Monica on the cheek.

"What did you mean when you said, *whatever comes?*" Jessica continued with her personal party and successfully circumvented Monica's query.

Mechelle Davis

Leaning toward Monica and giving her the shimmy Jessica continued. "Happy B-Day girl, now let's go have some fun you'll forget all about them and I guarantee you you will never forget this night."

Monica went that night upset thinking that neither, Eryka or Kim remembered her birthday. "I can understand Eryka, but Kim what did I ever do to her?"

"You're right, let's go." On the way out the phone rang again.

"Let it ring, Jessica said, we almost got you out the door, no turning back."

"Okay, but I still don't feel like I look good in this outfit."

With her arm around Monica's waist Jessica said smiling, "You're right, you don't look good, you . . . look . . . Ho-hot!" Monica was dressed to kill, in platinum pink, well-fitted, but not too tight dress. She gave just enough to have the eyes wondering and the mind wanting more. Complete back out to stop just at the V of her buttocks. The front fit tight to the rib cage, until just under her breast where loose, pleated material lightly stitched in red flirted with her firm breast and held on to her neck for dear life. Preventing accidental exposure was a diamond chain that extended perfectly across her cleavage.

Her six inch platinum pink sandals, lightly stitched in red hugged her ankles to not only compliment the dress but her well-toned legs. The rhinestones across the top of her sandals sparkled like the teardrop diamonds in her ears. Her hair flowed over her shoulders with big bulky spiral curls which made her look young, flirty, fresh and sophistication. Monica was eloquently dressed, almost too eloquent for the type of party she was going to and compared to her friends who were dressed in micro miniskirts, short-shorts, a blue Jean skirt and little to nothing tops. Unlike Monica they left little to the imagination.

"Great going ladies with leaving a little to the imagination!" Monica teased the three ladies as they arrived at the over-crowed party of students and non students alike. Monica could tell that everyone was having the time of their life. Observing the scene she was quickly approached by a tall man, very nicely built, with dark black hair, bluish green eyes, an expensive haircut, appearing to be at least ten years her senior, but she guessed 20 and dressed like he did not want people to know he is extremely well off. When he approached Monica, looking down at her gently with his warm eyes he said, "I have been waiting for you!"

Smiling, and coyly looking up at him she replied, "That's original. Strangely enough I have been waiting for you too." Stretching out her hand, "My name is Monica."

Flashing a perfect smile and using a seductive voice, he received her hand "Hello Monica . . . Quinn." Never letting his expensive suit touch the ground, he kneeled to one, knee still gazing into her eyes and holding her hand, "Will you marry me?"

"Sure, but first let's talk and get to know one another."

"Sounds like a great plan, would you like something to drink?" Though a partier, Monica was not at all a drinker.

Monica replied, "Sure, it's this way and proceeded to walk in the direction of the house, Quinn in another.

Monica paused at the second Quinn paused and slightly looked over her shoulder parting her lips just enough to display a smile but no teeth.

"It's this way." Nodding her head and gesturing her index finger in the intended direction.

Quinn returning the same flirtatious smile, but with a hidden agenda, "Umm, how about we go this way?"

"Toward the house, sure" Monica said with the same eager yet challenging smile.

"But the best drinks are in that direction," Quinn Replied. He gently took Monica's hand in his and led her toward the tennis court. With his touch came a breeze and a wave of heat. Monica smiled thinking this man look and smells heavenly, but my gut feeling tells me he is definitely a fallen angle. Ignoring her gut she enthusiastically followed then paused, "Maybe I should let my friends know where I am so they won't worry."

"It's okay; we won't be gone long." Quinn held tighter to her hand and began to talk to ease her. That uneasy feeling she had in her dorm room intensified, is he what the uneasiness is all about? Can't be, I have never met him before and he's too dam attractive to be harmful!

"You look pretty preoccupied for someone who becomes a little closer to legal today."

Mechelle Davis

Monica looked up into the face of devastation hiding behind a smile, with warning in her heart and love in her eyes.

"How do you know it's my birthday?"

Quinn smiled and looked down. "Well you're dressed to kill, you smell wonderful and you have this 'I am woman' look on your face." Monica smiled at the man that seemed to be saying all the right words and shyly glanced down and back up at the perfect figure before her. Continuing to gaze up at him with a smile she asked again, "How do you really know it's my B-Day?"

Quinn smiled back, "we have mutual friends and they told me."

"Mutual friends? Who?"

Quinn did not say, just smiled, and then the sound of his voice put even the most perfect musical note to shame. "Don't worry everything is fine, they helped me set this up." Monica instantly began to search her mind for someone that could possible fit in the same category as Quinn and herself, but her thoughts were interrupted with what her eyes saw. They arrived at the tennis court he had removed the net and replaced it with a table. There was soft light glowing from the table, surrounding the table and in the center, placed in a large and beautifully arranged were her favorite flowers, daisies but what impressed her most was what looked to be two oversized clothes rack he had over the table with a crystal chandelier suspended between the two.

"Someone is already here we should go." She played naive. Quinn replied, "Yes someone is already here, us! Tonight is your birthday, right?"

"Yes, but how did you know that? And why would you do all this for me before ever meeting me?"

"I do know you you just do not know me. I told you we have mutual friends and I have been waiting for you." Monica smiled uncomfortably as she detected impatience in his voice. She knew she needed to remove herself from his presence, but she was happy that someone had finally taken the time to put her first; she had felt so alone since Kim first went to college. Monica longed for the attention that he was showing her, she felt she deserved it and she did, just not from him.

"Come on," he said in a gentle, patient, confident voice. "You are a party girl, but I have a sneaky feeling that you have never been wined and dined. Am I correct?" Not answering Monica smiled and looked behind her to measure the distance from where she stood, through the small woods back to the house. She realized she would never make it in her hills. The sound of the music was closer than she actually was, with each passing moment her feelings of uneasiness intensified and she grew angry with herself for not following her instinct. Noticing Monica's nervousness Quinn assured her, "Do not be afraid, I won't hurt you. Come on, have a seat." He gently encouraged as he pulled her chair out for her.

Reluctantly she sat down, something inside of her said run, get away from him, and rejoin the party. *Is this what my uneasy feeling was about?* The question kept tugging at her stomach. This had to be it she thought as her heart continued to pound so hard that Quinn could hear it in her voice and see it in her throat. She would soon regret that she did not listen to her warning voice. She sat down and looked up into his trusting face and warm smile, but that did not ease her. He reached under the cloth that flowed to the ground and pulled out two slices of cake, one with a candle and one without. He lit the candle and placed the cake in front of her and the other in front of him.

"Carrot cake?"

"Uhm?" Monica questioned preoccupied with assessing her surroundings.

"Carrot cake, this is your preference, right?"

How does he know so much about me? Who are these mutual friends? Nervous Monica began looking around again, "So you never said who our mutual friends are." Not really expecting an answer, but trying to figure out how she would get away from him she started to take off her shoes. He looks extremely athletic, but it might be worth the try. Quinn begins singing happy birthday, and Monica hears him in her distant hearing, but is distracted by her thoughts. She looked over at the entrance thinking to herself, but the words escaped her lips in a whisper, "When did he lock that?" The sound of her pounding heart grew louder again, he notices her fear and it excited him. He places his hands on top of hers and she is startled "Don't be afraid, I promise I won't hurt you. Go ahead, blow out the candle and eat some cake."

"No thank you. I'm really not hungry."

Mechelle Davis

"Is that how you keep that magnificent figure? You look so beautiful, stand up, spin for me." She thought of screaming for help but knew it would be a moot effort for no one would hear her and what would she explain she needs help from, a feeling, a wonderful set up, a beautiful man who is being attentive, understanding, romantic and complimentary? Before standing, she bought time questioning him about their mutual friends while she slid her feet back into her shoes, strap under her heels.

"Go ahead model for me." She slowly rose from the chair keeping her eyes on him she stood and put her hand slightly out palms turned upward as if to say "see." He took his pointy finger and twirled it in a circular motion and she turned keeping her eyes on him.

"Why are you so suspicious of me? Come on, sit down, have some cake." Looking at the intensity in his eyes she slowly sat down, took a fork full of the moist cake and placed it in her mouth. She could not ignore the heavenly taste dancing on her tongue.

"Delicious, isn't it?"

Giving a nervous smile, "Yes it is. Why are you doing this, what do you want?"

"You, I want you. Am I frightening you? If I am, I apologize."

"Could we go back, I am sure that my friends are looking for me? They will come looking shortly."

"No they won't!" He said sharply, displaying a little irritation, but he quickly recovered. Not quick enough with confirmed suspicion, clearing her throat from the excess cake, she asked, "How do you know that?"

"I know that because my friends—our friends are helping me with this. We went through a lot of trouble planning this and you don't appreciate it."

Ignoring his comment Monica thought to herself, Robin? Jessica? The mutual friends and tears began to fall. She quickly wiped them away.

"Eat some more cake." He pushed her plate closer to her.

Monica placed another fork full in her mouth. Quinn removed the napkin from his lap, wrapped it around his pointy finger and wiped her tears. Speaking as if Monica's tears were from his encouragement of taking another bite, he gently replied with a smile, "Okay you've eaten enough; don't want to ruin that great figure!"

Mechelle Davis

He reached down and pulled out a roast beef sandwich with sauerkraut, sour dough bread and two pickles on the side and sat it in front of her. Looking at the sandwich she thought about Cameron and smiled. The two use to chew and make sour faces at each other. Then she realized the fattening sandwich was only something she and Cameron shared as a joke to mock Kim's healthy eating habits. Just as she begun to ask him how he knew so much about her, she thought of her brother again. Then thought better of it, *I am getting paranoid Cameron would never set me up with my Dad, my dangerous Dad!*

"Eat up and we can go." Monica had taken two small bites of her sandwich and began to feel lightheaded.

"Are you okay?" Quinn asked as he made his way around to her side of the table.

"Here let me help you with that." Quinn took her sandwich and put it back onto her plate. She was not sure if the music she heard was in her head or if it were real, Ashford and Simpson, "Always." She glanced over at the entrance and was not sure if she had seen Cameron or if her paranoia manifested itself into an actual person. She looked again there was no one there and the gate was unlocked. She did not know what to think her head was spinning faster than her heart was pounding. She called Cameron's name as she collapsed, Quinn caught her and danced with her limp body.

When she came to, groggy she noticed the music in the distance had stopped he was on top of her jamming himself inside of her with his hand over her mouth. She was not sure if it were the pain that brought her to, or if it were his clammy hands over her mouth or the smell of his hot mustard and sauerkraut breath that played the role of smelling sauce. Whatever it was it did not dull the pain that he was inflicting on her physically, mentally and emotionally.

He handcuffed her to a tree and went back for seconds and third's when he was done he placed an ice pack on her Virginia. During his break she tried to break free, but he had screwed some kind of clamp to the tree and hooked the handcuffs to it. She was completely at his mercy.

Next to her was a small basin with warm water, soap and a wash cloth. Quinn removed the ice pack and began to wash her with such care as if he loved her and was delighted to do what he was doing.

Mechelle Davis

"My arms hurt." Was all she said.

He agreed to free one hand but not before he made certain that she would not scream or try to attack him when he freed her left hand. Monica looked around and saw her clothes, undergarments and all, neatly folded on a tree branch. She agreed to cooperate. He completed cleaning her then redressed her, freed her right hands and when he went to put her left shoe on she picked up her right and pushed her stiletto deep into his eye. Pulled it out and struck him in the head. He screamed with such agony and as she ran she smiled holding her stomach from the pain of his harsh jabbing. She somehow found her way to an emergency room and upon entering she passed out at the entrance, blooding still flowing in heavy streams down her thighs.

Nurses and random patients rushed to her aid. Monica was laid on a gurney and even though her injuries were not apparent, she was treated with urgency. When she came to six hours later, fighting the air, all she could say was. "He raped me, over and over again and she was out again, when she woke four hours later the second time she was accompanied by a female detective, doctor and a psychiatrist.

"Do you know where you are?"

"Yes." Monica said in a voice that told of the pain she was feeling.

"Do you know who did this to you?"

"Yes . . . I mean no."

"Ms. Hargrove, Are you trying to protect someone or are you afraid? The detective continued with her questions. "You don't have to be afraid, if you know who this person is you should tell us so that he cannot hurt anyone else. We can protect you."

Monica looked at the detective and said, "I am sure I am not the first person he has raped, who told to protect me?" Purposely overlooking Monica's question the detective asked, "Is there anyone you would like us to call?"

"No," Monica said in a sad and hurt voice.

"You really should not go through this alone."

"I am alone and tonight I learned how truly alone I am."

"Ms. Hargrove, you have a large amount of GHB in your blood whoever did this nearly killed you. Who drugged you, who did this to you, what does he look like?"

Mechelle Davis

Holding her stomach attempting to nurse the residual pain the medication overlooked, "Pleasure and pain." She responded, "He looks like pleasure and pain."

"What do you mean by that? The detective asked, Monica did not reply.

"Miss. Hargrove, I understand how you must feel, but we . . ."

Monica cut her off, "Do you? Have you ever had someone you dreamed of your whole life come up to you and say all the right things, gain your trust and within a matter of minutes take it away? Have you ever had a gut feeling that something was not quite right and ignored it and when you did decide to pay attention it was too late? Have you ever been tied up, raped over and over again in every part of your body thinkable? Have you ever had a total stranger put his penis in your mouth and tell you to suck it like you love it? Do you know what it is like to lose trust in yourself to know that you will doubt or second-guess everything about whom and what you know or knew about you? Do you know what it is like to have someone take your virginity, for your first time to always be this horrific memory? Monica paused for a moment; her voice became calm and solemn. Last night was my birthday. 21 years prior I was born, 21 years later I died. Even if you do understand, I am sure your experience wasn't as nearly as traumatic as mine. She began to cry again softly, "he raped me; I lost my virginity and died in the worst way imaginable." Sobbing, "No Mam, you don't understand how I am feeling."

The three women stood quietly and their years of training and experience did not prepare them for such abuse as they see with Monica. They cried because they can see the unpleasant change in her even though they did not know her before. Their hearts went out to her while a steady flow of tears rolled down each of their faces. They were stunned by her outburst, expression of feelings so soon after her assault, a clear sign of self-destruction in any possible direction. The female detective forgot to take notes of Monica's statement, but the Doctor recorded it all.

The detective's years of experience taught her many things, but never to be prepared for such emotions. Monica's words will forever be burned in her heart and memory. She sat on a stool next to Monica's hospital bed and did the only thing she could think to do, clear her throat and continued with her questions.

"Ms. Hargrove I am truly, truly sorry for what happened to you. I know that there is nothing I can say to take away the emotional and physical pain you're in and feeling, sighing she continued, and I hope that you do not mean that you do not care if anyone else get hurt, so please tell me all you can. For starters, we found two types of blood on you, where did the blood come from?"

Dazed by her traumatic experience, Monica sat replaying her conversation to herself before she left earlier the night before. *Something isn't right, I should stay home. I'm not going!* Before her own thoughts were interrupted by Quinn's words, *"We have Mutual Friends. Don't be afraid, I won't hurt you."*

"Ms. Hargrove?" The detective's voice echoed in the back of her mind. "Where did the second blood type come from? Is it your attackers? Did you injure him? Did you come into contact with someone on the way here?

"Him—me—my stiletto."

"I'm sorry I don't understand."

"I gouged his eye out with my stiletto and then put a hole in his head."

"I will need your shoe for evidence."

Smiling Monica said, "You can have the whole night. He raped me, but it looks like we both walked away with some permanent scares."

"I can see that you are proud of whatever damage you have inflicted on him and your fighting may very well have saved your life and I applaud you for fighting back. Can you tell me his name? Miss Hargrove, in order to help you I nee . . .""

Monica cut her off. "I need to begin to put this night behind me that is the only need I really care about." With that Monica never said another word to anyone about it until months later when she confided in her parent's the horrible details that led to her pregnancy. She asked for their help and they were there every time she thought back to the last time she spent time with her parent's.

Monica heard a car pull up in a parking space right outside her bedroom window and ran to the window in anticipation, looking down she smiled the biggest childish smile as she waived.

Mechelle Davis

"Mom, Dad!" Monica exclaimed excitedly feeling like a child as she wobbled to her apartment door, down the stairs, and out the main door right into her Dad's arms.

"I thought you two would never get here, I am so glad that you are!" The Jenkins had arrived at 9 p.m., Tuesday, June 16, 1998, just as they said they would. Monica thought back for a moment to her own parent's as she seldom did to how their words meant nothing. She smiled at her parent's presence and because she was grateful that even in the short time of living with them she would forever have their qualities, moral and values.

The airport limousine driver unloaded the Jenkins things onto the sidewalk of the parking lot and though Dad had several bags Monica noticed that her mother's load was a little lighter than normal.

"I thought you and Dad were going to stay two weeks? How long are you here for?"

"We are going to stay two weeks . . . plus, I just packed light because I thought that after you've had that little bundle of joy that you might want to go shopping and get some after pregnancy clothes just in time for your birthday. Monica smiled, "Mom I really don't believe this little critter will arrive on time, but I can hope so don't fret I will buy clothes for the old me. I will never turn down a shopping spree?" She patted her stomach as she playfully talked to her belly, "come on little one hurry up out of there!" The baby kicked as a response, Monica quickly secured her Mom and Dad's hand and placed them on her stomach. All three stood outside with their hand on Monica's belly smiling with so much love in their eyes and heart.

The baby kicked again and this time Monica doubled over.

"Are you alright?" her Dad asked with concern in his voice and equally in his eyes as he stepped to her side and secured her in his arms.

"Yes, I have been having these pains for about a week now and Dr. Fudul said that they were Braxton Hicks he instructed me to stay off my feet.

"Sir, what floor shall I take these to?"

Monica chimed in though her pain, "Second floor on the right, the door is already open. Mom, Dad do you think you can get that driver to take us to the hospital? These feel far more different than the previous Braxton Hicks, I think something is wrong."

When the driver returned Mr. Jenkins gave Mrs. Jenkins a look and she took over supporting Monica. Mr. Jenkins said a few words to the driver and slid $200 into the driver's hand. Unfolding the bills to see the two crisp $100 bills the driver was more than eager to take them to any hospital they wanted to go.

"Are your bags packed?"

"Yes."

"Where are they?" Mrs. Jenkins asked as Mr. Jenkins attempted to keep Monica calm.

"1-2-3 breath, 1-2-3 breath," he instructed as he simulated the sound of a woman in a lot of pain.

"In the . . . front . . . Moocow Closet!" Monica screamed in agony as her legs gave way to the intensity of the pain. Briefly collecting herself, "Mom could you grab my purse off the chair in the kitchen?" Monica was now doubled over with her legs spread apart.

"Looks like we're having a baby tonight; happy birthday to Eryka." Mr. Jenkins said as he smiled and went through Monica's breathing routine with her.

"No Daddy it's too early!"

"Maybe for you, but I think this child would beg to differ."

"Could you call Mr. and Mrs. Simpson and have the parent's to be meet us at the hospital?"

Mr. Jenkins looked puzzled and Mrs. Jenkins cleared it up for him.

"They are the adopting parents."

They too were with Monica every step of the way. They paid for her apartment, all doctor expenses, clothing and food, but Monica would not accept anymore than that. She was comfortable living the nine month life she chose to avoid an abortion.

Monica had been out of school for longer than she wanted, the birth of her child geared more complications than she anticipated. The stitches seemed to be the worst part of it all. She was ever more grateful that her Mom and Dad were there to help her through her ordeal. She was surprised that when it was all over that she felt empty inside, she almost miss the movement and knew she would miss the sound of the baby's heartbeat during check-ups. She kept

Mechelle Davis

every ultra-sound and every appointment card to every doctor's appointment she wanted her baby to know that it was loved even though it wasn't made from love.

The Jenkins turned to look at Monica's bundle as the nurse wheeled the baby into the room, 10lbs, and 6 oz, 22 inches long, remarkably beautiful. With a strange subtle look of maturity and his massive size made him look at least a couple of months old instead of a couple of hours.

"Do you want to see your baby Monica?" The nurse asked with a gregarious smile and cheerful tone in her voice while she wheeled the baby over to her.

"No, please take the baby away!"

Mrs. Jenkins motioned for the nurse to wait as she chimed in. "Honey I know that giving your baby up was a hard decision, but to never have laid eyes on your child and to never have held your baby will leave you with regrets for the remainder of your life. Even if for a moment you will forever know the smell, and the softness of your baby's skin, the feel of the hair."

Mrs. Jenkins explained to Monica as she bent down and picked the baby up. Returning to an upright position her mother placed the baby in her arms, and when Monica looked down at the baby it had the most beautiful aqua-green eyes she had ever seen looking right at her. Mrs. Jenkins snapped the picture just as Monica softly kissed its lips. Monica smiled at the smell of milk on her baby's warm breath. She slowly removed the blanket it was swaddled in and stared at how big her small wonder is. Looking her tainted miracle over she smiled at the birthmark that looked like a stemmed rose, Mrs. Jenkins took a picture.

Pausing for a moment the three stripped the baby down, took pictures and redressed it. Monica slowly counted ten fingers and ten toes and sobbed uncontrollably as she cradled the child's head to her chest and under her chin. Rocking back and forth Monica gently moved her finger until she felt a soft spot; she rested her hands and again amazed that such a thin piece of tissue allowed her to feel the life that grew inside her. Right after Monica rubbed her cheek against the softness of her baby's hair until the nurse announced she needed to return the baby to the nursery. It was the shortest, longest hour of her life. Monica cried believing that she did not think that

Mechelle Davis

she would be able to go through with it after holding her beautiful baby.

Mrs. Jenkins wrapped her arms around her daughter and reassured her that she had three days to change her mind and if she did, she and Dad would support the child while she completed college. Though Monica's Dad never said a word he placed his massive hand on her leg and when she looked at him he smiled with tears in his eyes, not for the loss of a grandchild but the pain his daughter was experiencing. Monica felt hurt because she had never seen her Dad cry or even come close to crying. She quickly removed herself from her mother's arms and through herself into her Dad's she felt safe, protected, and loved. She prayed that she picked the right family a family that would raise her baby with the same presence of security and love that she accidently found in the Jenkins family.

The tap at the door caused Monica to open her eyes, when the figure stepped in, she asked, "Doc, do you know of any good abortion clinics?"

T he last month of the year went by quickly, so many things seemingly changed. Kim's sessions with Dr. Kowen were extended to Monica and Eryka who took every opportunity to have an ear. The relationship between Dr. Kowen and the three blossomed and Eryka was grateful to have her.

Dr. Kowen's Saturday appointment seemed to last forever she made a mental note not to charge her patient for the session because her mind being other places did not allow her to give her full attention. The day went by much too slow, she was overly anxious to see the girls walk across the stage especially in spite of all the tragedy they had experienced. Eryka's jealous attitude toward Kim diminished or at least appeared to have.

Kim stood at the podium, struggling with her words, choking down her sobs, unable to control her tears, she knew she had seen the familiar face and longed for it to return. Kim searched the crowd for Pete but he was gone as quickly as he appeared. Now that her parents are gone and she donated all of her inheritance, are her sister's still really her sister's? So many unanswered questions and uncertainties filled her mind replaced what she had rehearsed all of the ten minutes she normally would have needed before her speech. She felt abandoned and alone on what should have been the most important day of her life instead of feeling like this was the beginning she felt like it was the beginning to a horrible end and in some way hoped it would end as quickly and suddenly as it begun.

Monica recognized the face instantly; anger, fear, rage and images of that night swept her body and flooded her mind. She closed her eyes to gain composure and when she opened them he was gone. She quickly searched the crowd for his face, but he was gone. She was sure it was him, he was in the distance. Eryka saw the array of emotions that shown through on Monica's face and wanted to get to her to comfort her, but the dean of student's was sitting between the two. The smile she initially looked over to give her to say, 'We did it!' was replaced with genuine concern. From that point on the graduation seemed to take forever to end. She had her sister's conflictions on her mind and she wanted so badly to have a strong feeling as to what their conflictions were. Her ability to feel things previous or yet to come did not include people feelings and emotions. She was now saddened with the fact that she could not help her sisters she did not realize that she was being beaten down by the power or down pour of their sudden troubled emotions. She scanned the audience for what could have changed her sister's mood and saw nothing, she thought, I need to call Dr. Kowen to confirm Kim's final follow-up appointment; I think Monica and me need to see her too. The three smiled when they simultaneously spotted Dr. Kowen waving.

Eryka's attention was caught when the Dean announced, "It is an honor for me to present these degrees to three young women who have persevered, over the last six years, through the greatest tragedies that life has to offer, the death of their brother and shortly after their parent's. There is no doubt in my mind that these three women will be successful in whatever path they choose to take in life. They have showed that with a goal, self-discipline, passion, perseverance, dedication, and a profound love for others, anything is possible. In case you have not figured out who I am speaking of, it is my honor to present these degrees to Eryka Bronson; Bachelor's of Science Business Administration, Kimberly Jenkins; Bachelor of Accounting and Human Resource Management and Monica Hargrove; Bachelor in Chemical Engineering and Marketing, all three are graduating with honors." The crowd roared with cheers and applause as the three ladies accepted their hard-earned degrees and returned to their seats with their tousles now on the left.

Kim took her seat with a smile on her face as she watched Jessica accept her Bachelor's degree in Marketing and Political Science and make her valedictorian speech. Kim briefly thought back to the day she met her.

Mechelle Davis

After college the three went in their own directions, Monica to Miami, Kim to Atlanta Georgia to join an 18 month program with MLT program and then on to be accepted into and graduate from Harvard law School, and Eryka to Virginia. Each felt that they needed distance from the other to find out who they truly were without the other. Eryka and Kim celebrated at the graduation party with their friends, sang and everyone said their goodbye's. It was hard, but they promised that they would continue their morning talks and visit on holidays and birthdays.

Monica decided not to attend the after party, but returned to her room to prepare to leave the place she called home for the last five years. Eryka and Kim decided to join Jessica but the fun for Kim was short lived when she thought she saw the face she seen at her parent's funeral. Her attempts to relax were futile and Kim decided to join Monica in her dorm. Monica though elated to see Kim still had the look of horror, anger and revenge in her eyes and equally in her face. She could not share with Kim that she was for sure that the man who raped her was at her graduation; because Kim's still believes she is a virgin.

"Wow Monica, if looks could kill. It seems like you want to be by yourself I'll come back later or see you in the morning, you seem to want to be alone."

"No Kim it's not that, sit down. I don't want to be alone, but I do."

"What's wrong, this should be one of the happiest days of our life. We did it. Through the loss of Cameron, Mom and Dad, and my breakdown, we did it!"

Monica thought, and my rape, adoption, and abortion. She looked at Kim, "There is something I need to tell you, but I'm not ready I need you to give me a couple of days and forcefully encourage me to tell you. I can't deal with it on my own anymore and I need to tell someone."

"You sure you don't want to talk about it now?"

"I'm sure."

Kim went to her sister, put her arms around her and laid her head on Monica's. The two sat quietly for a moment Kim looked in her sister's face seeing pain she had not noticed before and decided to respect her sister's wishes. "Okay, you got it, in a couple of days we will have this conversation again in its entirety. Monica was grateful that Kim showed genuine concern because she was feeling completely alone. She hugged Kim and let out sobs that Kim remembered all too well as well as the feeling of wanting to be left alone in the company of someone you trusted. Kim now knew how her sister's felt the many occasions when Dr. Kowen showed up to her dorm door unrepentantly at the direction of her sister's; she wanted to have Dr. Kowen show up for Monica right now. Kim prayed that the two weeks that they would see Dr. Kowen would go by swiftly she knew that whatever was haunting Monica she would not completely share with her, but two weeks turned into four years.

Each had moved on with their lives, holding secrets and resentments for things never discussed attempting to start over and leave the past behind. The distrust was stronger than their relationship and their past was unfinished, leaving it behind was not an option either of them had. They soon learned that the three loud but silent family members they tried to abandon; pain, despair, and heartache came for a return visit and brought some additional unwanted family members with them.